O9-ABI-872

THE BELLS OF BICÊTRE

The Bells of Bicêtre

SIMENON

A HELEN AND KURT WOLFF BOOK

HARCOURT, BRACE & WORLD, INC., NEW YORK

*To all those professors, doctors, and male and female nurses
who, in hospitals and elsewhere,
struggle to understand and to relieve the suffering
of that most disconcerting of human beings:
the patient.*

G. S.

FOREWORD

When I was a boy, most of the books I used to borrow
from a lending library (they had black cloth bindings and a
pleasantly musty smell) boasted a preface, and I must
confess that, now that I have been writing myself for over
forty years, I sometimes wish that fashion had not vanished.
I remember with particular nostalgia certain novels by
Conrad, preceded not by one preface only but by a preface
to the second edition and even to the third, plus a foreword
and a note, a whole series of informal writings that delighted
me almost as much as the story itself.

For did they not provide a direct contact between the au-
thor and his reader, marginal to his work itself? Novelists
today are ready enough to explain themselves in newspapers,
on the radio, and on television, but they do not always reach
by these means those who read their work.

I do not propose to expound my intentions here, far less
to set forth any literary doctrine. I might, at a pinch, have
made do with the ritual formula that serves equally well for
films: "The incidents described here are purely fictional, and
any resemblance between the characters and any living persons is entirely coincidental."

In recent years this precaution has become indispensable, even though sometimes ineffective, since people today readily recognize themselves in works of fiction, particularly if they see any prospect of material profit.

This makes the novelist's position a difficult one. Twenty-five years ago, for instance, while I was in Paris, I was writing *Le Coup de Lune,* a novel that takes place at Libreville, in Gabon, and specifically in a hotel situated at the extreme edge of the town, close to the equatorial forest. Impossible to remember the name of the hotel, where I had stayed two years previously and which I was anxious not to mention. I therefore chose for my novel the most unlikely name: *Central Hotel.* Well, I had hit on the very one, and a few weeks later the proprietress of the Gabonese hotel turned up in Paris to sue me.

This experience, unfortunately, has recurred a number of times in various forms. How is one to find a plausible name which is not borne by somebody, somewhere in the world? And what if, when describing a provincial town, one is obliged to mention the prefect, the mayor, the police inspector? Suppose you make your character fat and bald, isn't the real man likely to be so too? Suppose his wife, in your book, is skinny and garrulous. . . .

For one of my latest novels, *Les Autres,* I deliberately undertook to invent a whole town, with its river, its law courts, its churches, streets, and shops. . . .

But how could I alter the setting of Bicêtre, where I had, none the less, to portray a doctor, interns, a hospital matron?

If, for instance, I were to depict the matron as dark-haired or redheaded, as a kindly woman or a martinet, should I be in danger of describing an actual person?

I declare that, although I have visited Bicêtre Hospital, I never met any of the characters described in his book. The same is true of my newspaper proprietor, my lawyer, my two academicians. I swear I have copied nobody!

My novel not being a *roman à clef,* I therefore repeat the time-honored formula: "Any resemblance with living persons is entirely coincidental." And I still regret the disappearance of last century's prefaces, which had a far keener individual flavor.

Georges Simenon

THE BELLS OF BICÊTRE

CHAPTER ONE

Eight o'clock in the evening. For millions of human beings, each in his pigeonhole, in the little world he had made for himself or had imposed upon him, a definite day was drawing to a close, a cold misty day, Wednesday the third of February.

For René Maugras, dates or times of day did not exist, and only later on was the problem of elapsed time to trouble him. He was still sunk at the bottom of a pit as dark as the abyss of ocean, deprived of contact with the outside world. He did not realize that his right arm had begun to twitch spasmodically, or that each time he breathed out his cheek puffed up in a ridiculous way.

The first message that reached him from outside took the form of rings of sound that spread and formed ever more distant waves. With eyes closed, he tried to follow them and understand them, and then something happened about which he was never to speak to anyone: he recognized these waves and felt a wish to smile to them.

As a child he used to listen to the bells of St. Stephen's Church, and say, gravely pointing at the blue sky: "The wings!"

His mother had talked to him about them shortly before

3

her death. He could not pronounce the word "rings," with which he described the bells because of the concentric circles of sound they sent out into space.

There were bells here too. He did not try to count the strokes, for he felt too numb. This numbness was not unfamiliar either. He had already experienced it, and for a while a certain confusion existed in his mind. Could he still be the eight-year-old boy who was rushed from school to the hospital at Fécamp and who, struggling and screaming, had a mask clapped on his face before being operated on for appendicitis?

There had been a gap then, and much later a strange taste in his mouth, a lassitude of his whole body and at last, when he had felt himself beginning to float, the rings of sound of the familiar bells.

He wanted to smile, now, because the idea that crossed his mind amused him. Without really believing it, he could not bring himself to reject it completely.

Wasn't he the small boy from Fécamp, just waking up in a hospital ward, and would not the first thing he saw be a fat, fair, rosy nurse, busily knitting? In which case, everything else must have been a dream. He must have dreamed, under the anesthetic, nearly fifty years of life.

Of course it wasn't true. He knew it wasn't true, that he was a man of fifty-four and that he left the little house in the Rue d'Etretat a long time ago. Nevertheless the confusion did exist for a certain number of minutes or seconds, probably seconds, and in spite of everything he felt impelled to make sure. For that, he merely had to open his eyes; and then something very strange took place, not in the least tragic, on the contrary almost comic: he did what was requisite to raise his eyelids, what one usually does, presumably by sending a message from the brain to certain nerves. And the eyelids refused to move.

He was not in pain. His prostration was almost pleasant,

4

somewhat as if he no longer existed as a person. He had no more problems or responsibilities. A single motive impelled him to go on trying: he needed to make sure, quite sure, that the fat, fair, rosy nurse was no longer knitting by his bedside.

Could his inward experiences be recognized from outside? The rings had dissolved in the distant air and he was conscious of another sound, which called up other memories. He was too weary to wonder what they were. A chair had creaked, as if someone had risen suddenly, and he must have managed to part his eyelids, for he saw, close beside him, a white uniform, a young face, dark hair escaping from under a nurse's cap.

It was not his nurse, and he shut his eyes again, disappointed. He was really too weary to ask questions and he preferred to slip back into his pit.

Was he to prove capable, a few hours or a few days later, of distinguishing between what he had really perceived through his coma and what he was told about afterwards? For instance, was there really a telephone in the passage, close to his room, and did he hear a woman's voice saying:

"Professor Besson d'Argoulet? . . . He's not at home? . . . Do you know where to contact him? . . . He asked me to let him know as soon as . . ."

He was to learn next day that there really was an old-fashioned wall telephone close to his door. The whole thing was still meaningless, and when it took on a meaning, it was to concern nobody but himself.

At half-past nine he was still unaware that it was half-past nine, and he woke up again more sharply and dramatically, as though after a nightmare, as if he had dreamed that he must at all costs cling to something solid. Only his strength had left him. His limbs were moving aimlessly, at random, uncontrolled. Then he tried to call out, to shout for help. His mouth opened. He was practically sure that he opened his mouth wide, but no sound came out of it.

5

He had to see what there was around him. His body was bathed in sweat, his forehead was damp, and yet he felt cold, his whole being was shaking uncontrollably.

"Don't worry. . . . It's all right. . . . Everything's going to be all right. . . ."

He knew the voice. He tried to identify it precisely, and suddenly he saw not only a face under a white cap, but a strange room with greenish-colored walls.

Standing beside the bed, Besson d'Argoulet—whom he called Pierre, for they had been friends for thirty years—was wearing a get-up which should have made him laugh: beneath his hospital coat, which was unfastened, he wore an evening-dress waistcoat and white tie.

"Keep calm, René, old fellow. . . . Everything's all right. . . ."

All right, obviously, for the Professor, who proceeded, somewhat absent-mindedly, to feel his pulse. Besson didn't happen to be lying there, in what was presumably a hospital bed, beside which a dark-haired nurse was bustling about. He'd not been mistaken, a little while back. He must indeed have regained consciousness for a few moments then, since now he recognized her.

"There's nothing seriously wrong with you, René. . . . That's confirmed by all the tests. . . . We shall have to bother you again with a few more, but it's got to be done. . . . I'm expecting Audoire at any moment. . . ."

Who was Audoire? A name that he knew, or ought to have known, since he knew everybody in Paris. The nurse had laid on a tray a syringe with a very long, thick needle. She seemed to be listening eagerly to the sounds in the passage, while keeping her eye on Maugras, and when a door was heard opening and shutting she darted forward.

"Above all, don't be surprised if . . ."

But he was, in fact, surprised, because he had just opened his mouth. It was not in order to complain, or to ask ques-

6

tions. Actually, he had intended to say, staring at the stiff shirt front and the white tie:

"Sorry to have ruined your evening, old man!"

He did not utter a single sound. He no longer had a voice. Nothing! Not even a groan. Merely a faint whistling or rather gurgling sound, as his cheek went on puffing and collapsing grotesquely. Like a child trying to smoke a pipe.

"It'll probably be a few days before you can speak. . . ."

There was a whispering in the passage. His senses were alert, some of them at least, for he caught a whiff of cigarette smoke.

"You trust me, don't you? . . . You realize that I wouldn't lie to you? . . ." Why ask him the question, when he was powerless to answer? He would gladly have said yes, to satisfy his friend Pierre. A halfhearted yes. A polite, indifferent yes, for nothing mattered to him now and he would rather have sunk back into his pit and, maybe, listened once more to the rings of sound of the church bells.

No, he didn't know Audoire. He had never met him. He would have known, for he had a good memory for faces and could unhesitatingly put a name to people he had only seen for a few minutes several years before. A doctor, presumably, for he was wearing a white hospital coat and a round cap on his head. His face expressed nothing. Maugras had seldom seen a face so serene and expressionless, indeed so commonplace, or such mechanical gestures.

The two men shook hands and exchanged glances without speaking, as if they had no need of speech to understand one another or as if they had already rehearsed the scene. Then Audoire, from the foot of the bed, spoke to René.

"You're quite calm. . . . That's fine. . . . We're going to do a few tiresome little things to you and then you'll go to sleep quietly. . . ."

So he was being spoken to like a human being, and he was almost surprised at that. True, he was meanwhile being treated

7

like an object. The young nurse had uncovered him and he was embarrassed to find that his thighs were bare and that he had a urinal between his legs, like an incontinent old man.

She kept a firm hold on one of his knees, which had begun to shake, and Professor Audoire took a syringe from the tray, not the big one with the long needle but a smaller one, and dug it into his backside. He felt nothing. He would have liked to tell them that too. Not because he was anxious. On the contrary, he had never in his life felt so indifferent, and he looked at the three of them as if their actions had nothing to do with him.

Something had happened about which he could remember nothing. He could not even recall where or when it had taken place. He frowned, or thought he frowned, for he was no longer sure of anything, now that his mouth was speechless and his limbs had ceased to obey him.

The two men in white stood waiting, watching him; the nurse still held his leg, keeping her eyes fixed on her wristwatch.

He didn't care what it was all about. It had to happen. He had always known it would happen, and the fact was that he felt relieved. It was all over now. He needn't bother about it any more. These other people ought not to worry about him.

They were all three waiting, probably, for him to fall asleep. Why? To operate on him? He felt no pain anywhere, but something had certainly gone wrong.

"Are you feeling all right?"

Maugras tried hard to put a smile into his eyes to thank Besson d'Argoulet, and the nurse, and the man they called Audoire, whom they treated with great deference. A big shot, like Besson, perhaps even more distinguished than Besson. What was his special line? He knew a great many leading medical people. He wondered, out of sheer curiosity, then his thoughts became blurred and he fancied he could hear in the distance the church bells' rings of sound.

8

The last thing he saw was a glance exchanged between the two men, as if to say: "He's off. . . ."

He was not dead, and there was sunshine in the room where Besson d'Argoulet, sitting in the nurse's place, was smoking a cigarette. The Professor was not in evening dress now, and he had not put on his hospital coat. At sixty, he was an extremely handsome man, with exquisite manners, who dressed with perfect taste.

"How are you feeling? . . . Don't try to talk yet. . . . Don't move. . . . I can see from your eyes that you've taken the shock very well. . . ."

What shock? And why did his friend Pierre feel obliged to adopt the unctuous tone he kept for his patients?

"I suppose you don't remember anything?"

He was tempted to answer: "Yes, I do!"

For he had suddenly remembered the Grand Véfour restaurant, the private room on the mezzanine floor, over the spiral staircase, where a group of friends—originally thirteen, now, owing to various deaths, only ten—used to lunch on the first Tuesday of each month.

How much time had elapsed since that moment? As far as he was concerned, it might have been a day or a week. It had not been sunny, like this morning, for he recognized from the quality of the light—a brittle kind of sunshine—that it was morning. He had not yet begun to worry about the exact time, but some women were sweeping and moving buckets about close to his room.

They had got together at the Grand Véfour, and through the bay window could see, under the fine rain, the court and arcades of the Palais-Royal. Besson had been sitting opposite him and almost everybody had been there, Clabaud the lawyer, Julien Marelle the academician, whose latest play was actually being performed at the theater across the way, Couffé, another academician, and Chabut. . . . He could have made

9

a list of them, putting each of them in the place he had been occupying, and he remembered Victor, the wine waiter who had served them for over twenty years, going around the table with a magnum of Armagnac.

He had left the table to go and call up his newspaper. The telephone stood between the men's and the women's washrooms. He had got Fernand Colère, his editor, who in spite of his name was as meek as a lamb.

When Maugras was away from the newspaper offices, if only for an hour, he invariably felt the need to telephone and give precise instructions, in a sharp, rather shrill voice.

"No! Don't alter anything on page one. . . . Cut out the third column on page three. . . . Tell the Ministry of the Interior we can't do anything about it, and that it's out of the question to ignore the incident. . . ."

Now, still smoking his cigarette, Besson d'Argoulet felt obliged to explain things to him:

"We were all at table, at the Grand Véfour. . . . You'd gone out to telephone, while the liqueurs were being served. . . . Then you went to the washroom and you must have been taken ill there, for when Clabaud went there ten or fifteen minutes later he found you unconscious. . . ."

Why these circumlocutions, this painstaking speech? He was being treated like a child, or rather like a very sick man, which indeed he was.

On one point the Professor was making a mistake, in spite of his self-assurance. And that was odd too, so odd that if he'd been able to speak, Maugras would have said nothing about it.

It was true that after replacing the receiver he had opened the door of the lavatory. He had stood in front of the urinal in the absurd posture which is familiar to every man. He had been thinking about Colère and about the actions of the Ministry of the Interior when, without any warning, he had begun to sway.

10

He remembered one sordid detail. He had clung with both hands, with all his might, to the slimy enamel of the urinal before letting go.

What had Besson just been saying?

"When Clabaud went in ten or fifteen minutes later he found you unconscious. . . ."

These words told nothing specific about the way they found him. Now he could visualize himself sprawling across the narrow stall, on the floor, trying desperately, not to get up again, not to call for help, but to do up his fly.

The mysterious thing was that he could really see himself, just as somebody else might have seen him; he could see himself from outside, just as Clabaud must have found him. Was such a splitting of personality possible?

"You certainly gave us a fright at first. . . ."

He was clear-headed and even, it seemed to him, more acutely so than in ordinary life. He noticed automatically what was going on around him, the inflections of the doctor's voice, his hesitations, even the unusual shape of his cuff links which represented some Greek letter, he did not know which, since he'd only studied Greek for a few months. As he discovered these, he was wondering whether Besson d'Argoulet was not feeling more uncomfortable than himself and if, whatever he might say, he wasn't still as worried as he had been in the washroom at the Grand Véfour.

True, Maugras could not speak and half his body was paralyzed. That, too, he had discovered by himself. Had his friend expected his reaction, or rather his lack of reaction, his calmness that was akin to indifference?

It really was indifference, as if what was going on in this rather shabby little room did not concern him, any more than his body now concerned him, and he felt no surprise on discovering a needle stuck into his arm, a rubber tube connected with a glass vessel half full of a transparent liquid.

11

His glance did not escape the doctor, who hurriedly explained:

"That's dextrose. Until you can take food by mouth, tomorrow or the day after, it's important to keep your strength up. . . ."

Presumably he spoke in that persuasive voice to all of his patients who were seriously ill. Maugras, who had only consulted him about trifles or for an annual check, had never seen him in this light.

"I suppose you're wondering why you're here and not in the Auteuil nursing home?"

Besson had sent him there once, four or five years earlier, for a series of tests after a bad attack of nervous depression. As usual he had been overworking, overdoing things in every direction.

"Well, that was where I had you sent in the first place, or rather where I took you in the ambulance. . . . You were immediately given the room you had before, and your wife hurried over. . . . Don't worry about her. . . . I've explained to her that you're not in any danger. . . . She's been very sensible. . . . I call her up several times a day, and she's only waiting for me to give her the word to come and see you. . . .

"Don't try to talk. . . . I know that's the worst part, the most demoralizing, but I promise you that in your case it's merely a temporary aphasia. . . ."

It had to happen. While his friend was speaking, René repeated the words to himself, as calmly as if they expressed some commonplace observation.

Why did it have to happen? He did not ask himself that. He even thought it was rather amusing. Perhaps words, too, were taking on a different meaning? Or was it that his lazy mind was getting them muddled? Instead of amusing, for instance, he would have liked to say relieving, but probably the right word did not exist. It was almost as if he were playing a game with himself, unknown to everyone else, while he appeared to be listening to Besson's speech.

He had been expecting a catastrophe for a long time now, perhaps he had always expected it, and during the last few months he had been so aware of its imminence that he had sometimes felt impatient because it failed to occur.

Besson d'Argoulet was beating about the bush because he was afraid of the syllables that he would inevitably have to utter: *hem-i-ple-gia*.

"Let me first tell you briefly why you're no longer at Auteuil. As soon as I diagnosed a probable thrombosis of the medial cerebral artery, I sent for my colleague Audoire, professor of neurology and chief consultant at Bicêtre Hospital. . . . You certainly know him by reputation. . . . It was he that you saw last night, and he then gave you a lumbar puncture. . . . Audoire wanted to have you within his reach, in the care of trained members of his staff, whom he can fully trust. . . . He has a couple of private wards at his disposal, one of which happened to be free. . . . And so that's why you've been here since Tuesday night. . . ."

Besson put on a joking air.

"I hope you'll forgive us, Audoire and myself, for bringing you to a place that's got rather a forbidding name. . . . Your wife, by the way, was distressed at first and I had to prove to her that you'd be better off here than in a private nursing home, even if the surroundings aren't so pleasant. . . ."

Maugras blinked, for no particular reason, as one blinks automatically, and his friend wondered whether it was a signal.

"Am I tiring you?"

He tried to convey, through features over which he had no control, the fact that he was not tired, and the doctor appeared to grasp his message.

The door to the left of the bed was glazed with panes of frosted, or rather of finely ribbed glass, that gave a distorted image, and from time to time shadows passed by, clumsy shadows, men leaning on crutches and yet moving noiselessly. It was rather mysterious. Perhaps they were wearing felt slippers?

Besson must have prepared his little speech, for he always picked up the thread of it.

"You know enough about medicine for me to let you know what conclusions we've reached, Audoire and myself. . . . I've got particular confidence in Audoire, who is far more highly qualified in this sphere. . . .

"Like everyone else, you know roughly what hemiplegia means, but like most people, you're probably unaware that there are various kinds, differing both in their causes and in their effects, each offering a definite clinical picture, with a specific prognosis for each. . . ."

Why so much talk? Wasn't he going to be told that his particular hemiplegia was the most ordinary kind, the least serious?

"In your case, the lumbar puncture makes it perfectly clear that there's nothing pathological, which means that it's a plain apoplectic stroke with . . ."

Besson frowned as though he were annoyed, and paused to light a cigarette.

"Are you listening to me?"

Maugras, as far as he was able, signaled that he was listening.

"You don't believe me. You think I'm trying to reassure you with claptrap. . . ."

But Maugras was not even worrying about that. What had happened was that he had crossed an invisible barrier and now found himself in a different universe. It even struck him as odd that this distinguished person, a Commander of the Legion of Honor, who was now sitting at his bedside and wasting time in futile explanations, was his friend, and that

14

they called one another *tu*. It was true that he himself was a Commander of the Legion of Honor too!

The difference was that one of the two was now a *hemiplegic*.

Like Félix Artaud, his best reporter, whom he used to send up the Amazon as readily as into Tibet or Greenland, who had interviewed every living Head of State, the great Félix Artaud, noisy, tireless Félix Artaud who could spend two or three nights in a row without sleep, who could drink a whole bottle of whisky without turning a hair.

Artaud had lain unconscious, like himself, at three o'clock in the morning, in a luxury hotel in the Champs-Elysées, where he'd been with an American girl.

A divorced man, he had no known relatives in Paris and it was René Maugras, his boss, who had been sent for, somewhat mysteriously, in the middle of the night. He had helped the hotel doctor and the nurse to pull on his friend's trousers, and he had driven behind the ambulance that took him to the American Hospital at Neuilly.

Artaud was only forty-five. He had been an athlete, an old Rugby player, always ready for a brawl. He had been looked after not by Professor Audoire but by a doctor whose name Maugras had forgotten, a redheaded little fellow, very thin, who wore a hospital coat that was too long for him, so that only his feet showed beneath it.

They had examined Artaud for hours on end, and he, too, had been entitled to his lumbar puncture and then to an electro-encephalogram.

Incidentally, had he himself had one of those while he was in his coma? He couldn't even ask that. He was at people's mercy now. They had to guess what he meant.

When he had gone into Artaud's room, the patient had a needle stuck in his left arm, connected, as in his own case, to a glass vessel.

15

On his next visit the reporter had no longer been in a coma, but his right cheek had been subject to a curious tremor and every time he'd tried to speak he could only utter a gurgling sound.

He had died on the fifth day, in the small hours, at about the time he usually went to bed.

Maugras had known another case, Jublin, the poet who was always to be found in the Brasserie Lipp, and who had had his attack on the sidewalk of the Boulevard Saint-Germain. Jublin must have been about sixty and he was to live on for six years, paralyzed, at the mercy of other people, in an invalid's chair.

And then there had been a famous film actor. . . . Well, well! Besson d'Argoulet, who was so amusing and so ironical at their Tuesday lunches, was now pompously demonstrating to him that his own case was different and that in a few weeks . . .

". . . a few months at latest. . . . Of course I'm talking of a complete cure. . . . You're an intelligent man and I'm anxious to explain it all to you in detail, for Audoire and I need your co-operation. . . . Just now, I'm well aware, you don't believe me. . . . You think that I'm just trying to encourage you and that I'm coating the pill. . . ."

René opened his eyes wide to explain that he wasn't thinking anything at all, that it was all the same to him.

Poor Pierre! This was a side of his personality about which Maugras had never thought. He knew the big boss who presided over official soirées, the skeptical Parisian who was to be seen at first nights, the gourmet of the Grand Véfour lunch parties, the man of letters who had indulged himself by writing, between a couple of reports to the Academy of Medicine, a trilogy on the private lives of Flaubert, Zola, and Maupassant.

He had heard him, at table, relate intriguing case histories and tales of tragedy.

16

Would he tell Maugras's own story someday?

He had never pictured him sitting, as he was now, beside a bed, fumbling for words, stubbornly trying to convince his patient, wondering through what crack he could force his way into that patient's mind.

"Don't exhaust yourself!" he felt like telling him.

The doctor had driven himself here in his English sports car. He lived in the Rue de Longchamp and had come down the Champs-Elysées just as the city began to come to life. Outside, the air was cool. Presently Besson would pick up his car in the courtyard of the hospital and drive off, with the top down, back through the Porte d'Italie to give his lectures on medical pathology at Broussais.

"I've found you a private nurse, Mlle Blanche, who once worked in my department and who's been taking care of you since Tuesday night. . . . You can trust her completely. . . . Another equally expert nurse will take her place at night. . . ."

He added, in a lighter tone:

"You've doubtless noticed that Mlle Blanche is pretty, which should help your recovery. . . . Tomorrow she'll start feeding you, with liquids at first, and after three or four days she'll make you get out of bed for a few minutes. . . . Well, you've had enough of that, haven't you? . . . I'd hoped to see Audoire here this morning. . . . He must have been kept by some urgent case, but he'll surely look in before midday. . . . And I'll pop over again at the end of the day. . . ."

Maugras clearly understood the glance his friend cast at the nurse as he went out. It meant:

"I've done what I could, unfortunately without much success. . . ."

He did not appear inordinately surprised at this. Perhaps it was fairly usual with hemiplegics?

He retraced his steps.

17

"You're going to have an injection that will put you to sleep for a few hours. Unless Audoire changes his mind, you'll be taken to the X-ray department for a cerebral arteriography. . . . Nothing dangerous. You won't even be aware of it, for you'll be under narcosis. . . . You mustn't bear us a grudge, old man, if we inflict all these petty torments on you, but in medicine as in everything else, in your newspaper too, there's a routine that has to be followed. . . ."

Maugras did not protest, felt no desire to protest. He bore nobody a grudge. He bore fate no grudge either.

Besson and the nurse whispered together in the passage, where the silent ungainly shadows kept passing to and fro. Somewhere on the right there must be a big ward, the inmates of which were allowed to walk about, and the passage appeared to be their exercise ground.

He was anxious for Mlle Blanche to come back, seized with sudden panic at feeling himself alone, as he had been in the washroom at the Grand Véfour.

And he was anxious for the promised injection to immerse him once more in that torpor where he might perhaps hear again those bells with their living rings of sound.

His eyes followed her when she came in again, fresh, alert, and smiling, and he reflected that she must be like that with each successive patient, that all of them followed her with their eyes with the same expression because she represented for each of them youth and life.

Had he been able to, he would have smiled at her as she lifted the sheet to give him his injection, so as to apologize for giving her so much trouble, and above all to apologize for his lack of faith, for being a bad patient, for having no wish to struggle.

For he did not want to struggle. What was the point?

18

It was still dark, but there was no way of guessing the time. His first sensation was one of anguish, for he thought he was all alone in the room, which was lit only by a blur of yellow light coming from the passage through the glazed door. What made him think he was alone was the fact that this door was standing ajar, as if he were under the distant surveillance of the nurse on night duty on that floor.

Turning his head a little, he discovered that he was mistaken, that somebody was asleep on a cot between his own bed and the wall. He could not make out the sleeper's features, only a head of red hair, and he remembered the night nurse who had been introduced to him the previous evening. She was an Alsatian girl, Joséfa, neither so pretty nor so smiling as Mlle Blanche. But her uniform concealed a plump, sensuous body, and the starched linen was taut over her breasts. He had an aunt, a sister of his mother's, whose flesh was as firm and vigorous, and she, too, had regular but coarse-cut features.

He had not seen Joséfa go to bed. He had not known there was a cot in his room. Perhaps it had been brought in while he was asleep, for he had passed out immediately after

19

his last injection. What sort of injection? They hadn't told him. They had given him several the night before, and each time they had written a few words or hieroglyphs on a sheet of paper fastened to the end of his bed.

Judging from the noises outside, the night must be drawing to a close. Many trucks passed down the avenue that led from the Porte d'Italie through the suburbs and finally became Route Nationale 7. He had driven along it hundreds of times on his way to the Riviera, but had never thought of finding out its name. He could not remember, either, whether it was every day or on certain days of the week that a market was held on the sidewalk, displaying not only foodstuffs but also booths with wearing apparel.

That was close by, barely a hundred yards from the hospital where he now lay. He had sometimes cast a glance, as he drove past, at the gray buildings surrounding a huge inner courtyard whose gate was guarded, like that of a barracks, by men in uniform. He had always thought that only old men and incurable invalids were sent there; they could be seen standing about the courtyard, alone or in small silent groups. And lunatics, too. Wasn't Bicêtre a psychiatric hospital as well as a poorhouse?

He felt no humiliation at finding himself there, nor fear. Although he still had a strange taste in his mouth, last night's narcotic had left his mind clear and lively, and, lying inert in his bed, he took pleasure in pursuing, for a while, the ideas that occurred to him, rejecting them, combining and then separating them again.

They were by no means tragic thoughts. Whatever those around him might suppose, he was not depressed but, on the contrary, he felt that he had never before enjoyed such serenity.

Only it was a peculiar sort of serenity which he could hardly have defined and which he had never expected.

20

How would he have reacted a few days before, even on Tuesday morning, if he had been told:

"In a few hours, you'll suddenly cease to be a normal man. You won't be able to walk. You won't be able to talk. Your right hand will be incapable of writing. You'll see people coming and going around you without being able to communicate with them. . . ."

He had never had a dog or a cat. Actually, he was not fond of animals, perhaps because he had never studied them closely or tried to understand them. And suddenly he remembered the look in an animal's eyes, presumably striving to express something and not being able to do so.

He felt no bitterness. And if he pursued his self-analysis he would discover that he felt no regrets. On the contrary! Deliberately, he recalled his previous way of life, up till that last Tuesday morning, and he was surprised at having led such a life, at having attached any importance to it, at having played a game that now struck him as puerile.

As though to give concrete expression to his state of mind he visualized a painting, seen in the days when he still had time to visit picture galleries. It was a painting by Chirico, representing a kind of synthetic figure, a tailor's dummy with a wooden head, suffused in a cold, lunar light.

And it was in an equally pitiless light that he now saw his last day as a so-called normal man. In Paris he had lived for some years in one of the apartments in that wing of the Hôtel George V reserved for guests making a long stay and known as the Résidence. This spared his wife the bother of housekeeping.

She had tried to run their house in the Rue de la Faisanderie. She had displayed good will and energy, but after a couple of years she had been on the verge of a nervous breakdown.

Not merely on the verge of it! She had actually had a nerv-

21

ous breakdown and, for weeks, had refused to leave her room, where she spent days and nights in the dark.

It was not Lina's fault; it was his fault for choosing her and imposing his own way of life on her.

She'd come to see him the evening before, after he'd been brought back from the X-ray department. He hadn't completely emerged from the fog of his narcosis and he had felt even more indifferent than he did now.

He had noticed, nevertheless, that she was wearing a black silk dress under her mink-lined gabardine. That was the fashion in their set, especially in Lina's set; by an inverted snobbery, women concealed their costly furs under an apparently ordinary material.

It must be about six o'clock. The darkness was beginning to lift and the fog could be seen clinging to the windowpanes.

Last night he had met the hospital matron, too, for it was she who had brought Lina in. He had taken a dislike to this sixty-year-old woman with her gray hair and her gray face, who seemed even more impersonal than Professor Audoire.

It looked like mimesis. Surely she was copying the great man? She stood there in the middle of the room, which was not a large one, and she had such a presence, like certain actors, that everything else ceased to exist. Her calm gaze inspected, measured, criticized.

She was a monolith who could well have borne the entire weight of the hospital.

Lina, awestruck, had hesitated before bending over him to kiss him. As he had expected, she had smelled of alcohol. She had probably drunk a couple of whiskies before leaving the Résidence George V and he was convinced that, on the way to the hospital, she had had their chauffeur Léonard stop in front of the first bar she saw, and downed another.

Once again, he didn't hold it against her. He was used to it. Only last Tuesday it had seemed quite natural to him, like

22

any of his own habits. They each had a separate bedroom and bathroom, while the drawing room provided neutral ground.

This arrangement had proved necessary, because they seldom went to bed at the same time, and Lina rose late in the mornings, whereas at half-past eight Maugras would get into the Bentley that was waiting to take him to his newspaper office.

He was always in a hurry. For years and years he had been in a hurry. He could never spare the time to look at the life of the streets. He scarcely knew if the weather was sunny or wet. Sitting in the back of the car he would get to work, glancing over the morning papers and underlining articles in red pencil.

He was an important man, and only last Tuesday he had been conscious of it. His gestures, his voice, his brief sentences, his way of looking at his interlocutors as if he did not see them, were all those of an important man; ministers would ring him up with a familiarity tinged with respect, and at moments of crisis the President of the Council would promptly summon him to Matignon.

Ministers, party leaders, bankers, academicians, stage stars were entertained every Sunday at his country house at Arneville, near Arpajon, a regular château or, more precisely, a folly built in the eighteenth century by a superintendent of finances.

"Good morning, *Monsieur le Directeur.* . . ."

It would start with the janitor and go on with the elevator boy and the doormen.

"Good morning, Monsieur Maugras. . . ."

When he reached the editorial rooms the tone would change and become less formal:

"Good morning, René. . . ."

There he'd find Fernand Colère, his editor-in-chief, who was the same age as himself and who had already been his colleague when, at twenty-five, he had edited the gossip column of a small paper, which had since died, called *Le Boulevard*.

Only last Tuesday he had been convinced that Colère was entirely devoted to him, that out of sheer admiration he had practically given up his life to him. After all, he could count on Colère to do anything for him! Colère would merely hang his head when, infuriated by some slip, some oversight, some mistake in the layout, the boss took it out on him with humiliating insults.

Suddenly he saw his editor-in-chief in a different light, akin to the light in Chirico's painting. He was no longer the fat, good-natured fellow, easygoing and a bit weak, but a witness who had followed closely on his heels for thirty years and who concealed, under apparent meekness, his envy and his hatred: the person who knew him best, who knew almost everything about him and who had taken note of everything.

Maugras had been surprised to see him come in almost immediately after Lina, who had brought him not only flowers but a slender crystal vase. The flowers, as usual, were his favorites, yellow carnations. There were only half a dozen of them, for he disliked bouquets. On his office desk, his secretary used to put a single flower each morning. Lina had guessed that the hospital would not have a vase narrow enough for six carnations, and she had brought one from the George V.

How long had they been living together? Seven years? Eight years? All that time, he had been sure he loved her. And now he had looked at her without emotion, just as he had looked at the matron or, later, at Fernand Colère.

"Pierre's been giving me news of you several times a day. . . ."

Pierre was Besson d'Argoulet. She called him by his Christian name too. She liked calling people by their Christian names, particularly if they were famous people.

"Up till now, he'd forbidden me to come and see you. Apparently Professor Audoire gave strict orders. . . . I had the greatest difficulty in getting through to your room. . . ."

Lina kept talking nervously; as soon as Colère came in she moved two steps closer to the window, to let him stand beside the bed.

"Well, René, what a fright you've been giving your friends! . . ."

Colère sounded insincere. They all sounded insincere, Besson, Lina, Joséfa, even Mlle Blanche, although she seemed closer than the rest.

On Tuesday, at the newspaper office, while he was being carried to the Auteuil nursing home, his editor-in-chief must have been hectically preparing an emergency front page, possibly with a black border, a headline running over five columns, and his picture, and an obituary notice.

Whom would they have asked to write it? No doubt one of the Grand Véfour set, preferably an academician, probably Daniel Couffé, whom he could easily picture setting to work in the dining room where they had just eaten lunch. It would be a rush job with a messenger from the paper waiting in the passage to collect the copy and hand it in as fast as it was written.

They must have kept the type standing, for it might come in useful at any moment.

"You know, René, it's no easy matter to get up here. . . ."

Almost what Lina had said.

"They've put up regular barricades downstairs. . . ."

He had almost forgotten that while he was lying here, in a coma or in a kind of daze, life had been going on, and people had talked about him, asked after him, tried to get in touch with him.

He felt neither pleasure nor distress at the thought, nor at noticing that Colère was also dressed in black, or in very dark gray, so as to be ready for any emergency. Had Lina thought of that when she chose her dress? Had she thought of the photographers who, if the end came suddenly, would pounce on her?

"They're only allowing me to visit you for a few minutes. . . . I hear from the doctors that everything's going well and that you'll be up and about in a few weeks. . . . So I'll just give you a rough idea of what's been happening, because, knowing the sort of man you are, you must have been worrying about the paper. . . ."

That was not true. He had not given a single thought to it.

"I assumed you wouldn't want any reference made to your little accident, and I gave the boys a call to ask them to say nothing about it. . . . I also called France-Presse and the two American agencies. . . . So far everybody's played the game. . . . And then I summoned the whole of the staff, from top to bottom, and I . . ."

Lina stood by, staring out through the fog at the gray rooftop of one wing of the hospital, which René could see from his bed. It was a mansard roof of gray slate, like a Louis XIV château. Actually, Bicêtre belonged to that period.

"Apparently on Tuesday night some fifty reporters and photographers invaded the courtyard and the entrance. . . . Although the press, the radio, and TV have been very discreet, telegrams have poured in constantly both at the paper and here. There have been so many telephone calls that they're complaining, downstairs, that the lines are always busy and that urgent calls are held up. . . ."

Did Colère imagine this would cheer him up? He was mistaken. Maugras remained utterly indifferent, and it was with equal detachment that this morning, in his twilit room, he strove to picture the details of his funeral.

A bell rang out, a single stroke. The half-hour. Half-past what hour? It came not from the hospital, where there must surely be a chapel, but two or three hundred yards away, beyond the avenue, where more and more heavy traffic was now passing, mingled with the suburban buses. Presumably there was a church or a convent over there, most likely a church, since convent bells usually have a shriller sound.

As the darkness grew less opaque, he began to hear sounds from the big ward at the end of the corridor, the door of which must be open. It was all confused and intermittent still. Sick men must be waking one after the other and tossing and turning in their beds, waiting for night to end.

A nurse went by, then another. From the side opposite to the main ward, he soon heard the sound of voices, the chink of cups on saucers, and then the smell of coffee reached him.

Presently Joséfa stirred, sat up in silence, and switched on a pocket flashlight to look at the time on her wrist watch. He saw her lie down again, stretched out on her back as if she were treating herself to a brief respite, and then at last she got up. He closed his eyes immediately, but he had time to note that she had slept fully dressed.

He guessed that she was folding the blanket and the sheets. A creaking sound told him that she was folding up the cot and putting it away in a closet, whose existence he thus discovered for the first time.

She leaned over him and carefully picked up his wrist to feel his pulse. She smelled of sweat. He recognized the smell peculiar to those who have slept in their clothes. He felt reluctant to make contact with the outside world, and pretended to be asleep.

At last she went out on tiptoe. A door opened and closed. There was the sound of water flushing and then, after a longish silence during which she presumably put on a little fresh powder, the door opened again and Joséfa went to join the night nurses who were drinking their coffee.

Thus he was beginning to discover the routine of the hospital. It was something to occupy his mind. Above all, it proved to him that his brain and his senses were not so numb as they had been the night before.

27

Another discovery: the dreadful twitch in his cheek had almost vanished. Under the sheet, he felt able to move the fingers of his left hand. He even managed to lift that hand, to bend his elbow, and a little later, to move his leg.

He tried the right side, however, without success.

Taking advantage of being alone, he attempted to speak, and emitted a shrill sound like a kitten's mew.

Fog, like yesterday's fog, became visible through the window and soon the slates of the roof could be made out. Two windows were lit up and behind one of them a woman seemed to be dressing hurriedly.

Cars drove into the courtyard and drew up at the foot of the central building, in which he was. Not far from his room there was a staircase with creaking treads. The church clock struck six and then the bells rang out for early Mass.

The world was coming to life around him, still in slow motion. Garbage cans were being dragged across the pavement. An electric bell rang faintly in the distance, or it might have been an alarm clock, while down below, on the ground floor or in the basement, the clatter of enormous saucepans sounded from the kitchens.

It reminded him of the newspaper office in the early morning, when a new shift came on in the linotype room, when the make-up hands took their places in front of the presses and the compositors in front of their machines, while in the editorial rooms the daytime journalists and typists relieved the night workers.

He did not know at what time the change-over occurred here. When he heard Joséfa's steps, he shut his eyes again so as not to be disturbed. She came up close to look at him. She no longer smelled quite the same. Taking advantage of the respite he was allowing her, she went back into the passage to light a cigarette.

He soon learned that the shift took place at half-past six,

when the patients were waked up. People started walking about everywhere at the same time, opening and shutting doors, and he discovered that his floor, which had seemed silent on previous days, was actually a lively, bustling place.

For several minutes he had been watching the shadowy figures of patients passing behind the glazed door when Joséfa, having finished her cigarette, came in and slipped a thermometer under his left arm.

He heard the sharp tap of rapid footsteps in the corridor, very different from the muffled, gliding sounds that went on all day. The steps halted outside the always slightly open door, which opened wider, and through his half-closed eyelids, which gave him the feeling he was cheating, he recognized Mlle Blanche in her smart town clothes.

She made a sign to Joséfa, who followed her out, and both of them, talking in low voices, walked down the passage to the cloakroom, where the nurse changed her dress and put on flat-heeled shoes instead of her high-heeled ones. She probably had a small car, which he pictured in some pale color, blue or light green.

When she came back she was alone. She took up the thermometer. He had not shut his eyes quickly enough and she noticed that he was awake.

"Good morning!" she said gaily. "I hear you've had a good night. If you're good, I shall try to give you a drink of orange juice presently. . . ."

Why talk to him as if he were a child? She was intelligent. She knew that he was too. If they had met anywhere else than in a hospital, she would have spoken deferentially to him and would not have dreamed of saying anything as stupid as "If you're good . . ."

He showed no reaction, merely followed her with his eyes while she consulted the sheet of paper at the foot of the bed

29

and noted his temperature on it. He was the only person who did not know what was written on that paper, although it concerned him more closely than anyone else.

In fact, he had become an object. Apparently tradition demanded that doors should be left ajar, not only his door but that of the main ward, the sounds from which he could hear.

And now a middle-aged man in a dressing gown of coarse purple wool pushed open the glazed door and stared at him with curiosity. Was this another hemiplegic, a convalescent? To judge by his vacant look, his slowly twitching head, he looked more like a mental patient. Mlle Blanche paid no attention to him and after standing there in silence for a few moments the strange figure moved off as he had come.

Trolleys passed, with enormous rattling cans. The door opened once again, to admit the matron, followed by a young house surgeon.

"Everything all right here? Has he had a good night?"

The inquiry was not made to himself. True, he would have been incapable of replying to it. Mlle Blanche held out the sheet of paper, fastened to a board. The matron read it and handed it to the house surgeon, who made no comment. They both went up to the stand that held the bottle of dextrose, and connected him to it again.

"Do you think," asked Mlle Blanche, "that I can send for the barber to shave him?"

He had not thought about his beard, which must have grown in four days, particularly as his hair grew thick and as he was dark, like his mother. Somebody else had thought about it for him, and he did not feel in the least grateful. He realized that these attentions were quite impersonal, that he was merely the temporary occupant of a bed and that the ritual would be the same for anybody. On such and such a day, the electro-encephalogram; another day, the lumbar puncture; yet another day, X-raying . . . later on, orange juice and a shave.

30

If Besson d'Argoulet had not been more his friend than his doctor, probably no one would have talked to him about his illness; he would merely have been told to be calm and confident.

Besson had told him as much as possible, with great kindness, and it must have complicated life for so busy a man to come all the way across Paris to the other side of the Porte d'Italie.

"Time for a wash and brush-up. . . . On my way here this morning I thought we might get you a small radio set. . . . I'm sure the Professor wouldn't object, and it might amuse you. . . ."

He had no desire to listen to the radio. He had no desire to be amused, and she had no business to try to think for him. He wasn't interested in the life that went on outside. He was satisfied with what was happening in his immediate neighborhood, with the comings and goings in the corridor, and the noises on his floor, which he was beginning to recognize.

Although he was not a tall man, nor a stout one like Colère, his body was well padded and he weighed a good hundred and seventy-five pounds. And yet Mlle Blanche, who couldn't have weighed more than a hundred, turned him over without difficulty, washed him from head to foot, and managed to change the sheet underneath him without disturbing him.

This washing period was the most trying moment of the day for him, and he kept his eyes shut, for he was ashamed. Physically, he was not handsome. He had never been handsome. As a young man, he had already had the same lumpish figure, the same slack features with a nose that looked half finished. It used to distress him. Since he had become an important man he had thought less about it, and, perversely, would not have minded being frankly ugly.

Here, however, while she washed and sponged him, he felt once more all the shame of his youth.

31

"I've got to give you an alcohol rub. . . . I thought you'd probably prefer eau-de-Cologne, and until you've been able to send for some I've brought you a small bottle. . . ."

He ought to have given her some sign of gratitude, but he could not bring himself to do so. She wouldn't understand him, nor would anyone else. People would imagine that he was resentful, or that he thought he was entitled to special treatment because he ran the biggest newspaper in Paris and a couple of weeklies. It was untrue. The truth was far more complex, and could not be explained.

Moreover he was annoyed because his bed and his room suddenly smelled of eau-de-Cologne instead of the faint but not unpleasant smell of sickness and medicine. It was almost as if they were trying to deceive him. Did he like the idea of being shaved? He wasn't sure.

"Now have a rest, while I call up the barber to find out if he's free. . . ."

The barber who shaved incurable invalids, paralytics, lunatics, and corpses! It was broad daylight. The fog had grown thinner and the sun was about to shine through. Two girls in blue aprons, who spoke to one another in Italian, invaded the room with pails and brushes, and without a glance at him, without curiosity, they performed their daily task.

When the barber appeared at last, the room was clean, there was fresh water in the vase that held the six yellow carnations, and fresh air came in through the slotted ventilator in the top of the window. The barber was an elderly fellow who himself looked like an incurable invalid. Perhaps he was one. His yellow finger tips smelled of nicotine; he had bad teeth, and he worked in silence with uncanny concentration.

"I'm not to cut his hair, am I?"

Mademoiselle shook her head. He seemed to be waiting for something, holding his little bag in his hand; she understood at last and pulled a note out of her handbag.

"I nearly forgot his tip. . . . Don't worry; we'll settle up later. . . ."

This detail impressed him: he was incapable, now, of paying for anything himself, and it felt rather as if he were completely out of money. He had several times had the same dream, of finding himself in a strange town, hunting through his pockets, and discovering that he hadn't a penny. . . .

His wife would not be up yet. Did she go out last night? She might have stayed in the flat, since it's not the thing to gad about in restaurants and night clubs when your husband is in hospital. In that case, she'd have invited at least one of her friends to keep her company, probably several. She was incapable of spending a single hour by herself, and the whisky bottle, surrounded by glasses, always stood ready on the table. She would take it with her into her bedroom and even, sometimes, into the bathroom.

She had asked him the night before, in a low voice, as if it weren't really her business:

"Wouldn't you like me to ring up Colette?"

She must have understood his sign, for she did not insist further. Colette was his daughter by a first marriage, born when he was twenty-three, so that she was now thirty-one, three years older than her stepmother.

The two women had never met, although this was neither Colette's fault nor Lina's. The fault was his.

When he got his divorce, it had seemed the handsome thing to do to leave the three-year-old child in her mother's care. Colette was already living in the country, at some distance from Paris, with an elderly relative who detested him. He had sometimes gone to see her, but without pleasure, for he had not been made welcome. The journey was a long one; he was going through the most difficult and crucial period of his career. . . .

Colette had been born lame. Operations had proved useless. Every kind of up-to-date orthopedic treatment had been tried in succession. Moreover, she unfortunately took after her father in appearance, having his figure and his rather shapeless features.

Once or twice a year she would visit him at the newspaper office, because she happened to be in the neighborhood, and since they both knew that they had nothing to say to one another such visits were painful rather than pleasant.

She neither asked nor accepted anything from him. She lived alone, in a working-class street in Puteaux, and worked in a school for abnormal children founded by a sort of apostle, Dr. Libot, with whom he suspected her of being secretly in love.

She was quite unimpressed by her father's career. And she had little contact with her mother, who had become a well-known actress and thus had realized her ambition, since at the age of eighteen she had studied at the Atelier Theater under Dullin.

Colette, in imitation of Dr. Libot, had made saintliness her career. He wondered none the less whether, with her clubfoot and her ungainly body, it did not give her a grim satisfaction to see him reduced to immobility and a ludicrous silence.

Had he suffered from the disapproval she had always shown toward him? For a long time, he had thought so. Surely parents were supposed to love their children, and children to love their parents?

He had no desire to see her. He had no desire to see anyone, not even Besson, who would make yet another effort to persuade him that everything was going well, and that he would become a normal man again.

They had said the same thing to Colette when she was young. At the time of her operation they had promised her she would walk normally.

34

Footsteps and voices rang out loudly in the passage, as a procession passed by.

"The Professor's visiting the ward," announced Mlle Blanche.

Audoire walked in front, a couple of yards ahead of the rest, his assistants and some thirty students, three or four of whom were girls. It was rather like a religious ceremony, if somewhat less hieratic. The patients must be sitting up in bed, and the little company would move on from one to the next.

A few years previously, Besson had insisted on Maugras's witnessing a similar ceremony, which took place three times a week in his department at Broussais. Most of the patients were confined to their beds, some of them were dying. Besson d'Argoulet had looked even handsomer and more impressive than at an official dinner, in his spotless hospital coat, with a white cap setting off his silvery hair.

Wasn't it a cruel sport? An unfeeling hand lifted up the sheet and disclosed a feverish body, malformations, bedsores, while the Professor, in his lecture-room voice, uttered his comments and the students took notes.

The group had passed slowly from one bed to the next and the patients' eyes had followed it, some of them expressing no human intelligence, only sheer animal terror. Each of them waited his turn, listening eagerly, trying to understand the doctor's comments, which might just as well have been made in Latin.

And yet Besson was a humane man. He knew most of his patients by name and would address them familiarly.

"Well, here's my old friend who's going to ask me a lot of questions again. . . ."

Sometimes he would give them a pat on the cheek or on the shoulder, particularly if he knew that the bed would probably be empty, or have another occupant, at his next visit. . . .

Maugras dreaded the prospect of seeing the white-clad group invade his room. His eyes must have betrayed him, for Mlle Blanche, attentive to all his reflexes, reassured him.

"Don't worry. The Professor never brings his students into the private rooms. He might come in with an assistant, but I doubt it. . . ."

If his calculations were correct, it was now Friday. He made a mental note of this, as he did of everything that he discovered about life in hospital. It did not concern him personally, but it served as a sort of exercise.

"He won't be long now," announced the nurse, after casting a glance along the passage. "On Fridays" (so he'd not been mistaken!) "the visit never lasts long. Tuesday's is the longest."

He made a note of that: Tuesday . . .

She tidied her hair in front of the mirror, and as this mirror hung above the washbasin, to the left of his bed, she brushed against him with her coat.

The Professor came into the room alone, while his students strolled down the corridor and dispersed in all directions, making almost as much noise as schoolboys leaving a classroom. Audoire gave him a brief nod, without bothering to smile at him like Besson, and his very first glance was a strictly professional one.

Mlle Blanche showed him the sheet of paper, which he promptly handed back to her as if there was nothing to be learned from it, as if the course of the illness was preordained once and for all. He muttered to himself, rather than to his patient, as he went up to the bed:

"Let's see where we are. . . ."

Maugras was wearing a pajama jacket with his initials, which must have been fetched for him from the Hôtel George V without his knowledge, but he was still deprived of his trousers. Audoire took a little hammer from his pocket and tapped Maugras's knees and elbows with it, after which he scratched the soles of his feet with a sharp instrument. He repeated the process two or three times, with a look of interest.

"Has he been given any Sintron?"

"Last night, at nine o'clock. I waited this morning till you'd seen him. I wanted to ask you, too, if I might give him a little orange juice. . . ."

The doctor shrugged his shoulders without replying, which meant, presumably, that he saw no objection, but that he thought it of no importance.

"Try a few passive arm and leg exercises this afternoon. . . . Not more than five minutes. . . . Three times a day. . . ."

He seemed to be avoiding Maugras's eyes, and the latter suddenly wondered if this was out of gaucherie and shyness. Without his hospital coat and cap, in some other setting, in a bus for instance or in the subway, he must look like some commonplace, dim little clerk.

Dealing with sickness, he was on his own ground. Dealing with a sick man, he felt less at his ease, and avoided contact. A joke flashed into Maugras's mind and he chuckled inwardly at it. Wouldn't the ideal thing, for some doctors, be sickness without any sick men?

"Has he tried to speak?"

"Not since I've come on duty."

"Say a few syllables. . . ."

And then Maugras was seized with panic, like Besson's patients when he visited them at the Broussais Hospital. Whereas he had been playing with ideas a minute ago, now the sweat broke out on his forehead. Hesitantly, he opened his mouth.

"Aaaaa . . ."

It was no longer the mewing sound he had made that morning, although he could not recognize his own voice.

"Don't be afraid. . . . Say something, whatever you like. . . ."

37

The first word that occurred to him was "Monsieur."

"Mon . . ."

Audoire nodded encouragingly to him.

The word came out almost normally.

"Mon-sieur . . ."

"You see! . . . You'll have to practice, even if it's discouraging to begin with. . . . You must use your left hand, too. . . . You're not left-handed? . . . It doesn't matter . . . you'll soon get used to it. . . . Nurse, will you give him a pencil and some paper? . . . See that he doesn't wear himself out, though. . . ."

He got up from the edge of the bed where he had been sitting, and went to the door. As he was about to open it, he turned around and seemed surprised to meet an almost hostile stare.

"I'll see you again this evening," he said quickly.

Mlle Blanche, too, seemed surprised and disappointed. Something had happened which puzzled her, which she could not define, and she found it hard to resume her smile and her cheerful manner.

She, too, felt that for no apparent reason, at a moment's notice, Maugras had become hostile.

How could he explain to them that they were disturbing him, that he had resigned himself, that he did not want their encouragements, that what had happened to him was bound to happen, that he accepted it, and with relief?

And since that was the case, what was the good of making him ridiculous in his own eyes by forcing him to bleat *"Mon-sieur. . . ."*

All they had succeeded in doing was making him want to cry.

But he would shed no tears in front of her, or anybody else. He chose rather to stare grimly at the ceiling.

CHAPTER THREE

He was allowed no respite and this irritated him, for he was convinced it was intentional, that it formed part of his treatment. It was rather like being in a spa, such as Vichy or Aix-les-Bains, where men who are usually touchy about their independence submit to a prescribed routine, and to the use of childish devices to relieve their boredom, from the glasses of water, measured to the nearest ounce, that they have to drink at some special kiosk, to the soft music played in lounges, the bridge tournaments and so forth, and the well-nigh compulsory visits to the casino.

They were doing their utmost to stop him from thinking. Whenever he was lying quietly in his bed with eyes half closed, amusing himself with his thoughts or his memories, Mlle Blanche would look at her watch, bending her head in a way that he was getting to know, and then he'd have to have another injection, or be turned over, or else, as had happened shortly before twelve o'clock, given a drink of orange juice.

He had wondered how she would manage this, seeing that his jaws and throat were as helpless as his arm and his leg.

Smiling, apparently convinced that he would take it as a

joke, she had brought a curious-looking cup fitted with a ceramic tube.

"The feeding cup! You'll see how convenient it is. Tomorrow you shall have some purée out of a spoon. . . ."

Still the same cheerful tone, which he could meet only with indifference and irritation, although he hated himself for this. He managed to swallow most of the orange juice, without enjoyment.

Afterwards, she turned the handle that raised the upper half of his bed. Another regulated the lower half. From time to time she changed his position. He was practically sitting up now, and for the first time he no longer had the urinal between his legs, although he still had a rubber sheet over his mattress, like a baby.

The sunshine was like spring sunshine. The air, filtered through the slots in the ventilators, was growing warm and smelled of motor oil, because of the traffic on the Route Nationale 7.

In his new position, he could see not only the mansard roof and windows of the right wing, but the tall windows on its first floor. They were uncurtained. He glimpsed white beds in a row, silhouettes moving slowly as they did along his corridor, and in contrast, the occasional bustling figure of some nurse. Men sat in chairs, strikingly motionless. Some smoked their pipes in silence, merely staring in front of them.

Were they, too, hemiplegics? Or was the right wing reserved for mental cases? He would find out later. He had plenty of time. The window closest to the central wing, where he lay, was the only one open, and an intern, sitting at a light-colored desk, was chatting with a girl, a nurse or a student, who burst out laughing from time to time and came to flick her cigarette ash out into the courtyard.

Mlle Blanche told him, as the trolleys with the huge saucepans went past in the corridor:

"I'm going to leave you by yourself for a moment. It's my

lunch time. You needn't worry. I shan't be far away. . . ."

Into his left hand, the one that functioned almost normally, she slipped the small pear-shaped bulb of an electric bell.

"If you need anything, don't hesitate to press the button. . . ."

At last he was alone. Not that he particularly longed for solitude. On waking up that morning, for instance, he had experienced a twinge of anguish before discovering that Joséfa was lying on a cot beside his own. During the day, it gave him a certain satisfaction to have Mlle Blanche sitting by the window or coming and going in the room.

Perhaps they were going to have to spend a long time shut up together, in an intimacy such as even married couples do not always know. He liked seeing her young, cheerful face, he was glad she was pretty and aware of her prettiness.

He would have disliked to remain cooped up with an elderly woman such as the matron, or some others he saw passing by, who gave the impression of performing an irksome duty or earning an arduous livelihood. It was his friend Besson who had chosen Mlle Blanche for him, and he felt sure that this choice also formed part of his cure.

That was precisely what embarrassed him and clouded his pleasure. People tried to think for him. Or rather, they imagined he must be thinking this or that, because it was taken for granted that on a specific day after his attack, a hemiplegic would be going through a certain stage, experiencing a certain state of mind.

He felt sure the order had been given:

"Above all, don't let him get withdrawn into himself. . . ."

They assumed that he was longing to die, whereas that was only a half-truth. He didn't care whether he died or not. Death, indeed, as he envisaged it, had its horrid side. The smell, in particular. And what was called the laying out. Decomposition. He felt mortified at the thought that he would inflict such unpleasantness on others. And finally, he had to

41

admit, there was the coffin. Although he knew perfectly well that he would no longer be aware of anything, he suffered from claustrophobia in anticipation.

As soon as he could speak, if he ever did recover his speech, or as soon as he had learned to write with his left hand, he would have to state his wish to be cremated. He refused to be surrounded with flowers, which give out a rather sinister smell in a death chamber. No candles, no draperies, no branches of box standing in holy water.

The ideal thing would be, when he had breathed his last, to be taken to the crematorium by unknown professionals, unseen by any of his acquaintances.

He accepted death, but not its trappings. It mattered little to him whether the end came in a few hours, on the fourth or fifth day as with Félix Artaud, or in a few years, as had been the case with Jublin.

He thought about it calmly, without terror or sentimentality. Was that what they were striving to prevent? Did they go still further and did Audoire, who scarcely looked at him, know him better than he seemed to?

This was very important. Important to himself. Not to anyone else. For other people, for the doctors, the staff at the hospital, his friends of the Grand Véfour, his colleagues on the newspaper, it would merely be an incident. The doctors would declare: "There was nothing we could do. . . ."

The two Italian maids would get the room ready for another of the Professor's patients, who might now be waiting his turn. His friends would murmur:

"Poor fellow!"

They would ask, as he himself had done on similar occasions:

"How old was he, exactly?"

To the under-forties it would seem quite normal, after all, that he should depart this life at fifty-four. Older men would feel a twinge of anxiety, which would soon pass.

As for Lina, she would turn to the whisky bottle in her despair, and, as had so often happened, the hotel doctor would be sent for to give her an injection and plunge her into a long sleep.

She would grow used to it. He was not indispensable to her. He wondered if his influence had not, indeed, been disastrous to her, and if she would not be happier and better balanced once she was widowed.

Only one of the three women who had played a part in his life had emerged unscathed: Hélène Portal, a journalist who still worked for him, and who had refused to marry him.

Anxious to preserve her individuality, she had never consented to live with him completely, and for years they each had a separate flat, with a separate group of friends.

This was the way he needed to think, deliberately, with nobody watching him or trying to distract him from his interior monologue. He was not searching his own conscience. Nor was he trying to draw up a balance sheet. It seemed at times as if he were glancing haphazard through a picture book, regardless of chronological order.

That morning, shortly before his orange juice and his feeding cup, he had visualized his seventeen-year-old self on the Quai Bérigny, at Fécamp. He had then just grown a mustache, which he was to keep for only a few weeks.

It was in autumn, late October or early November, for the Newfoundland fishing smacks, most of them still sailing boats, were beginning to come in.

He was wearing a gray overcoat flecked with red, bought ready-made and of poor quality woolen cloth, of which he was none the less rather proud.

The sky was heavy with rain, as it often is in that region, and the harbor water was almost black. Trucks stood along the quayside and cod was being unloaded, in bulk, the smell of it pervading the whole town.

Sailors who had landed that morning had gone off on the

arms of their wives, who had been watching for them from the end of the jetty, waving handkerchiefs as soon as the boat entered the channel.

Not all of them had wives and children. Many, who had spent months on the Newfoundland banks, were soon sitting around tables in the harbor cafés, drinking laced coffee or spirits.

Why did this picture, rather than another, flash into his mind? It was as flat and dull as a cheap postcard and had the same pitiless precision. He could picture every house front, the names painted over shops and restaurants, and the building, somewhat larger than the rest, that housed the offices of M. Firmin Remage, the shipbuilder for whom his father worked.

It amused him to hunt for the date: 1923! It was five years since the end of the war, ten since his mother's death, and a year and a half since he had left the Lycée Guy-de-Maupassant and gone into the office of Maître Raguet, the notary in the Rue Saint-Etienne.

For the past few months, moreover, he had been the Fécamp correspondent of the *Phare du Havre*, and he had in his pocket a press card with his photograph, from which he derived a certain pride.

That morning his father was standing between the trucks and the schooner that had come in with the tide, the *Sainte-Thérèse,* he remembered the name. All M. Remage's ships were called after saints. With a purple pencil in his hand, his father was counting the bales of cod that were being loaded onto the trucks.

If he happened to be standing on the quay too, instead of in the lawyer's office, it was because an accident had occurred on board the ship while it was still on the high seas. A man had disappeared in suspicious circumstances, and now the police were investigating on board.

He could see it all, the masts and the yards, the black

shapes of motor trawlers moored side by side; he fancied he could still hear the sound of hammering at the wooden hull of a boat being built on the Quai de la Marne.

His father had a faded blond mustache. He had the gentle, grave expression of a man conscious of fulfilling his allotted task. For paddling about in the slimy mud of the quay, he wore clogs, polished with blacking like shoes.

He was not M. Remage's chief assistant but one of the humblest cogs in the firm, employed in the bookkeeping department, and he earned less than the seamen.

René stood by a bollard, waiting for the police inspector to finish questioning the skipper so that he could interview him too.

He was young then. Apart from his appendicitis, he had never been ill.

Now that morning, in particular, he had suddenly been overwhelmed by a depression that seemed to him irremediable. He looked at the little gray town, the shop signs, the schooners and trawlers that he had seen in the docks ever since his childhood, the shipbuilding yard on the other side of the lock, the sea in the distance, unconcernedly swelling and sinking, and finally at his father, who bore his humility or his mediocrity with smug tranquillity, and in the space of one second he discovered the pointlessness of everything.

A meaningless world surrounded him and he felt that he no longer belonged to it, that perhaps he had never belonged to it. He observed it no longer from within but from outside, like a stranger.

"What's the point?"

He felt convinced, now, after all these years, that he had asked himself that question in those terms. What was the point? What had been the point of working so hard to learn things he could never assimilate, since he was to leave school before his final examination? What was the point of those dreary hours spent working for Maître Raguet, who spoke to him only in harsh contemptuous terms? What was the point of sending those reports to the *Phare du Havre*, where they'd be cut down by three quarters and where he'd be told, invariably:

"Shorter! You must learn to make them shorter!"

What was the point of living?

Several times since then he had experienced the same sense of emptiness, even when he was making the greatest efforts and achieving the most tangible success.

What was the point of living? What was the point of getting together at the Grand Véfour on the first Tuesday of every month with a dozen people whom he called his friends, and who meant nothing to him?

Each month one of the party drew up the menu and settled the bill. Apart from Dora Ziffer, the only woman among them, who indeed had joined them only by accident, they were all prominent people of considerable means. They had met halfway along the road to success, some of them still at the outset.

If they met so regularly, was it not in order to reassure one another, to measure, week by week, the distance they had covered? Did not each of them secretly make comparisons between himself and his companions? So much so that they competed as to who should provide the rarest and most costly meal?

In the secluded atmosphere of the mezzanine dining room, they congratulated one another, with copious shoulder-slapings and embracings.

"Well, old fellow! How's Yolande? And how's your play going? . . ."

Or your novel. Or your business. Or else the country house you're building, your villa at Cannes or Saint-Tropez.

Three of them had already gone. From now on, the ranks would thin faster, for they were all reaching the dangerous age, and during these noisy lunch parties, for all their good

46

humor and their often childish jokes, they would be watching one another and thinking:

"He's aged, all of a sudden. He won't last very long. . . ."

Had his turn come to leave an empty place at table?

"He'd been working too hard. Burning the candle at both ends. . . ."

"Just lately he seemed to be in a hurry to live, as if he'd had a premonition. . . ."

Besson would inevitably offer a medical opinion.

"His blood pressure was too high. I used to warn him. I begged him to worry less about the paper. . . ."

"What's going to become of Lina?"

They would exchange knowing looks. They all knew that Lina was unhappy, and slowly drinking herself to death.

Would they discuss Lina?

"Do you think he loved her?"

"At all events there was nothing he wouldn't do for her. . . ."

"I wonder if she wasn't always rather unbalanced. . . ."

"She's a good one. . . ."

"He tried to make her over, the way he wanted her, same as he had done with Marcelle. . . ."

"By the way, what's become of Marcelle?"

"She's on tour. . . . She doesn't seem to get any older. . . ."

"She can't be far from forty-five. . . ."

"Fifty-two. She's two years younger than he is. . . . I still remember the birth of their child. . . . They were very poor and the baby slept in a drawer because they couldn't afford a cradle. . . ."

"A girl, wasn't it?"

"She was born crippled. . . ."

"He never cared to talk about her much. . . ."

The conversation would not go on much longer on that note. They would soon change the subject, and discuss the

47

wine or the dishes in front of them, Julien Marelle's play or Clabaud's latest speech, or the forthcoming elections to the Académie Française; Besson d'Argoulet was being considered as a candidate on the strength of his three books on Flaubert, Zola, and Maupassant: he was already a member of the Academy of Medicine.

Was the effort of living really worth while? Living for the sake of what? For his paper, for a couple of weeklies that pandered to the worst public taste, for the radio station of whose administrative council he was chairman?

For his Sundays at Arneville, which were like a less intimate version of the Grand Véfour lunches, except that there was more talk there of politics and finance?

For his flat in the Hôtel George V, as impersonal, for all its luxury, as a railway station or an airport?

He took advantage of Mlle Blanche's absence and his solitude to continue skimming through his mental picture book, and once again he saw the beach and harbor of Fécamp, on the morning the *Sainte-Thérèse* docked; the scene was in black and white, or rather in black and gray. There were colored pictures too, but it was this one, the picture of the Quai Bérigny, which haunted him most today, perhaps because it was the most significant and the one which, despite the lapse of years, retained an intimate connection with his present life.

His life? If his lips had obeyed him better, he'd have been tempted to smile. Not necessarily an ironical smile, but one of affection for the young man in the shabby overcoat who had grown a mustache in order to look more important.

The scene seemed quite close at hand. Time had passed quickly, and he wanted to take stock of what was left of it.

In the main ward, people were eating. It was rather impressive, for nobody spoke and the only sound was the scraping of spoons and forks against plates. The nurses, on the other

48

hand, in their private sitting room, were presumably chatter-
ing, talking about their patients perhaps, and since he was a
man in the public eye, a Paris VIP, as it were, Mlle Blanche
would probably be cross-questioned about him.

Would she complain that he was unco-operative and un-
grateful? Would she produce intimate details about him,
about his body for instance, or his behavior?

What's the point? as he had already reflected on the quay
at Fécamp.

And yet he felt quite comfortable under the sheet; a sun-
beam had reached one corner of the room, and puffs of air
drifted in through the ventilator.

Unfortunately, it soon came to an end. He recognized her
step. She paused for a moment to light a cigarette, possibly
to put on the cheerful expression that formed part of the
treatment.

As she came in she asked laughingly:

"Did you miss me? I hope you didn't need anything?"

Without asking his leave, she removed the towel that covered the urinal, raised the sheet, and slid the receptacle between his thighs. Even this no longer depended on him!

The first session of passive exercises ordered by Professor
Audoire was a disappointment. He had not expected a mir-
acle, nor any spectacular form of therapy, but all that happened was that she lifted his paralyzed arm a few inches and
then laid it back on the bed, and did the same with his fore-
arm, then his wrist, and finally his lifeless leg. At first his eyes
involuntarily betrayed his fear, a purely animal fear of the
unknown, and Mlle Blanche reassured him:

"Leave it to me. . . . I promise it won't hurt you. . . ."

She sat down on the edge of the bed and when she dealt
with his right leg his penis was uncovered. This embarrassed him all the more as, without any trace of erotic fancy,

49

probably for purely mechanical reasons, he had a partial erection. She appeared not to notice. Like a drill instructor she counted the movements:

". . . five . . . six . . . seven . . . eight . . ."

At twelve, she stopped and pulled up the sheet again.

"That's enough for today. . . . You're not tired?"

He shook his head.

"Shall I give you a pencil and paper?"

He accepted meekly, without enthusiasm, without delight.

He would do whatever was required of him, but he put no faith in it. If only they would stop treating him like a child! She began again with exaggerated cheerfulness, while he stared at her with curiosity.

"We're going to have a little talk together. I shall ask the questions and you shall write the answers. You'll see how quickly you get used to writing left-handed. . . ."

She laid a writing pad on the bed, and held out a pencil.

"Since yesterday, flowers have kept coming to the office for you. I didn't want them to be brought up without consulting you. Some patients like flowers in their room, and others don't. I warn you there are a great many, and they must have cost a small fortune. What'll you decide?"

The first pencil stroke he made was clumsy and crooked, the second already firmer, and he managed to trace, in a stiff scrawl, the word: NO.

"Would you like me to get the cards that were sent with the flowers?"

He had no wish to know who had sent them. Since the previous day he had not once glanced at the six yellow carnations his wife had brought. But as Mlle Blanche insisted, and was not satisfied with a shake of the head, he once more traced the same word on the paper.

"What shall I do with the cards? Shall I keep them for you for later on?"

He hesitated, began by writing *JE,* then feeling too lazy to put down a whole sentence he crossed out the *JE* and summed up his thought with a single word: *FICHE.*

This meant: *Je m'en fiche* (I couldn't care less).

She gave a little frown at first, and then laughed.

"What a strange man you are. . . . One doesn't know how to approach you. . . . Are you always like that? . . ."

He was listening attentively, perturbed at first at hearing on the stairway the same clatter of footsteps as at six-thirty in the morning, when the day shift came on. This time the steps were accompanied by raised voices, and his instinctive fear was like the terror of a dog on a chain. He thought he had discovered the hospital routine, and this unexpected din nonplussed him.

"It's visiting time," she explained. "Patients can see their friends and relations every afternoon at two o'clock. . . ."

Men, women, and children coming from the outside world, with the voices and gestures of the outside world, invaded the floor, passed in front of his door, poured into the main ward. For the next two hours he was to hear them, to see them strolling down the corridor with their invalids.

"Let's go on with our little game. . . . Let's see! . . . What question shall I ask you? . . . Unless you'd like to ask *me* one. . . ."

No! This time he did not write the word, merely shook his head. In any case the questions he wanted to ask her would be too complicated. She would think he took some special interest in her, and that was not the case. He was interested in her in so far as her answers would reply to the questions he was asking himself.

While she had been sitting beside him on the bed, exercising his limbs, he had wondered, for instance, why she had chosen to spend her life among sick people.

He had seldom met a young woman with such freshness,

such poise, such zest for life. She gave the impression of moral as well as physical cleanliness. Her whole personality was healthy and direct.

She must be about twenty-five, the average age of the girls who worked on the newspaper, and he assessed the difference between these girls and his nurse.

The most attractive of them were somehow stamped by their profession, and lacked spontaneity, as if instead of following their natural rhythm they had adopted a foreign one. They were not in their right atmosphere. They lived a feverish, hectic, artificial life.

Why, and in what circumstances, had Mlle Blanche chosen her profession? He could understand how his daughter Colette had done so. But not Mlle Blanche. He wondered what her real personality was, where she went at half-past six in the evening, when she left Bicêtre in the little car he imagined her driving.

She wore no ring. Had she a fiancé or a lover? Did she live with her parents, or alone in a flat which she attended to after her day's work?

Did she go to the movies, to dance halls? Did she spend her evenings with other young people?

An absurd recollection flashed into his mind, while she put away the pencil and paper. Two years before, there had been a young typist on his newspaper, a girl with the long narrow face, commonplace and yet mysterious, that one sees on plaster images of the Virgin.

She bore the ludicrous name of Zulma, and she kept somewhat apart from the other girls in the office, who had nicknamed her the Madonna and teased her unmercifully.

Maugras knew her only through having dictated a few letters to her in the absence of his own secretary. He had looked at her with some curiosity, as he was now looking at the nurse, then had thought no more about her.

It was the fashion at that time, in the night clubs of Montmartre, to devote one or two evenings a week to strip-tease acts by amateurs. After a first night at some theater, some friends had taken him to one of these shows, and the third young woman to appear was none other than Zulma, the Madonna from his office, in her neat tailor-made suit, her face ashen, her light blue eyes staring into vacancy as she began taking off her clothes.

He had withdrawn into a dark corner so as not to embarrass her. The precaution was unnecessary, for she saw nothing, absorbed in the process of undressing, in the gradual uncovering of her pale body.

The previous numbers had aroused laughter. But, watching Zulma, everybody was silent, and the atmosphere was one of nervous tension, almost of anguish, as if they all felt that things might go wrong.

Her movements were awkward and jerky. From her vacant gaze, her expressionless face, it was clear that she was performing a kind of rite, almost a kind of exorcism, which concerned herself alone.

Maugras did not know if the girls were provided with certain accessories before being sent on the stage. At all events, when her last undergarments were removed, she was seen to be wearing at the base of her belly a triangle of silver sequins that looked like fish scales. A silvery star quivered at the tip of each of her breasts.

She had worked for a month longer at the newspaper office before handing in her notice. Nobody knew what had become of her.

Why did he think of Zulma, who had nothing in common with Mlle Blanche? He liked the nurse's mouth, her full lower lip, the curve of her cheek and the nape of her neck. But he did not desire her. If he had been capable of desiring a woman, in his condition, he would have chosen to make love with Joséfa, who would have resisted laughingly before parting her knees.

53

What might have happened if, seven or eight years earlier, he had met Mlle Blanche instead of Lina? Would he have noticed her in ordinary life? He asked himself the question, without really bothering to answer it.

The telephone rang in the corridor. Somebody unhooked the receiver. A woman's head appeared in the doorway.

"It's for you," the nurse was told.

He followed her with his gaze, thoughtfully, vexed with himself, and vexed at once again being roused from his introspection. She was back in a moment.

"Mme Maugras is on the phone, asking whether you'd like her to come and see you this afternoon. . . ."

Just the same as when he'd been in his office! She never went to see him there without calling up first to ask permission.

He lay still for a long moment, hesitating. Lina hated sickrooms, funerals, even weddings. She thought duty required her to come to Bicêtre, because it was the proper thing to visit a sick husband.

The previous evening, although she had not asked permission from him, she had got it from the doctors. If she came back today she would form the habit, and she would turn up at the hospital every afternoon.

Finally he shook his head.

"You're sure?"

She seemed surprised, somewhat embarrassed.

"In that case, I shall tell her you're feeling tired. . . . No! That might worry her. . . . That you're expecting the Professor at any minute. . . ."

When she came back, Mlle Blanche was absorbed in thought. Sitting down in her chair beside the window, she looked out for a long time before asking him:

"Have you been married long?"

He showed her five fingers of his left hand, then two of them.

"Seven years?"

Had she noticed, the day before, that his wife had been drinking? Had she, being a nurse, realized that something was wrong, that Lina's feverishness was not natural, that the look in her eyes betrayed a latent unease, as though she felt that she belonged nowhere?

After several minutes' silence, the nurse asked another question, still looking out over the courtyard.

"Do you love her?"

Had she forgotten that he did not have the use of his vocal chords? His silence surprised her and, when she remembered to turn toward him, he nodded once again.

Actually, it was true and yet not true. Neither Lina nor he knew how things stood between them. Only two months previously, after a supper party to which they had been together —which seldom happened nowadays—they had had a violent quarrel.

She had been drunk. He himself had drunk more than usual, although far less than she had, and he thought he was being quite calm.

Never mind what they had said to each other. The meaning of the words did not matter. Each of them was convinced of having ruined his life for the sake of the other. Lina, however, interpreted her thoughts differently, accusing herself of having made him suffer, which was an indirect form of self-pity.

Next morning he had gone off to his newspaper as usual. He never went home for lunch. Normally they did not meet again until the evening, in some bar or restaurant, only returning to the hotel if they had to dress.

By eight o'clock that evening she was prostrate in bed, with the hotel nurse sitting beside her in the darkened room. They never referred to that night again. None the less the word *divorce* had been spoken for the first time and, for the first time too, he had glimpsed hatred in his wife's eyes.

55

"Because you run a big newspaper and people lick your boots, you think you're a great man and are entitled to do whatever you like. . . ."

She had chosen the most wounding words. A few minutes later she was groveling at his knees, asking for forgiveness and accusing herself of every sort of sin. . . .

On nights such as these, the slightest thing brings one to the verge of suicide. He might perhaps have killed himself if he had had a weapon within reach. Life seemed as pointless and absurd as on that morning at Fécamp.

Ever since that gray morning when the *Sainte-Thérèse* had docked, he had worked with such fierce intensity as to alarm Besson d'Argoulet, who advised him, at each consultation, to take his work less seriously and to delegate some of his responsibilities.

What would be left to him if he hadn't taken things seriously, even without believing in them?

It was like Mlle Blanche's question: "Do you love her?"

He could only reply yes. Perhaps it was the truth. Perhaps that was all the love of which a man was capable.

For the past two months they had almost shunned one another, Lina and he, they had avoided being alone together and, above all, they had avoided talking of themselves. She had begun to drink more heavily. He worried about it, dreading a new fit of depression which might be more serious than the first. The look in her eyes terrified him, the look of a hunted creature or one in the grip of an obsession.

She seemed to be evading a thought which she was desperately concealing from him. And hadn't he, too, all his life, been evading something? Ever since Fécamp. Ever since for the first time he had felt emptiness surrounding him.

Was Mlle Blanche still thinking about Lina as she sat there in silent reverie?

They were both motionless for a long moment, during which he lost consciousness of the comings and goings in the corridor, noisy though these were. He was very far away. He could not have said what he was thinking about. He had forgotten he was lying in a hospital bed, and it was with a start that, through blurred eyes, he saw Besson, elegant and self-assured, come into the room.

"Well, how are we today? Depressed?"

The doctor's eyes pursued his, trying to probe him.

"Your wife called me up as I was leaving my office. . . . She was worried by your refusing to see her today. . . . I reassured her. . . . I explained that for the first week you'd have your ups and downs. . . ."

They were at it again! They knew, day by day, what his mental state as well as his physical state must be. Why didn't they write it down beforehand on the chart at the foot of the bed, at which Besson merely cast a casual glance before coming to sit down beside him?

Mlle Blanche, who had risen when the Professor came in, waited a minute in case he needed her, then discreetly left the room.

"Let's get down to business, old fellow. . . ."

Besson uttered this remark with the bogus joviality of some boulevard comedian, and Maugras looked at him as he had looked at Audoire, with the same cold penetration, discovering that the great man, with all his medals, was after all merely a figure of fun.

CHAPTER FOUR

"You're well enough now for me to have a serious talk with you. . . . I had a telephone call from Audoire just now. . . ."

From the moment Besson appeared, Maugras was aware that he had come with a definite purpose, and these words confirmed his intuition. The two doctors had telephoned one another about him. Lina, too, had rung up Besson. There was a conspiratorial world about him to which they all belonged, including the matron and Mlle Blanche. As for him, he lay inert in his bed, at the mercy of people who compared notes about him, discussed his case, and passed judgment on him.

Besson had played the funny man, just now; he had made his entrance as the hearty, back-slapping type. Now he assumed an anxious tone, with a touch of gruffness, and the whole thing had been planned beforehand. It was all a pre-arranged scene, in which he had promised his colleague that they should each play his own part!

Once again, this was how parents treated children! When persuasion did not work, the mother would say to her husband:

"You try! You've got more authority than I have. Perhaps if you shake him up a bit . . ."

Besson was shaking him up.

"If you were a fool, I shouldn't speak to you as I'm going to do. With some patients we have to cheat, because they're incapable of understanding. That's not the case with you. . . ."

He felt scarcely any curiosity about the rest of the speech. He was looking at the man himself, with fresh eyes, as though he had not known him for thirty years.

"Audoire isn't pleased with you. . . . He feels that you're not co-operating, that you're withdrawing into yourself, that you persist in shutting yourself up in your illness. . . . And yet you must know that it's difficult, if not impossible, for a doctor to cure a patient against his will. . . ."

When was he being lied to and when was he being told the truth?

"Of course I understand your attitude better than Audoire, because I've known you longer than he has. . . . I can easily imagine the repercussions of a traumatic experience such as you've had on a man as intensely active as yourself. . . ."

He was wrong about that for a start, yet it did not prevent him from being pleased with himself and spinning out his phrases as if he were making a speech to the Academy of Medicine.

"What you must get into your head, you see, is that you're not the first person to be in this situation. . . . Audoire has seen plenty of others, in this very room, and he knows all about a patient's reactions. . . . Admit that you've not believed what Audoire and myself have been telling you. . . ."

What had they told him so far? That he would not die. That he would recover. That he wouldn't be a helpless invalid for the rest of his days. That in a few weeks or a few months at most he would resume his place among the human beings leading their hectic lives on the other side of the window.

But he didn't care!

"I explained to you briefly yesterday the difference between one kind of hemiplegia and another. I'm convinced that you've got some worry at the back of your mind, none the less. . . . Do you imagine, by any chance, that you've got a cerebral tumor? . . ."

Besson waited for his reaction and, as he did not stir, assumed the knowing look of someone who has guessed right.

"That's it, isn't it? I bet you've been thinking of our friend Jublin. . . ."

To be quits with him, Maugras shook his head.

"Jublin's case was completely different from yours. . . . Do you want me to give you technical details? . . ."

Once again, no! He didn't want it to go on any longer. What was the point, since he'd accepted the same fate as their friend? He barely listened, he heard Besson's voice, the words he uttered, without paying attention to them, and whole sentences got lost because he made no attempt to give them a meaning.

"Listen to me, René. . . . I won't say we weren't anxious about you the first day, and even the first night. . . . Everything depended on a certain number of tests and analyses. . . . That was why Audoire was eager to have you close by, although you'd have been more at home at Auteuil. . . ."

Far from it! He'd not have been at home anywhere.

"Your pulse rate was sixty, which was reassuring, and if it interests you, it's now sixty-eight, which is normal. . . . As for your blood pressure, it hasn't risen above twenty, which is scarcely higher than your normal blood pressure. . . .

"I'm boring you, but it's essential that you listen to me, so that you'll have no doubts left in your mind. . . .

"For two days, you knew nothing about what was going on around you. . . . After that you had only vague or distorted impressions. . . . So I'll tell you briefly what we did. . . .

"First we injected a phial of Neutraphylline, and then we proceeded to clear the respiratory tracts. . . . All this is the usual treatment. . . . The object is to prevent congestion of the lungs. . . . To guard against any risk of broncho-pneumonia we administered a million units of penicillin. . . ."

Maugras remained remote.

"Your cholesterol is normal at two sixty, better than mine, which is over two eighty. . . . As for your glucemia . . ."

He had completely ceased to follow, and Besson would have been astonished to learn why he was staring at him so intently. Actually he was trying to rediscover, in the professional bigwig of today, the young medical student he had once known.

Once again a picture flashed into his mind, like the one of Fécamp, except that this picture was in color and in motion, with some blurred passages as in amateur movies.

His memory was less certain with regard to its date. 1928, 1929? He could have sworn that they were still living in the Rue des Dames, his first wife Marcelle and himself, in their little room on the fourth floor of the Hôtel Beauséjour. It belonged to what he thought of as the Batignolles period, because of the nearby boulevard. His successive homes were the best landmarks for fixing events in time.

And yet he had the impression that his daughter was already born, that he had even spoken to Besson about her malformation. Now two or three weeks before Colette's birth they had moved into lodgings in the Rue des Abbesses, close to the Atelier Theater, where Marcelle had gone on playing small parts until her pregnancy made it impossible.

It didn't matter. He had been writing news items for the *Boulevard*, which was a paper chiefly concerned with the theater. Actors, journalists, night prowlers used to meet in

61

those days, after the show, in the Brasserie Graf, next door to the Moulin Rouge. The room was noisy and brightly lit, and he always sat in the same place, close to the door, from which he could watch people coming and going along the Boulevard de Clichy.

Julien Marelle, whose first play had just been put on, had introduced him to a young lawyer, Georges Clabaud, son of a State Councilor, who was at that time articled to a famous solicitor. Clabaud, who was later to become fat and chubby, was then very thin, and already showed a mordant, ironic wit, passing ferocious, and almost always amusing, judgment on all and sundry.

And through Clabaud . . .

It amused him to retrace the sequence of chance events, while keeping his eyes fixed on Besson d'Argoulet. What he was privately calling to mind was the formation of the Grand Véfour group.

Clabaud lived at his father's, at the far end of the Boulevard Raspail, an irregularly shaped house with unexpected staircases and mysterious corners, and passages interrupted for no apparent reason by steps up or down. The young man had a low-ceilinged room on the mezzanine floor where he entertained his friends.

Somebody, Maugras did not know who, had brought along one evening a medical student from Bichat, whom Clabaud later introduced to his friends at Graf's.

"You'll see! He's an ambitious fellow, for all his quiet ways, and I'm convinced he'll get ahead. In any case it's just as well to have a medico as a friend. . . ."

That evening they'd been eating onion soup at the far end of the room. Mistinguett had been sitting at the next table with a man who looked like a lawyer or notary; after the meal he had scribbled columns of figures on the back of the menu card.

Besson had been a good-looking man even in those days,

slighter than today and without such a fine presence, but with the same way of listening to his own words, with an occasional pause to make them more impressive.

By and by, if he was left in peace, Maugras would try to reconstruct the whole development of the Grand Véfour group. The period had been a complex one. Changes had been swifter and more unpredictable in the lives of each of them. They were all at the start of their careers, and now one, now the other took the lead. The rest would watch him enviously. Sometimes they lost sight of one another, and then met again by chance two or three years later.

There was as yet no question of stability. Every man's destiny was still uncertain, and among those whom Maugras knew at this period many had dropped out, suddenly disappearing from circulation just as Zulma had done.

Besson d'Argoulet had certainly not been as smooth, as impressive as today. But whereas he had a clear picture of Mistinguett and her lawyer at the next table, he could not visualize Besson precisely. Probably because they had aged together, he could only see him as a man of sixty.

". . . As for the injection, apart from sedatives to make you sleep at night, what you've been given, if you want to know . . ."

But he had no desire to know.

". . . what you've been given, if you want to know, is an anticoagulant called Sintron, intended to prevent the formation of further blood clots. . . ."

He did not hear the rest, for Besson insisted on telling him the result of the encephalogram and the arteriograph.

"So much for the clinical picture. If there's anything you've not understood, or if you've any questions, I'll give you a paper and pencil. . . . No? . . . Just as you like! . . . You do believe that I'm telling you the truth, don't you, and that there's definitely no question of a cerebral tumor? . . ."

They were on different planes. This was a dialogue between

63

deaf men, in so far as it could be called a dialogue. Besson was talking about tumors and arteriographs whereas René, if he'd had a question to ask, if it had been possible to ask any man, even a friend, such a question, would have inquired:

"Are you satisfied with yourself?"

Wasn't that, in spite of appearances, far more important than anything else? Was a man like Besson d'Argoulet at peace with himself? Did he feel that he stood on stable and solid ground? Did he believe in the importance that he claimed for himself, in the reality of his achievement, his lectures at Broussais, his reputation in the world of medicine, his decorations, his flat with its exquisite furnishings and its works of art, his position in the fashionable world of Paris?

The question might be put to other people too, and not merely to the members of the Grand Véfour group.

Weren't all their activities, like his own, merely a form of escape? Did they not feel, if only occasionally, a sense of having betrayed something?

Betrayed what? He did not know, and this was not the time to try to elucidate so vital a problem.

"After which, let's get down to your state of mind. . . ."

Was Besson at last going to consider the issue that really mattered? Maugras had a gleam of hope, and also of surprise, for this would alter the picture of his friend which he had been mentally tracing. Hardly a flattering portrait. He was convinced that Besson, as soon as ever he set foot in Paris, had had a precise idea of his career, of the goal to be reached and the means to be used, that he had been resolved to do anything to that end.

His people were not rich, although better off, more bourgeois than the Maugras family. His father was a country doctor at Virieux, in the Isère. Pierre was educated at the lycée at Moulins before entering the medical faculty in Paris.

He was a brilliant student, as they say, and he became the

favorite pupil of Elémir Gaude, a famous psychiatrist of the time, Charcot's successor at the Salpêtrière Hospital.

Was it purely by chance that he married his boss's daughter? Among all the girls he met, was she really the one he loved? Could he swear that no element of calculation had entered into his choice?

At the age of thirty-two, thanks to his father-in-law, he had become departmental head first at Bichat Hospital and then at Broussais Hospital, and he had switched over from psychiatry to internal medicine. Psychiatry was unremunerative; as a medical specialist he had almost immediately acquired a clientele in the fashionable world.

Was it accident, again, that he was present at all dress rehearsals, and gradually won himself a place in the smart set of Paris? Who knows? Perhaps it was with an ulterior motive that, long ago, he had attached himself to their group? Among those who met around the tables in the Brasserie Graf, surely there might be some future celebrities?

And if, at thirty-four, he became one of the youngest faculty members with tenure in France, if three years later he obtained a chair, and finally, on Gaude's death, he was elected to the Academy of Medicine—did it have nothing to do with his father-in-law?

In René's mind, as he lay inert in bed with his eyes still fixed on his companion, it was not the facts that mattered, nor the intentions. What he would have liked to know was this: was his friend aware of them? It was a question of sincerity, and also of clear-sightedness.

He had often asked himself this about other people, particularly about politicians, when he was still leading a normal life. According to his mood, he had found different answers, but the question had not seemed as urgent as it did now.

"A hemiplegic's initial reaction, as Audoire could tell you more authoritatively than I can, is one of more or less complete depression, the almost certain expectation of death or, if that does not occur within the first few days, of permanent invalidism. . . . Immobilized, often deprived of speech, the sick man imagines himself doomed to remain forever cut off from the world. . . . Admit that you've thought that yourself. . . ."

It was true, but not in the way Besson expressed it.

"The result, whether in the case of an educated man or a more simple-minded individual, is a kind of mistrust of the doctor and of everybody else around him. . . . We might call that the first phase, the most painful one. . . . It's vital to come through it as fast as possible. . . . And that's where you're disappointing me. . . . It seems to me and to Audoire, and to those who have been looking after you . . ."

All those, in short, who surrounded him with a sort of freemasonry, who simulated cheerfulness and confidence while observing him with cold detachment, who whispered behind doors, passed one another mysterious reports and exchanged telephone calls!

". . . it seems to us, I repeat, that you're not trying to get well, that you are being hostile to us. . . ."

Not hostile. Indifferent. Even that wasn't the right word. He saw them differently from the way they saw themselves. His problems were no longer the same as theirs. He had gone beyond them.

It would have been pointless to try to communicate, and the little comedy that Besson had been putting on for his benefit, while Mlle Blanche smoked a cigarette somewhere or other, perhaps in the courtyard, unless she was standing behind the door, that little comedy had the opposite effect to that which they had anticipated.

The more Besson talked, the more remote Maugras felt from them.

They were tackling the problem from the wrong end, be-

66

ginning in the washroom at the Grand Véfour, without suspecting that it was necessary to go much further back, as far back as Fécamp. Just as, in Besson's case, it would doubtless be necessary to look in his native Allier for the roots of the man he had now become.

"I'm not saying there are not special cases, or that all patients react in identical fashion. . . . None the less it's useful for a fellow like you to know what the effects of your illness are likely to be. . . . It'll help you to get rid of the mistaken ideas you're undoubtedly fostering. . . .

"Anguish and depression then, in the first stage, and often, too, to give you the whole picture, a sense of inescapable fatality. . . . *It was bound to happen.* . . . Almost all patients go through this crisis, convinced that they're doomed, in spite of the doctor's reassurances. . . .

"In many cases this certainty is accompanied by a sense of relief, or of morbid resignation. . . . I shouldn't tell you all this, you understand, if you were an ordinary patient. . . ."

Maugras resented the accuracy, or rather the near-accuracy, the apparent accuracy of his analysis. If it all seemed true at first glance, it was untrue nevertheless as far as he was concerned.

"I've known cases where the sick man considered that he was undergoing a well-deserved punishment, that he was paying for sins he had committed. . . ."

They were still trying to do his thinking for him. They were searching his heart. They were trying to lay bare the darkest corners of his consciousness.

"So now you know that you're not an exception and that you're following the usual curve of your complaint. . . . And the time has come to stop wallowing in gloom and to start co-operating with us. . . .

"You've had orange juice. . . . Two or three days more,

and you'll practically be taking normal food. . . . Those passive exercises that must have seemed so childish are none the less an important step toward rehabilitation. . . .

"From now on, if you really wanted to, you could speak whole sentences, though you might get some of the words confused. . . .

"I'm not saying you won't need patience, but by next Monday you might be surprised to find yourself standing up by your bedside. . . .

"It's essential to believe in it, to have some trust in us, instead of looking incredulously at us as you now do. It's up to you to decide that you're going to be as you were before. . . ."

Poor Besson! Beads of sweat were gleaming on his brow and he had forgotten to light his cigarette.

"About the eighth day, usually, progress becomes noticeable, often spectacular. Until then, I'm asking you, both as your friend and as your doctor, to trust Audoire and myself. . . ."

He rose as if exhausted, and reverted to his initial tone as he concluded:

"That's all I wanted to say to you, old man. . . . All our friends are waiting to be allowed to come and see you, and they're constantly calling me up for news of you. . . . You think you've been deserted. . . . Nothing of the sort. . . . You see there are lots of us who rely on you, Lina first of all, who needs you badly, as you know. . . ."

He held out his hand with a smile. He seemed moved. He probably was. Actors too feel genuine emotion as they recite their parts.

What was the point of distressing him? Maugras drew his left arm from under the sheet and held out his own hand.

"I won't ask you to make any promises, but I beg you not to let yourself go deliberately. . . ."

Deliberately!

As he went out, Besson had lingered for a moment with his hand on the doorknob. He'd had his back turned, but René had known, without seeing his face, that he was out of countenance. He had been vexed with himself; he still was. If he had been able to, he would have called back his friend and apologized for his behavior.

There was no discussion in the corridor between the doctor and Mlle Blanche, who promptly came back into the room. A gesture, a glance exchanged as they met would have been quite enough.

For a moment she seemed to search Maugras's face for some confirmation of defeat. She, too, was disappointed. She bustled about more than was necessary, tidying up, emptying the ash tray, preparing the next injection.

What was that phrase of Besson's that had struck him chiefly?

"You're not co-operating. We cannot cure you against your will. . . ."

Those were not the exact words, but that was the meaning, and it reminded him of his mathematics teacher at the Lycée Guy-de-Maupassant.

"Are you with us, Maugras?"

He used to give a start, and the teacher's apostrophe invariably called forth laughter. Monsieur Marengrot was quite right. Once again he'd drifted away without being aware of it. The most disturbing thing was that he'd have been quite incapable of saying what he had been thinking about.

"You favor us with your physical presence, but you refuse to belong to the class. . . . Try as I may, I cannot possibly teach you mathematics against your will. . . ."

René couldn't help it. At the beginning of each lesson he promised himself to follow it attentively and he was more surprised than anyone on hearing the inevitable:

"Are you with us, Maugras?"

His reports bore such comments as: *Lacks concentration*.

Does not try hard enough. An intelligent but inattentive pupil. . . .

He hated distressing Mlle Blanche. What could he write on the pad to reassure her?

"You never take your eyes off me. . . . You follow the movements of my lips, and yet I defy you to repeat the sentence I have just been saying. . . ."

That was his English teacher, who disliked him and resented his stubborn look.

Lack of will power. Another comment on his report. Had he not shown will power all his life long? Was he not entitled, today, to display a different sort of will, the will to resist?

Anyone entering the room just then might have taken Mlle Blanche and himself for a couple who had quarreled over some trifle. For the first time that day he heard the bells, to which, during the busier intervals, he paid no attention. True, they were ringing a full peal.

As weddings do not usually take place in the middle of the afternoon, he assumed the bells must be for a funeral or perhaps for a christening. Are bells rung for a christening? He could not remember.

Besson, like himself, had thought of their friend Jublin. Knowing that Maugras would inevitably connect his own case with the poet's, he had forestalled him.

It was irrelevant that Jublin had suffered from a brain tumor. The physical side of the question was not important. The vital point was that Jublin had lived on for those five extraordinary years, which René almost envied him.

Unfortunately, even if he were to remain paralyzed down one side of his body and were never to recover his speech completely, his case would be different from Jublin's.

Jublin must have joined the group about 1928, shortly before Besson d'Argoulet, in any case when it still met at the Brasserie Graf. He was a tall cadaverous fellow who, at a fancy-dress party given by a painter in his studio in the Boulevard Rochechouart, had impersonated Valentine the Bone-less, the famous quadrille dancer from the Moulin Rouge, as painted by Toulouse-Lautrec.

His face, which was of a chalky whiteness, remained imperturbable even while he was uttering the most extravagent remarks. He was four or five years older than Maugras; he had taken part in the Dadaist movement and had then joined the Surrealists.

He spent his life in cafés, confining himself to no particular group or district in Paris, equally at home in the Deux-Magots, Boulevard Saint-Germain, or the bars of the Champs-Elysées and the bistrots of Montmartre; he knew everybody, whereas nobody really knew him.

Nobody, for instance, could have said where he lived or what he lived on, and it was by pure chance that Maugras discovered him in a sort of glass cage in the printing works of the Stock Exchange where he earned his living as proofreader.

He never spoke about his writings, although two or three volumes of his verse had appeared. Later on, when critics began to take notice of him, a Left Bank publisher had taken him on as reader, in order to give him more leisure time.

How had he found himself, after the war, in the Grand Véfour group? Had not the group itself been formed somewhat haphazardly?

Besson d'Argoulet had laid its foundations without knowing it. Maugras had just been awarded the Legion of Honor, and Besson, who had already been decorated, had been allowed to confer the insignia upon him.

Besson could not resist such things. He adored ceremonies, honors, titles, decorations, and what he must have enjoyed most about his position of authority was to walk through the wards at Broussais Hospital, followed by scores of respectful pupils.

They had long since deserted Montmartre and the Brasserie

Graf. There was no longer any homogeneous group. Each of them had gone his own way, and they met casually, as chance and the social life of Paris dictated.

"Hello! What are you doing these days? . . ."

Many successful men frequented the Grand Véfour, under the arches of the Palais-Royal. Maugras, when he became editor-in-chief, used often to lunch there, at a table that was reserved for him in the ground-floor dining room. One day Besson had called him up at his office.

"Are you free for lunch next Tuesday?"

He had said yes, without thinking more about it, and when he got to the restaurant on Tuesday he was surprised to hear the proprietor say to him:

"The other gentlemen are expecting you upstairs. . . ."

They had prepared a surprise for him. Pierre Besson had collected some of their oldest friends, those who had reached the top, to celebrate his honor. They had decided to invite only men.

By chance Marelle, the playwright, who was incapable of saying no, had met, on alighting from his taxi, one of the most ruthless women journalists in Paris, who was also the ugliest: Dora Ziffer, who combined dramatic criticism with reports on the law courts for a newspaper of the extreme left wing.

"In a hurry?" she had called out to him.

He had told her about the surprise lunch party. She was of their generation, and had collaborated on the now defunct *Boulevard*.

"D'you mind if I come up for a moment?"

Eventually, of course, she had sat down with all the rest. The meal was over and liqueurs were being served when somebody pointed out:

"Come to think of it, we're thirteen at table. . . ."

The rest was somewhat confused in his mind. The point had been reached when, after a good meal and too much good wine, everybody was talking at once, with flushed cheeks.

"Why shouldn't we meet here once a month?"

"The Thirteen Lunch Club!"

They had not taken it very seriously. And yet the tradition was still going on, years later. Jublin had been one of them, and you never knew whether Jublin was speaking in earnest or in fun, whether he was a genius or a joker. For it was in this light that they thought of him at the Grand Véfour until his cerebral hemorrhage.

They did not imagine him married, but leading a bohemian life, moving from one lodging to the next, or in the picturesque disorder of a bachelor establishment.

At the hospital to which he was taken, a woman turned up, to everyone's astonishment: a dumpy little woman in her forties, modestly dressed, who asked:

"Where is my husband?"

Not only was Jublin married, but he lived in a respectable middle-class flat in the Rue de Rennes, not far from the Gare Montparnasse.

Maugras went there only twice. The first time it was too soon. Jublin, who was not yet resigned to physical decay, refused to see anyone, least of all his old friends.

Maugras could still picture the little dining room with its flowered wallpaper, and a green potted plant in one corner, where Mme Jublin explained in a low voice:

"You must forgive him. . . . He's grateful to you all for coming to ask after him, but he'd rather be by himself. . . . He's gradually getting used to it. . . ."

She said this with a strange serenity.

"Later on, perhaps, he'll need company again. . . ."

Jublin had been married for twenty years without anyone's suspecting it. The night wanderer who haunted Graf's and the Deux-Magots and the Brasserie Lipp had a home base, a flat which might have suited some lower-grade civil servant. He had a wife too, one of those women who all look just alike as they go shopping around the neighborhood in the morning.

If Maugras went back to the Rue de Rennes on a later occasion it was for a definite purpose. He knew that Jublin had no money. The couple lived on his scanty royalties. Now there is a certain medal awarded each year by the Municipal Council of the City of Paris to some writer, painter, or sculptor, which is accompanied by a check for a million "old" francs.

After a few telephone calls, Maugras had got his way. He remembered standing for the second time at the door of the flat. A shrill tinkle echoed inside. The door opened noiselessly and Mme Jublin, wiping her hands on her apron, stared at him in surprise without recognizing him.

He recalled the slightest details, like those of that morning at Fécamp. The visit had taken place at five o'clock in the afternoon on a rainy day in the beginning of winter, when the street lamps and shop windows had begun to light up and the figures of passers-by looked black against them. The landing was dark. A single lamp was burning in the sitting room, diffusing an orange glow. A voice that he did not recognize suddenly said: "Come in. . . ."

It was Jublin, who emerged from his study in a wheel chair which he propelled himself. His legs were covered by a tartan rug. It seemed to Maugras that he was looking at him with only one eye, and this made a strange impression on him. Mme Jublin immediately moved to her husband's side as if to protect him.

"Well, old man? . . ."

There was a twinkle in his eye. His expression was not at all dramatic but, as usual, mischievous and ironical!

"Is it my carcass that's upsetting you?"

It had needed an effort to understand him, for he could not pronounce certain consonants and some of his syllables were confused.

"I've come to . . ."

Through an open door he caught a glimpse of a study with

74

a couple of logs burning in the fireplace. The whole scene was dimly lit, with large patches of almost total shadow. From time to time only Jublin's twisted face stood out against the semidarkness.

"I've come to tell you that the City of Paris . . ."

Then his friend said mockingly:

"Don't inform me that it's offering me its medal?"

"That's just it. . . ."

"That means I'm about finished. . . . Don't be upset . . . I'm expecting it. . . . It's kind of these gentlemen, for I've not done anything for them. . . . Pity they always wait till it's too late. . . . Remember the list of prize winners. . . ."

"Don't overtire yourself, Charles," his wife warned him gently.

None of his friends had ever called him Charles. In fact, they did not know his first name, which never appeared on the cover of his books.

"That medal is like a sort of secular extreme unction. . . . I'm not going to refuse it on that account. . . . The money'll be useful to my wife. . . ."

Jublin died the following spring and it was learned that he had written with his left hand, in the solitude of his almost absurdly commonplace flat, his best poems. Not merely his own best poems but, according to an increasing number of critics, the best poems written during the past fifty years.

He had spent five years shut up with a woman of very ordinary appearance and possibly of very ordinary intelligence too; he'd had plenty of time to think, to look through his mental picture book, his horizon bounded by the gray house fronts opposite, to the accompaniment of the clangor of buses and taxis in the Rue de Rennes and the whistle of trains from the Gare Montparnasse by night.

His wife was still living, in the same flat, where nothing had been changed, where every book, every object had remained in the same place, including the pipe that she used to fill and light for him. The wheel chair had not left its former occupant's favorite corner of the room.

She worked for her living. Maugras had offered to take her on the staff of his paper. He would have found her a quiet job. Others wanted to take an interest in her. She politely refused all offers, with an air of embarrassment.

She chose instead to work as cashier in a shop in her own street, a short distance from the flat, from those few cubic yards of still air where Jublin, when he was weary of prowling around bars and cafés, knew that he would find her.

Could René have told Besson, just now, that he envied his friend's lot? Where was Lina now? It didn't matter. And it didn't matter if she was drinking, either.

There was no Rue de Rennes in his own life. There was no dumpy, commonplace little woman, doing her marketing in the neighborhood each morning. Neither were there any books, any lines of poetry that men would go on saying to themselves.

Besson ought not to have spoken to him about Jublin.

He closed his eyes without realizing it. Nor did he realize that Mlle Blanche, uneasy at seeing him lie motionless so long, had come to bend over him. He gave a start when he heard her say, in low muffled tones:

"Are you crying?"

CHAPTER FIVE

His last thought, the night before, while Joséfa, thinking him
asleep, was unfastening her brassière under her uniform, had
been:

"If only I wake up in time. . . ."

He'd been feeling drowsy by then. Wasn't it odd that no
sooner was he freed from one routine than he felt the need
to set up another? The hours of each day were neatly dove-
tailed, marked by various washing and nursing processes, by
the doctors' visits, by the comings and goings in the passage.
Some hours were pleasanter than others.

His best moment, since he had come here, had been when
he woke up on Friday morning, the half-hour he had spent
alone, listening to the sound of the bells and the hospital
noises.

He wanted to repeat the experience, to make that early
morning half-hour, still as it were intact, his own special half-
hour.

His sleep had been restless. Twice the nurse had risen to
cover him up, but he had only a hazy recollection of this. Now
that his eyes were open, there was still something hazy about
his mind and senses.

He did not feel as lucid as on the previous morning. This lethargy, indeed, was almost pleasurable. He did not know the time. He waited, only afraid it might still be the middle of the night.

He listened for more than a minute, puzzled by a monotonous sound which seemed familiar but which he could not immediately identify, and then he discovered that it was rain pattering against the panes and running down a water pipe not far from his window.

At Fécamp, when he was a small boy and they lived in the little house in the Rue d'Etretat, rain water used to be collected for washing—it's softer, his mother used to say—in a barrel that stood in one corner of the yard, and it used to make a very special sort of music.

He scarcely remembered his mother. He could picture her only as an invalid, sitting in her wicker armchair beside the kitchen stove, and he could still hear the sound of her coughing fits. He'd been seven when she died of tuberculosis. Many people died of it in those days, and they called it consumption.

He was surprised later on when his father told him that she had been ill for only two years, and that before that she used to take him out like other mothers, at first in his pram, then, holding him by the hand, along the streets and on the jetty on the days when it was not too windy, and that later on she used to take him to the nursery school every morning, and fetch him again when school was over.

He felt hot. His body was damp. He wondered if they hadn't given him some fresh drug that induced this torpor, this uncertainty in his perceptions. He tried hard not to go to sleep again before having heard the church clock strike. He hoped it would strike six, like the day before, so that he would have his half-hour.

His neck felt so stiff that he could hardly turn his head to make sure that Joséfa was lying on the cot. In the haze of

78

yellow light that filtered through the glazed door, he saw her sleeping peacefully. Her hair had fallen across part of her face, and every time she breathed out, her lips parted as if they were swelling.

It was disquieting to watch anyone asleep, especially a woman whom one scarcely knew. He always found it touching to watch Lina in her sleep. Her less lovable characteristics vanished and so did her age, and Lina seemed to become a child again, a little girl who hadn't yet lived, inexperienced and defenseless.

Joséfa had unbuttoned the top of her uniform, consciously or in her sleep, and he could see the bluish lace on her slip, which only half covered her breasts. Firm and fleshy, these seemed to swell like her lips, to the same rhythm.

She was lying on her side, facing him, with one hand thrust into the moist warmth between her thighs.

Erotic fancies stirred in him. Lina, too, used to sleep like that sometimes, particularly toward morning, and when they shared the same bed, Maugras used occasionally to be wakened by the sound of a rhythmical panting that grew faster until it was finally stilled.

Was this the case with Joséfa? She was more highly sexed than Mlle Blanche, and she must need men. She would probably find herself a man during the day, and she would give herself in a wholesome, natural way, violently but gaily, without bothering about sentimental complications.

He was glad to hear the bells which, today, preceded the six strokes of the clock. Was it by chance that he had wakened at the same time as the day before, or could it be the automatic working of his subconscious?

He found some difficulty in breathing. This did not worry him; on the contrary. If he was less well, if complications ensued, that would prove to them that he had been right.

As regards Besson, he might have been mistaken yesterday,

79

and he felt some remorse for that. He had thought of his friend as an ambitious, cynical schemer. But had not others formed the same opinion of himself? He, too, had had a brilliant career, even more astonishing than Besson's, considering his starting point.

Were not some people convinced that when he left Fécamp he was already bent on conquering Paris?

He kept looking at Joséfa, fascinated by the hand that, in her sleeping innocence, she pressed against her private parts. He was thinking of several things at once: of Joséfa, of women in general, of Lina, and of the sixteen-year-old boy at Fécamp who bought his first pipe less to give himself self-confidence than because it was a symbol to him.

He couldn't have accounted for the ambition that he cherished then, or a few months later, and it would greatly have surprised his present friends. Not only had he no thought of living in Paris, where he had never set foot, but the very name of the capital city terrified him.

His goal was a modest one, and lay close at hand. He pictured himself spending his life in Le Havre, where he had sometimes gone on his bicycle to saunter, head in air, along the busy streets and sit at the terraces of cafés.

He wasn't going to stay at Fécamp as local correspondent for the paper from which, by a fluke, he'd obtained his press card. He would go to Le Havre and become a proper journalist. Every morning, with his pipe between his teeth and his hands in his pockets, he would make his way to the editorial office, where he'd take his place, well satisfied with himself and his job, at peace with the world.

Logically, that was what should have happened. And it took at least a couple of accidents for things to turn out differently.

He'd waited to do his military service before sending in his application. A few weeks before the medical examination he was taken ill. For no apparent reason his heart began to beat precipitately, while his legs went limp and his body was bathed in sweat.

He had gone to see Dr. Valabron, their family doctor, who had looked after his mother. Opinion was divided about Valabron, for he spent a good part of his time playing cards in cafés, and was slovenly in his appearance.

The doctor ordered him to rest for a few weeks and take some drops three times a day; such complaints, he said, are quite usual among adolescents who have grown too fast.

For two months he did nothing but read, take leisurely walks, watch the boats in the docks, and send his newspaper the local news that he got each morning from the police station.

He retained few memories of this period, two or three at most, including one of the beach, with the haunting noise of the undertow and the sound of his shoes on the shingle, and the crabs in the pools left by the tide.

When he appeared at the Town Hall for his medical examination he was surprised to find that the army doctor, looking grave, spent more time over him than over the rest, asked him a great many questions about his mother, and finally rejected him as unfit.

"The M.O.'s a fool!" Valabron declared. "I can guess what he's diagnosed, some congenital heart trouble or other. Well, I brought you into the world and I'll swear your heart's as good as anyone's."

Valabron did not go into details. As for René, there was nothing more to keep him at Fécamp except his father, who was drinking more and more heavily and whom he scarcely saw even at mealtimes.

He went to Le Havre. There were no openings, the editor told him, which was not surprising, since a staff of three was enough to run the paper.

He tried Rouen, but he had no luck and got no encouragement there. What was left, except Paris?

He couldn't be said to have chosen this course deliberately. On the contrary, he had held back; he'd done his utmost to stay in the provinces and lead the humble life to which he believed himself destined.

Even in Paris, hadn't it been his dream to become someday an editorial secretary, a sort of journalistic functionary with regular hours and a monotonous job?

Now they were beginning to stir in the main ward, and the clatter of garbage pails broke out in the courtyard. Life was beginning to stir around him, and he missed no detail of it, which did not prevent his mind from flitting from one thought to another, while he kept his eyes fixed on Joséfa, hoping that she would not wake up too soon.

If ever he became physically normal, or near-normal, again, he would enjoy making love with Joséfa, even if only once, for she represented one of the two types of women that had always attracted him. By some incomprehensible contradiction he had always, throughout his life, chosen women of a different, almost opposite type.

Was he afraid of women? This seemed the most plausible explanation of his behavior. He was convinced inwardly that it was false, but, at fifty-four, he was still unable to formulate any other.

He could only feel the explanation, which wasn't the same thing. Wouldn't his friends laugh at him if he confessed that in spite of his age and his numerous experiences, woman still retained her mystery, her glamour for him, and that he was still inclined, when he thought of love, to use the words of the catechism: the act of flesh?

It was not only in connection with woman that his early religious teaching had left its mark upon him, and he remembered the Abbé Vinage, a young man of under thirty, saying to the children assembled in the sacristy:

"Everything counts for eternity, nothing is lost, not even our most secret thoughts, and one day we shall find every minute of our lives being weighed in the scales. . . ."

He had been through the usual ceremonies of christening, first communion, and confirmation. He had gone on attending High Mass on Sundays and had taken communion at intervals. It was not until he was about eighteen that he gradually stopped going to church, without any sort of crisis or definite break.

When, toward his fifteenth year, his sexual desires became too strong, he spent several evenings hanging around the brothel which then stood close to the harbor and whose red lamp impressed him so powerfully that his heart beat faster when he saw it in the distance.

The house stood all by itself between the two docks, where masts and yardarms creaked all night long, and fishermen prowled around it, heavy-footed and often unsteady of gait.

It had two entrances, one under the lamp leading into the main room where customers sat at table among women in short shifts, the other, more discreet, reserved for "gentlemen."

It was this door that he had pushed open one drizzling night and he had sensed the hesitancy of the proprietress, Mme Jeanne, who was still an attractive woman.

He was so nervous at that point that he longed for her to say he was too young. Eventually she smiled and called one of the girls. He "went upstairs," as the saying was.

Perhaps that was the clearest recollection of his whole life, even clearer than the morning when the *Sainte-Thérèse* docked: the woman sitting on the edge of the bed, her legs parted as though for a sacrifice, her wax-white skin, with the dark triangle of hair from which he could not take his eyes.

He had been to confession next day, and for months he had lived in terror of the disease he might have caught. He went back, none the less. Indeed, during the whole period of his adolescence at Fécamp, these were the only women he knew. It had never occurred to him to have a girl friend like most young men of his age, nor to pick up one of the girls from the canning factory when they left work in the evening.

Was this the result of a certain laziness in him? Or shyness? Fear of ridicule? The prospect of not proving equal to the occasion?

Nevertheless his ideal had existed, in flesh and blood, and he could say without exaggeration that he had been in love, after his fashion. In love with a woman of thirty-five, Mme Remage, the wife of the shipbuilder for whom his father worked.

Wasn't Mlle Blanche a little like her, in a younger and livelier version? Mme Remage had been a Chabut, the only daughter of the Chabuts who owned the Galeries Nouvelles at Le Havre, the biggest store in the town.

The shipbuilder and his wife lived in a new villa on the Yport road, at the top of the cliffs. They had two children, whom you could often see playing on the lawn as you went past the garden.

Her name was Odile. He frequently came across her in the town, where she went to do her shopping, with her car and her chauffeur in attendance; she was always calm and smiling as if she had nothing but pleasant thoughts. From her face, with its clear complexion and firmly outlined lips, there emanated an inward joy and peaceful trust in mankind and in her fate.

What was she like now? An old lady, whom he had never seen again, and thus he could treasure his old picture of her.

Did she really possess that serenity which he ascribed to her on the strength of his memories? Clean and clear-cut; those were the words that sprang to his mind when he thought about her, as about Mlle Blanche.

With one difference, though, which was probably due to

his no longer being the same age. As a young man he had tried to imagine Odile Remage making love, to picture her in the attitudes taken for his benefit by the girls in the brothel. He could not do it, although she had two children—two daughters, now married and with children of their own, practically old ladies themselves.

In the case of Mlle Blanche he was able to do so, although almost reluctantly. Was it his early religious teaching which had left him the nostalgic longing for a certain purity?

Joséfa had removed her hand, and the uniform was slightly crumpled where it had lain. He guessed that she was about to wake up. The rhythm of her breathing had altered. A quiver ran over her face, like the ripples on the surface of a pool when the wind rises.

He felt hot. The window was no longer black. The rain was falling more heavily and the water was running down the pipe with a noise like a brook. Cars drew up in the courtyard, doors were slammed, and people hurried toward the main entrance.

He recognized the same sequence of sounds as the day before, the steps on the stair, along the passages, in the wards, which he knew only through his hearing.

The smell of coffee reached him in due course and shadows passed by on the other side of the door.

Today, Joséfa leaped out of bed while he was not watching. He was sorry about that. When he turned his head toward her, his eyes open, she was already fastening her uniform, which was creased, as was her cheek.

She showed no embarrassment at having been watched in her sleep.

"Did you have a good night? Have you been awake long? Do you need anything?"

To her, this cohabitation seemed quite natural. Not to him, except when he considered it rationally. None the less he felt as if she had surrendered to him some part of her private life. She thought so little of it that she barely turned away to fasten her stockings to her garters.

Was he naïve enough, at fifty-four, to be still affected by such simple gestures?

"I'm late this morning," she said as she heard the half-hour strike. "The other nurse must have arrived. . . ."

She patted her hair and hurried outside, leaving the door ajar. He didn't know if he was satisfied or disappointed with his half-hour. There were so many questions to which he wanted to find an answer, those questions that one dismisses or avoids in normal life, but that take on supreme importance when one is lying in a hospital bed.

He did not want to go away before having answered them. "Go away" was a tactful euphemism. A thought had struck him the evening before, when he was alone with Mlle Blanche in the twilight.

She had not switched on the lamp as on previous evenings, perhaps because she had just witnessed his distress and wanted to give him time to recover, perhaps because she herself was disturbed by seeing a man of his age in tears.

For to her he must seem almost an old man. They had remained for a while in the half-darkness, with only the light from the passage filtering through the ribbed glass. For a moment he identified himself with Jublin in the seclusion of his flat in the Rue de Rennes.

Had Jublin taken advantage of those five years of solitude to undertake an assessment, an audit, as it were, of his whole life?

Now he was in the same position as his friend, he was convinced of that, in spite of Besson's optimistic reassurances, and he wanted to get his life into focus.

Not to confess his sins, nor to examine his conscience. "Father, I accuse myself. . . ."

No! But to evaluate, with all possible detachment, what was left of fifty-four years of a man's life.

The Abbé Vinage had asserted with conviction:

"Everything counts. . . . Nothing is lost. . . ."

And yet there were entire periods of which he retained only a vague and somewhat distasteful memory. Just as he could not succeed in picturing Besson as he had known him in the old Brasserie Graf days, so he felt unable to identify himself with what he had been at certain periods.

His busy existence had been pointless. He felt ashamed of some of his enthusiasms, as of some of his moments of dejection, which seemed to him now futile and ridiculous.

If everything has its value, if nothing is lost of our actions or even of our fleeting thoughts, ought he not to find within himself some deeper traces of the past, rather than these scattered mental images? He had not chosen them and he was surprised that they, rather than any others, should have occurred to him.

He tossed about, in discomfort. Yesterday, under the influence of twilight, he had played with an idea that had quickly appeared preposterous or at least impracticable, and in any case implied excessive self-importance. To retrace one's life year by year, with detailed accuracy, like those biographies of famous men where everything is clear, logical, and orderly!

In his case nothing was clear or orderly, everything was tangled up, including the thread of time. He kept his eyes fixed on the half-open door. A few moments earlier he had been longing for absolute solitude, and now he was in the throes of vague anxiety because Mlle Blanche had not yet appeared!

Her hands were cold, her hair was wet. She seemed absentminded, as if she had come in so hurriedly that she had not yet had time to adapt herself to hospital life. She was redolent of the world outside. Her eyes soon lit up affectionately, however, and she seemed glad to see him again.

"What a downpour! And the wind's blowing, in the bargain. At one street corner I had to stop because I couldn't see anything through the windshield."

So she did drive a car. It was the first time she had referred to her life outside the hospital. Perhaps she hoped to revive his interest in it.

She had put the urinal under the sheet and the thermometer under his left arm, and for a brief moment their two faces were so close that dark hair brushed René's cheek.

While she busied herself with her usual morning task of tidying up, he had time to return to the problems that preoccupied him. He corrected his earlier thoughts, which proved the difficulty of being sincere with oneself.

He had recalled his visits to the Fécamp brothel as though they had gone on until he left the town. He had not faced the whole truth. Of course it wasn't as if he were making a confession, or a statement under oath. None the less, he had cheated.

In fact, he had tried to efface a certain picture, that of the house between the two docks, with himself standing irresolutely in a patch of darkness while a drunken man, a great strapping fellow in a sailor's cap, came out and moved away, gesticulating and talking to himself.

Maugras had been just about to cross the road when he had heard steps approaching. He'd waited for the coast to be clear. And just as the newcomer passed under the street lamp he had recognized his father, with his coat collar turned up and his hat pulled down over his eyes, making his way to the "gentlemen's entrance" and, after a few whispered words to Mme Jeanne, disappearing inside.

There was nothing extraordinary about it. His father, at this period, had been a widower for the past ten years. None the less René paced about the quayside, distressed and disheveled, before going home, and he was lying in bed with his eyes wide open when he heard the door open and close again.

He had not gone back to Mme Jeanne's. No, he was cheating again. He had gone back once, when the wind was blowing a full gale and he hadn't the courage to bicycle the eighteen miles there and back between Fécamp and Le Havre. For it was to Le Havre that he had gone after that, when desire was driving him almost crazy.

Mlle Blanche picked up the thermometer, looked closely at it, and her face betrayed her surprise. He knew his temperature was up. He had suspected it ever since he awoke. His sluggish feeling was not like that caused by the drugs on previous days. It reminded him more of the attacks of flu he had every autumn, and the upper part of his chest felt congested.

"Are you in pain anywhere?"

She took his pulse, sitting on the edge of the bed in an attitude that was by now familiar to him. Her lips moved while she counted its beats. She tried to conceal her anxiety. She seemed so uneasy that a few moments later she disappeared on the pretext of going for a cup of coffee.

During her absence the door opened noiselessly, slowly, and the patient he had seen the night before, the old man in the purple dressing gown, came in once more to stare at him. There was something alarming about his expressionless face. If he was a mental patient, as Maugras supposed, there was nothing to stop him from coming up to the bed and . . .

Then, to his relief, he recognized the nurse's step outside; she merely pushed the visitor out, patting him on the shoulder just as one might pat an old dog on the back.

This incident made him wonder how they managed in the main ward. To judge by the figures he saw going past, there must have been at least forty beds, and there were only a couple of nurses to look after them. At night, a single night nurse was on duty in a corner of the passage.

And he had a nurse all to himself for twenty-four hours

out of the twenty-four. Mustn't this seem, to the others, an extravagant luxury? When they passed his half-open door, wasn't there envy as well as curiosity in the glances they cast through it? Did they wonder who was the fortunate occupant of the private ward? Had they discovered it through the staff, and did they talk about him among themselves?

He wonderd why Mlle Blanche did not start washing him, and soon understood when the matron came in, not casually in the course of her rounds, but in response to a summons. She immediately took hold of his wrist, scanning his face attentively.

His eyes must have been glittering, his cheeks flushed. He had been awake for less than an hour; it was hardly daytime, and he already felt less well, drowsy, his breathing more and more difficult.

He took no interest in watching the rain beating diagonally across the panes, nor in listening to the wind banging a shutter somewhere.

He couldn't help it, but he was not sorry for what was happening. It proved that he had been right yesterday, rather than Besson d'Argoulet with his artificial optimism. Would Besson now come hurrying over?

"I'll give you a hand," the matron said to Mlle Blanche.

A hand for what? He cast a mistrustful glance at her. He didn't like her. Particularly when she asked him:

"Don't you want to have your bowels moved?"

No! He only wanted her to go away. She did not go away. She helped Mlle Blanche to wash him and change the sheets, by which time the intern, who must also have been sent for, appeared with his stethoscope around his neck.

Glances were exchanged, as at the start of his illness. Of course, he was not in on the secret. What was happening had nothing to do with him, even if it was happening to him, in his own body.

The stethoscope, still warm from contact with another

chest, was laid against his bronchial tubes, his lungs, his heart.

The intern smelled of stale tobacco. He stood up, whispered a few words to the matron, and then all three began to turn the handles of his bed. His legs rose very high. His head was hanging down and mucus slid down his throat and into his mouth and he was unable to spit it out.

They went on whispering in a corner. When Mlle Blanche returned to the bedside they were alone in the room once more, and she took hold of his hand, not to feel his pulse now but as a friendly gesture.

"Don't be afraid. . . . Professor Audoire rather expected this. It happens in fifty per cent of cases. . . . You've got a slight inflammation of the trachea and it's given you a temperature. . . ."

She did not tell him how high.

"The Professor can't come right away. . . . He had an emergency operation at six o'clock this morning. . . . He's still in the operating theater. . . ."

He wondered where this theater was. On the ground floor? On the same floor as his own room? Thus, at dawn, while he was looking at Joséfa's bosom and thinking about Fécamp, while the bells were ringing and the church clock striking, an unconscious man, a man who had been temporarily or forever deprived of awareness of his existence, was surrounded by ghostly masked figures performing, as it were, a slow and tragic ballet.

It wasn't over yet, since Audoire was still busy. What sort of operation? Was it some hemiplegic, having his tumor excised?

He was seized with real panic. He would not allow them to operate on him, to cut his head open. His hand clutched the nurse's hand and he would have liked to speak to her, to tell her he forbade them to operate on him without his knowledge, to implore her to stop them from doing so.

It was too easy. An injection would put him to sleep and

then they'd only have to take him away on one of those wheeled beds on which he'd already been taken downstairs twice, by the main elevator.

He had already known he was at their mercy; now he realized how much so.

"Don't get excited. . . . I know it's not comfortable. . . . You don't remember, but when you were in a coma you stayed in this position for two days. . . ."

Was his temperature rising? He felt hotter than ever and was surprised that it was happening so fast.

He still felt indifferent about dying. Not quite. Once again, he was lying. In any case he would rather die there, with Mlle Blanche beside him, than in the operating theater, with his skull cut open.

"I expect the Professor will give you another dose of penicillin and then this little trouble will clear up. . . ."

She was growing impatient too, glancing repeatedly at the door and then at her wrist watch. He was dribbling now, and from time to time she wiped his face.

At last the door opened to admit an unfamiliar-looking Audoire, an awe-inspiring, almost terrifying Audoire, who no longer reminded one of an ordinary little man in the subway.

He was all in white, with trousers like pajama trousers and a very thin, transparent gown without buttons, fastened at the back with cords, and he was wearing boots of greenish rubber.

His forearms were bare, like a butcher's, and they were very hairy. A mask hung under his chin. The matron came in after him, with the intern. There were suddenly a great many people in the small room, and the atmosphere grew tenser.

Audoire sounded his chest for a long time, twice over, with an expressionless face; he lifted René's eyelids, felt his limbs, scratched the soles of his feet again. . . .

"Open your mouth. . . ."

He thrust in a metallic object which might have been merely

a spoon and which none the less frightened Maugras. Everything frightened him that morning. It wasn't like the other times. He was at their mercy, he had no defense against them.

They understood one another without saying a word. One glance from the Professor to the matron and the latter hurried out, returning shortly after with an instrument which he had no time to examine.

"Don't be afraid. . . . We're going to clear your trachea and your upper respiratory tracts. . . . It's not pleasant, but it won't last long and it'll relieve you. . . ."

They were pinning him down, like a dog at the vet's. Perhaps he was looking at them with a dog's eyes? He saw faces very close to his own, and he struggled before being hurt, before even having anything done to him.

An instrument forced his jaws apart and a tube was thrust down his throat. He felt it going down. He wanted to signal to them that he was choking, that he couldn't bear it any longer, that he couldn't breathe. . . .

Those ten or fifteen minutes were the most unpleasant he had ever experienced in his life. He had really felt just like an animal and he realized that he had behaved like one too, first by struggling, then, as he lay inert, by staring at each of them in turn with wild eyes.

They set a kind of pump going, and he felt sure that his lungs were being sucked out. Then, without letting go of him, they introduced a rubber tube first into one nostril, then into the other, and this time it was his brain that seemed to be being removed.

At last they set him free. Only Mlle Blanche still held his hand, and her face was a blur. Not only had he stopped reacting but he felt completely emptied, sucked dry, incapable of a single reflex. He had even lost all curiosity and stared at them with dull eyes, without even wondering what they were doing or saying. The only more or less clear idea that he still retained was that of the operating theater, to which he was determined not to be taken.

The matron went out again and came back with a syringe and a vial. The Professor himself thrust in the needle and slowly injected the fluid without taking his eyes off the patient's face.

What were they afraid of? Of his fainting? Of his heart's stopping? Or were they watching him so closely to make sure he'd go to sleep? He clenched his teeth so tight that he heard them grating, and then he was suddenly seized by convulsive movements of the arms and legs, as he had been earlier. Both arms? Both legs? He did not know.

He tried to push them away, to get out of bed, to escape from them. A glance from Audoire brought the others to his aid and the injection was continued with René once more pinned down on his bed.

He did not fall asleep. The syringe was empty. The Professor stood up again, and handed it back to the matron.

"That's over," he murmured, wiping his forehead. "We're not going to torment you any more. . . ."

Did it hurt him to hurt other people? It seemed so, from his obvious uneasiness. He accepted a cigarette from Mlle Blanche. She must know when he needed a smoke.

"Don't worry if you feel less well than yesterday. It's a very ordinary complication. . . ."

The nurse had already told him that. She had not been entitled to do so. It was the doctor's business to decide what the patient might or might not be told. This world was governed by an even stricter hierarchy than the outside world.

"Now that your respiratory tracts are free you'll be able to breathe without difficulty. . . . You've often been treated with penicillin, I suppose? . . . That would explain why the first injection had so little effect. . . ."

If it was penicillin that he had been given now, why did he

feel so numb? He gave up, overcome with weariness. He no longer looked at them. He could still hear the rain on the windows, the water running down the drainpipe, and there came a point when it all seemed to be playing a tune in his head.

He was so tired! For such ages now, for years and years, he had been tired, and had kept going all the same in spite of the temptation to let himself drift, to stop struggling, to give up once and for all.

They were still talking. The voices grew more remote. The door opened and closed again. He did not know why, this time they had closed it instead of leaving it ajar. Was it a bad sign? He didn't know, either, whether they had left him alone.

They had hurt him badly, and above all they had frightened him badly. And they had taken away the little confidence he had left in himself, and in the potentialities of man.

For ten minutes, which had seemed endless to him, he had been merely a terrified animal, held down on his bed by alien hands. If he could have bitten them he would have done so.

And that made him unhappy. It was the first time since he had come here that such distress had overwhelmed him.

A cool hand stroked his forehead. But it was a hand which, a short while before, had helped to pin him down. The hand of somebody who was nursing him for pay.

He wanted to go to sleep.

CHAPTER SIX

He did not sleep very much. Although he lost consciousness several times, and dreams mingled with reality, he remained most of the time in a half-drowsy state, his eyes closed, deliberately withdrawing from his surroundings with the more or less acknowledged intention of punishing Mlle Blanche.

The two Italian women came to do their cleaning, and knocked against the end of his bed with their broom. The intern looked in shortly after the clock struck eleven, stood looking at him, a yard away, and then went off without saying a word. The matron, whom he recognized by her odor if not by her massive presence, came in too, and connected him to the dextrose vessel.

There was no mention of shaving today. His cheeks and chin must be a dirty gray, and by an indirect association of ideas he thought of his father, his grandfather, and his friends from the Grand Véfour.

Thus a very ordinary starting point was enough to set going a train of thoughts which in normal life would have seemed absurd to him. Everything depends on one's point of view.

He told himself, ironically, that his point of view was that of a man lying upside down. But it did not follow that what came into his mind was unimportant. He'd find that out later on.

It struck him that his contemporaries had known three different worlds. Whatever the social level in which they were born, they had had grandfathers with long beards, frock coats, and top hats, and grandmothers in leg-of-mutton sleeves. They had seen their mothers in long dresses, with hair piled high in chignons, their fathers had worn mustaches, and each of them had had at least one uncle who boasted huge side whiskers.

Men always used to carry walking sticks. When the first motorcars appeared, moss and grass still grew between the paving stones in the streets; women used to creep furtively out of their houses with little spades to collect the droppings left by horses on the road.

This period merged in his mind with that of the Great War, when the lighthouse beam did not shine, the gray coast-guard vessel lay at anchor in front of the jetties, and the glass around the gas lamps in the street was painted blue.

The next period lasted until the Second World War. It seemed brighter and sunnier. Women wore short dresses and had more freedom. He had begun to discover Paris, he was slowly making a way for himself there, and he never tired of watching life on the Grands Boulevards.

It seemed to him that they had taken life, and their individual problems, more lightly in those days. But wasn't that because they'd been younger? Had they not felt that they were playing a game, that their actions did not commit them to anything?

The year 1940 broke up the group. Some of them left for the unoccupied zone, for England, or for the United States.

And when the Allied troops marched in along the Champs-Elysées, a roll call of the friends revealed gaps. Some had died in concentration camps, one had been shot by the Committee of Liberation; some had become heroes and others, considered collaborators, dared not show their faces.

The Grands Boulevards had ceased to be the heart of Paris. The Champs-Elysées had assumed that role; cars thronged even the sidewalks; at a moment's notice you could fly to New York or Tokyo.

Why did the atmosphere seem to have grown darker again? Because of the threat of the atomic bomb, the faster pace of life? Girls wore the same blue jeans as boys, and it was said that both boys and girls considered love as a form of physical exercise.

Those of his friends who had remained afloat had won prominence or fame. They felt the need to meet every month, to watch one another, to stick together, but never, during those Tuesday lunch parties, were the real questions asked.

Was the only bond between them the fact of having lived through these three periods, of retaining the same memories, the same nostalgic longings?

Perhaps things had always been like that. Men who were their age in the middle of the nineteenth century had witnessed equally spectacular political and economic changes, equally drastic transformations in dress and manners.

If the question bothered him, it was because he was anxious to distinguish between his own personal evolution, for which he was responsible, and the general evolution of the world.

Somebody, a woman, came to the door and spoke to Mlle Blanche. A quarter of an hour later the door opened and he recognized a smell of hot meat that he had almost forgotten. The nurse's lunch was brought her on a tray and she ate in silence, sitting by the window. From the sounds, he could follow the movements of her knife and fork and of her jaws.

He was not given any orange juice. About one o'clock the Professor, before leaving the hospital to go home for lunch, came in to have a look at him. Maugras peeped through half-open eyes as he went toward the door and saw that he was wearing town clothes, a dark suit of a rather ugly brown, as badly cut as if ready-made.

Two hours earlier he had felt vindictive, furious at having been held down forcibly on his bed, bitterly resentful of his own panic. Now he blamed himself alone. He had behaved like a fool, making no effort to master physical suffering, to endure like a man the petty torments, to use their own terms, that they had inflicted on him.

Hadn't he been as foolish as the patient who dreads going to the dentist's and who shakes with terror as soon as he is seated in the chair, before even opening his mouth? This had happened to him, as to everyone else. Each time, when the treatment was over, he had forgotten his fear and his few minutes' pain.

It was the same with his illnesses. He was used to saying with some pride, as though it were to his credit, that he had never been ill. On reflection, he discovered that he had spent several days in bed every year, not to mention his appendicitis and the heart trouble in his youth.

A hundred times, on passing from the waiting room to the consulting room in a doctor's office, he had broken out in a cold sweat at the thought of a pessimistic diagnosis, and as he pulled off his shirt he had wondered whether the hour had not struck when sickness would become his condition.

This was his own private expression. He knew what he meant by it. You can be ill without realizing it, you can harbor a serious complaint for years and still be a man like other men.

Then, on account of a mere trifle, a feeling of faintness, a pimple, a sore throat, or a tightness in the chest, you consult a doctor. You go into his office as a normal being. You watch his reactions during the examination. And, when the verdict has been reluctantly uttered, you've become a sick man who will never again see life in the same light.

Was this the case with him? Besson d'Argoulet had tried,

kindly at first and then impatiently, to show him that his thoughts and his states of mind corresponded to the customary phases of his ailment and that there was nothing unprecedented about them.

Why, from Besson, did he jump to his father, who at the age of eighty-four was still living in the house in the Rue d'Etretat where he himself was born?

He had repeatedly offered to bring his father closer to Paris, now that he had retired, to buy him a little house in the country, with a garden, or to rent a modern flat for him at Fécamp where a maid would look after him.

His father had refused, had gone on doing his own housework and cooking his own meals, just as when René was a child.

As a small boy, when he got back from school and let himself into the empty house with his key, he would find on the kitchen table a penciled note with a list of provisions to be bought in the neighborhood.

Before beginning his homework he had had to peel the potatoes, prepare the vegetables, and put the soup on the stove.

It had never occurred to him to envy his schoolfellows, who could play in the streets until dark.

His father did not complain either. Was it because of the period in which they lived? Were the poor more resigned then, because they knew they could do nothing to change their lot?

His father envied nobody. He entertained no hope of climbing up a rung or two in the social scale. He would go on with his bookkeeping until age put a stop to it, he would count the bundles of cod being unloaded from the boats, the provisions and the bags of salt being loaded when the boats sailed.

They lived a drab, quiet life together, in the house where nothing was ever shifted from its place.

Then, at a time which Maugras could not determine exactly, his father acquired the habit of coming home later and later, with a smell of gin about his mustache.

Soon the evening meal had to be delayed an hour so that he could have his game of cards at Léon's, a tavern on the quayside.

He did not become a drunkard, but the hours he spent at the café had become increasingly important to him, and he ended by going back there after his meal.

He acquired a fixed stare. He would stumble over words. From time to time he would indulge in a fit of sentimental weeping as he looked at the wicker armchair.

René had been taught that children do not criticize their parents. The Abbé Vinage in particular had instilled into him an ideal image of family life, like those in children's picture books.

He was fond of his father, no doubt. Nevertheless the boy had begun to discover, somewhat to his distress, that his father was not intelligent, that his view of life was a restricted one, that his resignation and gentleness were perhaps merely stupidity.

At the time of his leaving Fécamp, his father was drinking more and more heavily, and two or three times René had to undress him and put him to bed, while he repeated:

"Your mother, you see . . . If only God hadn't taken her away from me. . . ."

It was his only protest.

"Why her? . . . What harm have I ever done God? . . ."

They had kept him on out of kindness at Remage's, where the former boss had been succeeded by a son-in-law; at sixty-eight he had an attack of delirium tremens. It was not until later on, when he had been three weeks in hospital, that his son heard of it and paid one of his rare visits to Fécamp.

René found a wizened, thin old man, looking more stubborn than ever, in a ward where other old men were vegetating.

"Why have you come? . . . You shouldn't have bothered. . . . You've got more important things to do. . . ."

He wondered now whether his father, instead of delighting in his success, was not secretly mortified by it. Each time that, on René's insistence, he had come to spend a few days in Paris, he had looked with indifference or with a thinly veiled disapproval at his son's surroundings.

"You're happy, aren't you? . . . Good! . . . Someone's got to be happy in this world. . . ."

He had had a relapse. For a week he had hovered between life and death. After this narrow escape, he gave up drinking.

He did nothing nowadays but his housework, his marketing, and a daily walk around the docks. His doctor—no longer Valabron, who had died long ago—allowed him two glasses of wine a day, and he looked forward for hours to the moment when he should drink them.

What made him cling to life? What gave him the strength to give up his only pleasure, knowing that in any case he had not much longer to live?

This disturbed René, who, since coming to this place, had faced the thought of death without fear or regret.

He had everything, and his father had nothing. But it was his father who, at eighty-four years of age, hung on, and who was quite likely to last for a number of years longer. Why?

Someone came to get the tray. Mlle Blanche came up to the bed. Had she been taken in? Did she suspect that he was not asleep, but only pretending? Had that, too, been anticipated, was it one of the normal symptoms of which Besson had told him? Did all hemiplegics start cheating on the fifth day?

For it was his fifth day of sickness, and he could scarcely believe it. It seemed like an eternity since a man called René Maugras had collapsed on the wet tiled floor of the washroom at the Grand Véfour.

It was Saturday, and he wondered if Besson would come to

see him anyway. It was unlikely. On Saturday morning he merely paid a hurried visit to the wards at Broussais, and often his wife sat waiting for him in the car.

They lived in a huge flat in the Rue de Longchamp, close to the Avenue Foch and the Bois de Boulogne. It contained paintings of Renoir and Gauguin, a couple of Cézannes, and one of Monet's finest works.

These had not been bought by Besson. From the very beginning of his career, old Gaude, his father-in-law, had been a passionate lover of painting and had acquired, for next to nothing, these pictures which were now worth a fortune. He had been the painters' friend. He used to visit them in their studios, on leaving the Salpêtrière Hospital. To be in even closer contact with them he had bought an old mill on the bank of the Loing, near Barbizon.

This mill, La Bluterie, had been enlarged. Besson had made some alterations and added a wing. At the present moment he was probably driving along Route Nationale 7 with his wife beside him.

Yvonne Besson was one of the most cheerful persons Maugras knew, and one of the most forbearing. She was well aware that her husband had affairs, that he could not see a pretty woman without desiring her. He did not lack opportunities and, with increasing age, it had become an obsession with him.

Was it his illness that made Maugras sniff out the weaknesses of his old acquaintance, the chinks in their armor? Besson's sexual successes were the subject of much gossip. It was said that most of his women patients succumbed, that it had become a compulsion with him, just as drink was with his father.

On meeting some woman, René himself had sometimes been tormented by the thought that he would never possess her. Was this what Besson felt, on a somewhat different scale? This, surely, was what he was aware of, and humiliated by?

103

The more dramatically now that his physical powers were waning.

He had confided in Maugras one evening after dinner, when the ladies had retired to powder their faces, leaving them alone together:

"You see, René old man, now that I'm not sure of bringing it off, I manage to get hold of them in places where I've an excuse for interrupting. . . ."

In his consulting room, or between two doors, or in his private office at Broussais Hospital? Had Mlle Blanche been through it? Would she have to go through it?

Besson d'Argoulet was a famous man. He enjoyed all the satisfactions of vanity to which anyone can aspire. Not a year passed without his receiving a degree of Doctor *honoris causa* from some foreign university, and he presided over medical congresses all over the world.

But all that he cared about was that some woman, met by chance, should yield to him, that he should lift her skirt or bare her bosom, trembling all the time lest he should prove unable to carry through what he had started.

Maugras had been mistaken in supposing that his friend pursued honors in order to reassure himself. What he needed most was to display his virility, perhaps also to make sure that his charm still functioned. . . .

Maugras regretted the trend his thoughts were taking, which involved painful memories for him. He himself had never been very virile. He had already been aware of it when, as a young man, he emerged from the house between the two docks at Fécamp. He remembered a woman watching him, once, when his dread of failure drove him to frantic exertions. She had been young, with a pretty piquant face and a pleasing body.

"It's because you try too hard. . . . If you didn't think about it so much . . ."

He was not impotent. At all events he hadn't been, a few

104

days earlier, but his powers were somewhat below the average. The fact was that he was not sure about this; he had never dared question his friends on this subject and when they told of their exploits he had always suspected them of boasting.

He could only go by the way women reacted toward him.

On the whole, they were fond of him. Often they would begin by looking at him with curiosity, as though wondering what it was about him that was unlike other men.

Was he really different from others? They made him think so. But didn't everyone consider himself different from other people?

Why did most women soon assume a protective, sometimes a maternal attitude toward him? At Fécamp it was understandable enough. He had been a mere boy, and the sight of a naked body was enough to set him trembling.

But since then? Hundreds of people were dependent on him. He held one of the most prominent positions in all Paris, made daily decisions that influenced public opinion to a considerable extent, whether about politics, literature, the theater, even the stock market.

Why did Lina not feel secure with him? Why could he not make her happy? And why did a woman like Mlle Blanche look at him with an expression of pity?

He could not keep his eyes closed indefinitely. That was hardly fair to the nurse. She looked after him to earn her living, of course, but she also gave him something of herself. Moreover, he had been dribbling. He felt a wet trickle on his face, and he was very thirsty.

As he stirred noiselessly, almost imperceptibly, she hurried to his side.

"Have you had a good sleep?"

She wore an amused look, as if to let him know that she hadn't been taken in but didn't hold it against him.

"Where were you off to this time?"

Knowing that he could not reply, she went on talking none the less, while she wiped his face and then dabbed it with eau-de-Cologne:

"I bet it was a long journey . . . and it can't have been an unpleasant one, for I saw you smile several times. . . ."

He had been unaware of this, and he wondered what might have made him smile.

"Professor Besson called up to apologize for not coming today. . . . He knows about your trouble this morning and he says you're not to worry. . . ."

Besson had driven past the hospital, barely a hundred yards away from it, on his way to the forest of Fontainebleau. Had he cast a glance toward the gray stone buildings, and had he talked about him to Yvonne?

Were Yvonne's cheerfulness, her poise, her good nature entirely sincere?

"Poor old René! D'you think he'll recover the use of his limbs and his speech? For a man like him it must be dreadful. . . ."

Never mind what her husband replied. At this moment Maugras was not interested in his own health, but in other people. He felt the need to scratch beneath their surface, convinced that if he succeeded he would see more clearly into himself.

Can one possibly know?

Clabaud, the lawyer, had been allowed in. Had he applied to the office or to the matron? Had he asked anybody's leave to visit him?

It was unlikely. Almost all his friends had reached the stage when there is no more queuing or calling at box offices, when one telephone call takes the place of days or weeks of correspondence.

They no longer formed part of the general public. They

belonged behind the scenes, they knew things of which other people were ignorant, and were kept in ignorance, because it might be dangerous for them to know.

Clabaud must have asked his way in quite coolly, like a man who is confident of getting through all barriers. He might have got through unnoticed, for it was visiting time, and moreover Saturday, so that there were even more people in the stairs and passages than on other days. It was like the crowd leaving a movie house.

Clabaud gave a gentle tap at the door and immediately pushed it open without waiting for a reply. Mlle Blanche looked at him in surprise, then, not knowing if she ought to interfere, cast a questioning glance at Maugras.

"Well, old boy, so they've put you with your legs in the air?"

Did he think his friend had lost weight, that he looked poorly, particularly today since he was unshaven and feverish? He showed no sign of it, held out his overcoat and hat to the nurse, and sat down astride a chair.

"Don't worry. . . . I took the precaution of calling up Pierre. . . . He told me that although you weren't a very co-operative patient, you're nevertheless getting on nicely. . . . He'd like you to start seeing people. . . ."

To take his mind off things!

"It seems odd to me to find you here. . . . Of course it must seem even odder to you. . . ."

He examined the greenish walls, the vessel of dextrose and its rubber tube, the urinal draped in a towel, and finally Mlle Blanche, who seemed reluctant to leave.

"I shan't stay more than a few minutes," he promised her. "I don't say I can take your place, but if he needs anything I won't fail to call you. . . ."

He was nearly bald, corpulent, but so tough and broad-shouldered that he did not look like a fat man.

He had not come without a purpose. The proof was that with his customary self-assurance he had dismissed the girl.

He had been President of the Bar and he, too, could be in the Académie Française if he wanted to, or rather if he had not made certain implacable enemies there through his bitter tongue.

Five or six years earlier he had been unquestionably the most famous barrister in France, and scarcely a week went by without his photograph appearing in the newspapers.

Since then he had had to reckon with a newcomer, Cantille, who was considered a youngster, being only forty-two.

The two men's photographs now appeared alternately. Spectacular cases were no longer Clabaud's monopoly, and it had happened two or three times that they had confronted one another in court, one pleading for the defense, the other prosecuting in the name of the State.

Did Clabaud resent this, like the aging male in certain animal species, sea lions for instance, who finds himself being ousted from the leadership of the herd by a younger, more aggressive, and more powerful creature?

"By the way, Pierre sends his apologies. . . . You know how things are. . . . The weekend's sacred, particularly for Yvonne, who'd be upset if she couldn't join her children and grandchildren at La Bluterie. . . ."

Clabaud himself had two sons and a daughter. One of the sons was married and the daughter was engaged. It was not from his friend that Maugras had learned this. As if by some tacit agreement, or out of reticence, none of them talked to one another about their private lives. This went back to the days when they used to meet in cafés and nobody knew who had children and who hadn't.

Later on they began to visit one another's homes, almost always in the evening. The children were in bed, or if they weren't they were kept out of the way, somewhere else in the flat.

So that it came as a surprise to receive, from time to time, a wedding invitation.

Clabaud lived on the Quai Voltaire, opposite the Louvre; below him there was a dealer in rare books and prints, and on the other side of the gate an antiquarian who specialized in remote antiquity. The flat was old-fashioned and austere, like Mme Clabaud herself, who bore some resemblance to the matron.

Was her husband still in love with her? Could he possibly be happy with a woman who domineered over everybody around her? He was one of the few guests at the Tuesday lunch parties who were not known to have had any love affairs.

He had a very big practice and one of his sons worked with him. Every morning he was up by six. He liked to say that his trump card was to need only four or five hours' sleep.

Besides his role as a trial lawyer, he was legal adviser to a number of important firms, and this was far more remunerative.

Of all their friends, Clabaud was the only one to lead a more hectic life than Maugras. For Maugras's interests were all connected with his profession. As head of a newspaper and founder of two weeklies, including one woman's magazine, he naturally took an interest in broadcasting and frequented people involved in current events.

Like Besson, Clabaud attended every dress rehearsal, and this was understandable enough. He was a passionate lover of the theater, and knew all the classical plays as well as any pensionary of the Théâtre Français.

The extraordinary thing was that he found time to satisfy other passions, which amounted to manias. For instance, he had written an exhaustive study on the old houses of the Marais district, and he had taken the trouble to visit all the Romanesque churches in France in order to write a voluminous monograph on them.

How much of his life had he given to his three children?

Maugras, indeed, had not taken much interest in his own daughter.

Today, he realized with surprise that children formed, as it were, a world apart from the rest of the world. In the passages and in the wards, this afternoon, there were as many children walking about as grownups, and the nurses had to restrain their exuberance.

"I know you're not allowed to talk yet. . . ."

That was certainly not what Besson had told him. Besson must have said that he was suffering from aphasia and that he would be deprived of speech for a long time, perhaps permanently.

Clabaud had had a heart attack two years earlier, and had stayed in a nursing home for a week. Nothing serious, he had been told. Just a warning. Since then he had given up smoking.

What was his reaction on seeing Maugras, his junior by four years, in a worse condition than himself?

He gave no indication of it, but appeared as easy and self-assured as if in his own study.

"I don't know if you've been following the latest news. . . ."

He glanced from the bedside table to the small table off which Mlle Blanche had eaten her lunch.

"I see you've got no radio. . . . D'you read the papers? . . . Your own, at any rate? . . . No? . . ."

This seemed to puzzle and disconcert him.

"If I'm not mistaken, you're leaving the admirable Fernand Colère a free hand. . . ."

Clabaud was losing no time. He had come with a specific object.

"Speaking of Colère, I gave him a call this morning. . . . D'you remember the Campan business? . . . No, of course not. . . . There's such a gap between the time when a case

110

first hits the headlines and the time when it comes to court that everyone's forgotten. . . ."

Automatically, Maugras searched his memory. It was a professional reflex. Campan . . . Campan . . . He seemed to remember that it had meant a front-page photograph: a tall, slender fellow with an air of breeding. . . .

"It was two years ago. . . . The antique dealer turned burglar. Remember? . . ."

The headlines at the time had been: The Arsène Lupin of the châteaux.

For nearly a year, châteaux in Touraine, Anjou, Normandy, almost every province in France had been visited by a burglar who picked out the most precious objects with amazing flair and had not once been taken in by a fake or an imitation.

In each case he had appeared to be familiar with the place, to know where the various objects were to be found, whether he was liable to meet servants, and whether there were dogs.

One night, two policemen were guarding the Chartres road, because of some trivial incident, the theft of a car that had just taken place in a neighboring village. A powerful car had appeared at the top of the hill. The driver had hesitated, slowed down for a hundred yards or so, then, suddenly changing his mind, had charged forward, and the policeman who was waving a light in the middle of the road had been knocked down like a ninepin.

He had been killed on the spot. As for the driver, he would presumably have got away undiscovered if, at a bend in the road some twenty miles farther on, he had not run into a small car.

This had been completely smashed up, and the occupants, a couple and their baby, had been killed. The man responsible for these four deaths was found lying gravely injured at the foot of a tree where he had hurtled through his windshield.

He was Henri Campan, thirty-eight years old, an antique dealer in the Rue des Saints-Pères. It was soon learned that he belonged to a well-known Bordeaux family, that his father had been a general, and his maternal grandfather a Senator for the Gironde.

In the car had been found ancient coins and *objets d'art* stolen that very night from a château in the Loire district.

Maugras now thought about Campan as he had thought about Besson, Jublin, Clabaud, and all the rest. Two years ago, the story had appeared to him merely as an admirable news item and he had exploited it to the full, like the rest of the press, publishing an exclusive interview with the burglar's mother, who was still alive in the Dordogne.

But now he was asking himself questions about that thirty-eight-year-old man, about his solitary activities, about the exceptional concourse of circumstances that had made a murderer out of him.

He guessed what Clabaud was going to ask him. Clabaud was Henri Campan's counsel and was concerned with winning his case or at least getting the mildest possible sentence.

"I'm sorry you can't meet him. . . . He's a strange fellow and his case has its puzzling psychological aspects. . . . I've managed to have him examined by a psychiatrist, but I've got to be prepared for the official expert to try to break down his conclusions. . . . You know how they do things in the law courts. . . ."

Maugras had understood. He didn't need to listen to any more, except out of curiosity, to see how his friend would set about it.

"I took the liberty of having a word with Colère about it, thinking he would be keeping in touch with you and getting your instructions daily. . . . He tells me this is not so, that he's only seen you for a few minutes since your accident. . . . The case comes up at Orléans on Wednesday and, as usual, everything will depend on the opinion of a few jurymen. . . .

"According to the light he's shown in, Campan can be considered either as the most heartless of villains or an irresponsible victim of fate. . . . That's the line I'm going to take, of course, and the more I study the case, the more I'm convinced I'm right. . . .

"The greatest danger, in a case like this, lies in the reaction of the public, the atmosphere of the trial. . . . In other words, a paper like yours can have a great influence. . . . I'm not asking you to take sides. . . . I've never ventured to do that. . . . All I want is a sort of friendly neutrality. . . .

"For instance, don't say too much about the policeman's widow, who's sure to burst into tears in court; don't publish her photograph going into the Courthouse; don't put too much stress on the couple with the baby, particularly not on the baby, which would be quite enough to get my man the death sentence. . . ."

Maugras did not feel indignant. If he had had such an inclination, it would have asserted itself long ago. Hitherto, until he had come to see the world from his bed at Bicêtre, he had taken such things for granted, as Clabaud did.

"You'll admit I've never taken advantage . . ."

It was true. And in return the barrister had sometimes helped him in a tricky situation.

"Yesterday evening, at the Michodière Theater, I ran into one of the Schneider brothers, Bernard, I think. . . . I always mix them up. . . . The one who has a racing stable and who longs to get into the Jockey Club. . . ."

It was not Bernard but François, the eldest of the three brothers who owned 90 per cent of the shares in his paper. Bernard was the one who spent most of the year in the United States.

Before the war, they had had big interests in Indochina. They had got out just in time, and had set up oil refineries in France and elsewhere.

"I said nothing to him about it. . . . I almost forgot to

tell you, he sent all his best wishes for your prompt recovery. . . ."

So that he could telephone on the slightest provocation! François Schneider preferred to have his connections with the paper kept dark, and he seldom set foot in the office that was kept for him next to Maugras's own. None the less he lived in perpetual fear of being compromised by the paper.

"Tell me, René. . . . Don't you think the last Parliamentary report was a bit biased? . . . Some of my friends were surprised at it. . . ."

Or else a front-page article about some international misunderstanding was likely to cause a drop in prices on the Stock Exchange. . . .

Clabaud had thought of everything, including his friend's paralysis. Having finished his speech, not without a discreet allusion to the powerful people he might have approached, he drew a paper out of his pocket.

"On my way, as I promised Colère this morning, I looked in at the editorial office. . . . He scribbled a note for you. . . ."

The page bore the words: "O.K., boss?"

Of course, that was what they called him. He'd almost forgotten it. Since being here, he had thought about all manner of things, except the paper which, only a week before, had been the essential factor in his life.

The barrister seemed sure of him. After all, they had known each other's ways for the past thirty years.

"I gather you can write with your left hand. . . ."

He had made sure of that from Besson. He had left nothing to chance. He was determined to win his case, not for the sake of Campan, about whom he cared little, but in order to keep even with his fellow barrister Cantille, who had just secured acquittal for a parricide.

He had his gold fountain pen ready, and he slipped his wallet under the paper to enable René to sign.

"Thanks, old man. . . . If it amuses you, when you feel like reading, I can send you a copy of the dossier. . . . You'll see there are things in the case that nobody would have dared to invent. . . . What makes it even more complicated is that Campan is a homosexual, and . . ."

There was a knock at the door. Mlle Blanche talked politely to some unseen person, then she came in herself and announced:

"It's your wife."

Why did he think for a moment that she meant Clabaud's? Of course it was his own. The barrister stood up, his hand outstretched.

"How are you, Lina my dear?"

Maugras was still lying head downward and Mlle Blanche came up furtively to wipe his nose and mouth and make him more presentable.

"Not too tired?" she whispered.

What could he reply? If she had stayed behind the door and heard it all, she must have understood.

CHAPTER SEVEN

They were alone together in the room, and as always when
this happened they both felt ill at ease and tried to conceal it.
This had been their predicament for years now. It had begun
in the Rue de la Faisanderie, at a time when they were still
sharing the same bedroom; then it had shown only in their
silences or in casual remarks so remote from their real preoccupations as to be worse than nothing. They avoided one
another's eyes and when inadvertently their glances met, each
of them forced a smile.

It was still raining. There were drops of water on Lina's
overcoat and on her dark hair, which hung straight down,
following the narrow oval of her head, the tips folded into
one large curl that touched her shoulders. Like Clabaud, she
had glanced first at his raised legs and he realized that she
felt a slight shock on seeing him thus, head downward, which
must alter the look of his face.

"Hello, René. . . . I'm not disturbing you? . . . Had
you finished with Georges? . . ."

Mlle Blanche had left the room after the lawyer, and was
staying discreetly outside. She seemed somewhat reluctant to

116

leave him, as though she guessed that this latest visit, too, would be an upsetting one.

Lina was standing; her open coat disclosed a Chanel suit which she wore chiefly on weekends. She had not been drinking, at any rate not more than one indispensable glass.

She had probably got up about midday. Had she been out last night? Most likely. She must have rung for Clarisse, her personal maid. When they went to live at the Résidence George V, where service was provided, he had insisted none the less that she keep Clarisse, for she could not bear being alone.

She needed somebody to talk to. Not him; she could not talk to him. Anybody else, if need be a barman whom she did not know.

What had she eaten? An egg, a slice of ham? She seldom had a proper meal. She ate less and less nowadays, not for the sake of dieting, since nothing made her fat, but because she had lost her appetite.

What told him that she had had only one drink was the fact that her hands were trembling like a drug addict's, as they did in the early part of the day. A single whisky did little to steady this tremor. Only gradually, as the hours passed and the drinks followed one another, would she gain self-confidence and recover her vitality, and even a certain unassumed gaiety.

He had often heard her laughing with Clarisse when he came home in the late afternoon to change, but as soon as he arrived they would grow serious again.

What was she afraid of? For she was afraid. For a long time he had been trying to understand why, without success. Explanations occurred to him periodically, always the same explanations, which seemed to him plausible at the time; then some gesture of Lina's, some chance remark, or a scene such as they had been having with increasing frequency, would raise the question again.

She had not called up to know if he wanted to see her to-day. That meant that, like Clabaud, she had something to ask him and, seeing the woolen suit, he guessed what it was.

"You must be feeling bored, poor René, now that you're getting a bit better. . . . Wouldn't you like me to send your radio? . . . Won't they let you read yet? . . . In a day or two, perhaps they could fix you up with television? . . ."

He knew that rather colorless voice, that droop of the lower lip when she was speaking without conviction, without thinking about what she was saying, merely to avoid being silent.

Of course, it must be unnerving, talking to a person who cannot answer you and having to watch the expression in his eyes. It had not struck him before. Would not this account for a certain self-consciousness in the attitude of everyone who came to see him, including the doctors?

There were inevitably moments of silence. No interlocutor can go on talking without a break. Only Clabaud had more or less succeeded, and it was his profession.

Lina did not know what to do with herself, whether to remain standing or to sit down.

"May I smoke?"

He nodded, and presently heard the characteristic snap of the gold cigarette case, the click of the lighter that matched it.

"In spite of the rain there are just as many cars rushing out of town as in springtime. . . ."

She had fine hazel eyes, but there was a perpetual feverish glint in them, as though she could never relax, as though some thought were tormenting her which she persisted in keeping to herself.

He would not think about it now. There had been no transition between the two visits, and Clabaud's had left him with a taste of shame.

It was not exactly shame, nor yet disgust. He was surprised, shocked, as if he had just discovered something, as if he had suddenly been brought face to face with a reality that he had always refused to look at.

He wanted her to have gone. If he could have spoken he would have said:

"All right, my dear. . . . Go ahead . . . have a good time. . . ."

She would, once again, look at him as if some guilty secret had been disclosed. For she had a sense of guilt. Sometimes he thought he knew why. He felt guilty himself, in a different way, but that was not a problem to be broached when one had a temperature.

Was he still feverish? Not to any distressing extent. He felt like a dog in its kennel, watching people go past and sniffing at them from a long way off.

"I don't know what to decide. . . . Marie-Anne called me up at two. . . . You know what she's like. . . . She makes plans and then she's surprised when other people don't adopt them enthusiastically. . . . I told her that . . ."

It didn't matter what Lina had told her. The result would be the same, and not only because Marie-Anne was, indeed, an autocrat.

Everybody who was anybody in Paris called her Marie-Anne, as if she were the only person of that name in the world. Her full name was Marie-Anne de Candines. She was a countess. Her husband had died ten years before. He had not amounted to much in her life, except to give her his name, and she had always behaved as if he did not exist.

He had been a fair insipid fellow, one of the last men in Paris to sport a monocle and to divide his time between his club, the fencing school, and the race course.

She was a Jewess, distantly related to the Rothschilds. Her father had been a banker. He was dead too, and her mother, aged nearly eighty, still led a busy social life in her estate on the Cap d'Antibes.

Marie-Anne was the ringleader of all those who followed

a certain way of life and flaunted certain tastes. She gathered around her, in her town house near the Alma and her country house at Candines, the young and the not-so-young, writers male and female, film people, couturiers, pretty girls who were on the stage or who wanted to be, a couple of painters, and a certain number of homosexuals.

She had had several long-lasting liaisons and made no secret of them. It was well known that a certain diplomat still visited her frequently and spent the night with her, although she was close to sixty. He did not belong to the set, and kept away from it.

"I adore queers!" she often declared. "They're the only men who understand women, the only ones who aren't bores in every sphere except sex. . . ."

He wanted to tell Lina:

"Hurry up! . . . She's waiting for you. . . ."

His wife was always like that; she was so afraid of being misunderstood or misjudged that she took an age expressing the slightest thought.

"They're all going to spend Sunday at Candines. . . . Marie-Anne's starting off at five o'clock. . . ."

It was half-past three. Allowing for Saturday traffic jams, Lina would take nearly an hour to reach the Place de l'Alma. Why didn't she get along, then?

"I told her I'd rather stay in Paris in case you needed me. . . ."

The phrase was a tactless one, as she noticed herself, and she reddened, hurriedly adding:

"You might want to see me tomorrow. . . ."

This was ambiguous. Why should he suddenly need her? If anyone called up the George V urgently summoning Lina to Bicêtre, it would not be himself. It would be Mlle Blanche or the matron, and it would mean he was dying, or dead.

As for wanting to see her, she knew they spent their time

avoiding one another, since that was the only way for them both to keep sane.

Why had she refrained from drinking before coming? Because on her first visit she had realized that he could smell her breath. Because she knew that he had suddenly guessed.

He never criticized her, nor did he look at her with the slightest hint of censure. When her nerves were overstrained she would scream at him:

"I can't even think without your knowing!"

Against whom, against what was she fighting, all by herself, instead of accepting his help? It was not true that he knew everything. The proof was that he still could not understand her, and felt as miserable as she did.

He smiled at her. Even so, he had to watch his smile, for she was apt to interpret it as ironical or indulgent, and indulgence exasperated her more than anything else.

He nodded, and hunted with his left hand for the pad which Mlle Blanche must have left within his reach, and for the pencil. He groped for it. She understood, rose and handed him the pencil, which he had been unable to find.

"Can you manage to write already? I bet that within a week you'll be talking as well as ever. . . ."

She knew he was going to say yes. She'd been convinced of it before she came. Her visit was a mere formality. She could simply have telephoned, but she hadn't liked to do this, because it would have meant making her request through the nurse. She had chosen, instead, to come across Paris in the storm.

"I shan't even need to take Léonard, so he can have the day off. . . . Marie-Anne wants to take me in her car. . . ."

The Château de Candines was near Verneuil, in the Eure-et-Loir, surrounded by hundreds of acres of forest.

He wrote down: *Go.*

What could he add? *Have a good time* would be too long.

He hadn't the energy. He expressed his wish in a gentle, affectionate glance. As he might have expected, Lina was upset. Did she think he was laughing at her? That he misjudged her, imagined she could not spend a day without her friends?

"You know, René, if I decide to go, it's more for Marie-Anne's sake than for my own. . . . I've been glad of her company often enough not to let her down when she happens to need me. . . ."

Oh no! Marie-Anne did not need Lina. But she, too, hated being alone, and was only happy when she had her little court around her.

"There's something else I nearly forgot to mention. . . . You've probably been thinking about it too and I wanted to set your mind at rest. . . . About tomorrow's lunch, at Arneville. . . . Last Sunday I heard you asking some friends to come again next week. . . . As the papers haven't mentioned your accident, I thought I'd better call them up. . . . Don't worry. . . . I gave them no details. . . . I just said you weren't feeling well. . . ."

That was not true either. She would have told everything, everything she knew, including the place where he had been found lying unconscious. She couldn't help herself. She would clutch at anyone and anything, the telephone, the chambermaid, the concierge at the Résidence, with whom she'd have a long gossip each time she went in or out.

The concierge must already know that she was going to Candines for the weekend, that she had gone to talk to him about it, that she wasn't quite happy about it, that she didn't like going so far away but that she could get back to Paris in an hour and a half if anything happened. . . .

Marie-Anne's friends were fast drivers and all had Ferraris, Aston-Martins, or Alfa-Romeos.

He wanted to shout: "Why don't you go!"

No: to say it kindly, wearily. Didn't she understand that this was not the right time to start him thinking about certain subjects? For years now he'd been almost managing not to think about them, rather as if something in the depths of his being, perhaps his instinct of self-preservation, thrust aside a dangerous problem.

He did not want his illness—his death, maybe—spoiled. He needed peace. She would need it too, especially as she would go on living. Wouldn't she automatically find that peace when he had gone?

That was not certain. It might be too late. Her hands were shaking more than when she came in and he felt sorry for her. She needed a drink, quickly.

She'd go and have one when she went out. She would go into the first bistrot she came to, and the customers would wink at one another when they saw her climb out of a chauffeur-driven Bentley to toss down a drink at the bar. She'd stopped being ashamed of that. So much the better! If only he'd set about things differently. . . .

No! He rubbed that out. He switched off, refused to let himself be disturbed by a worry he knew only too well. Another smile. A kind, encouraging smile.

"You're sure, René, that you . . ."

Oh yes, yes! Go. . . . Tell them that you found me lying head downward, that it gave you a shock, that I was looking resigned, or impatient, whatever you like. . . . Tell them whatever you like, your glass in your hand and your eyes glittering more and more. . . . But for heaven's sake, go!

She seemed to have understood. She hunted for an ash tray and crushed out her lipstick-stained cigarette end.

"I hardly dare wish you a good Sunday, René. . . . It would have been fairer if it had happened to me. . . ."

He closed his eyes. He couldn't stand any more. She leaned over to put a kiss on his forehead.

"Till Monday. . . . I'll phone Besson on Monday morning. . . ."

He heard her move away, heard the door opening, the footsteps and voices of the visitors in the passage.

He raised his eyelids to welcome Mlle Blanche, who came in wearing a graver, more anxious look, and gazed at him as if she were sorry for him without quite understanding.

She had guessed that something was wrong between Lina and himself just as, on the occasion of the earlier visit, she had guessed that Lina had been drinking. Did she wonder which of the two was responsible?

"Are you feeling sad?"

A vigorous shake of the head, so vigorous that his reaction surprised her.

"Tired?"

It wasn't quite that, either. He was tired, true, but that did not date from today, nor from his entry into the hospital.

Depressed? That was nearer the mark, although the term did not express everything. She must not worry about him. In any case, surely she knew that according to Besson he was merely following the course of his illness, as clearly defined as the graph of his temperature?

He watched the rain falling and was glad of it, because it gave a greater intimacy to the room, in which he liked to see Mlle Blanche coming and going. They were getting to know one another. Had she, too, been sorry that their tête-à-tête had twice been interrupted that afternoon?

She must wonder what were his exact relations with his wife, what bonds still existed between them, why and how they had decided one day to spend their lives together.

She was not alone in asking herself that question. All their friends asked it, or had asked, especially the women, who watched Lina with curiosity. Some of them looked at him afterwards, compassionately.

They were mistaken. He had no regrets. He loved Lina. He needed her as much as she needed him, and he would do anything in the world not to lose her.

Better think of something else, anything else, with one's eyes fixed on the nurse's white uniform, and he hunted through his head like a child hunting among its toys, choosing which to play with.

Actually, there was no question of choice. Some thought arose irresistibly, almost always an unexpected thought, and sometimes they occurred two at a time without any necessary connection between them.

They were questions rather than thoughts. He asked himself unending questions, sought for the answers.

Mental images that he thought he had forgotten sprang to mind too. Georges Clabaud in his black lawyer's gown, a briefcase under his arm, leading him through the vestibule at the Palais de Justice toward the Second or Third Chamber, where an important trial was taking place.

It was before the war. He was already editor-in-chief but of a less important paper than the one he now directed. People had fought for seats. Many fashionable women were there, including Marie-Anne de Candines, with whom he was not yet on familiar terms.

Clabaud had gone to get a chair from somewhere in the background so that Maugras could sit close to counsel's bench, apart from the general public, as if he were one of those officiating.

At one point a young woman barrister who was sucking peppermints handed him her box, motioning him to pass it to the defendant.

Did Clabaud believe in Justice? Besson d'Argoulet, for his part, did not believe in medicine, at any rate not in the same way as most of his colleagues and still less in the way that sick men do.

"We cure a good number of our patients, but most of the time we don't know how or why. . . . Every time we think we've made a discovery, new questions arise, so that it seems more like a step back than a step forward. . . . In a hundred years or in five centuries, our descendants will speak of us as we speak of African witch doctors. . . ."

Was this skepticism mere affectation on his part? Did Clabaud, when pleading a cause or when discussing his clients in private, take his role seriously? Was he acting a role?

Maugras, at fifty-four, was in a better position than most to know men and society, since his profession enabled him to see behind the scenes.

During the five days that he had lain here, with the near certainty that he would not get up again, he had been trying to understand himself, to reach some opinion about himself at last.

Lina's visit had proved to him, once again, that he was wide of the mark, scarcely any more advanced than when, as a child, he listened with terror to the Abbé Vinage's words at his catechism class.

"Our actions, our speech, our thoughts follow us. . . . Nothing is lost. . . ."

Now, in the courts where Clabaud spent the best part of his time, a man might be judged in a single day, or in two or three days at most, with the crowd, all around, playing somewhat the same part as the students that surrounded Besson or Audoire when they solemnly made their rounds of the wards.

"I was his schoolteacher. . . . At the age of eleven, he already showed a tendency to . . ."

"I am the family doctor. . . . I was there at his birth. . . . At three years old . . ."

Then the concierge, the office boss, or somebody or other else would contribute some scrap of truth or error.

The man would sit alone between his two police guards, his chin in his hands, with vacant gaze or with too fixed a stare.

Maugras had no policemen by his sides. There was, indeed, the matron, who would soon be coming to see him and who might well be cast for that part.

126

Audoire would be the presiding judge, self-assured, impassive, unassailable.

And Besson? One of the assessors. There was always an assessor with rosy cheeks and silvery hair, smiling benevolently after a good lunch.

Lina would not be in the courtroom. Her friends would have told her that her nerves would not stand it. She'd be waiting for news to be given her by telephone, as the case proceeded.

"No! He doesn't look depressed. He seems to have lost interest in what's going on around him. . . ."

And Mlle Blanche? Wasn't she the young woman barrister who handed the defendant peppermint drops?

"That's the way I like to see you, relaxed, almost smiling. . . . It's time to take your temperature. . . ."

They felt at ease together. The wards and corridors had got rid of their visitors. Night was falling. The sky was still rainy. The nurse looked at the thermometer and seemed pleased.

"The Professor was right. . . . You're almost down to normal. . . . If he were here he'd probably allow you a little purée, but I daren't take the responsibility. . . . We'll leave it till tomorrow. . . . Are you hungry?"

He was not hungry. He was calm. He was trying to reckon the time he still had to spend with Mlle Blanche before Joséfa came to relieve her. And then it was pleasant, too, to know that Joséfa was lying by his side, and to watch the quiet rise and fall of her bosom in the morning. . . .

You could still hear cars driving past, people leaving Paris, like Besson, like Lina, like almost all their friends. . . .

While he stayed here.

He had missed his morning half-hour, and he had missed Joséfa's awakening, although the bells had rung a full peal.

127

The folding bed had already been put back in the cupboard, and what roused him from sleep, from a dream that he was to try in vain to remember for the rest of the day, was the noisy opening of the door, and a woman's voice cheerfully announcing:

"Good morning, monsieur! . . . My name's Angèle, and I've come to take Mlle Blanche's place beside you today. . . ."

It was almost broad daylight. The woman was a small, rotund person, bursting out of her uniform. Her vitality seemed explosive in that room, usually so calm and still. She had a good-natured, vulgar face, and one could imagine her swapping picturesque insults with the dairy woman or the fishwife.

He felt a twinge of resentment as he looked at her, for Mlle Blanche had really been guilty of a kind of treachery in not warning him the day before. She had not dared tell him that she wouldn't be coming, that she, too, was having her Sunday off.

And yet it was on the day before that she had shown herself particularly understanding with him, and they had never got on so well together as during the second half of the afternoon.

Had she been afraid of his protesting, or trying to make her change her mind? Or of his getting excited and spending a bad night? Had she felt unwilling to introduce her private life into the world of the hospital?

"She's gone to the country, like everyone else!"

He could not speak. It was inwardly that he made his bitter comment. Because it was Sunday, he was being neglected, left to the mercy of a stranger.

Angèle, since that was the name of this dumpy woman who had just burst in on him, did not waste a moment. She fixed him up with the urinal.

"D'you want the bedpan? . . . All right, I won't press

128

you. . . . Some of them need it as soon as they wake up. . . ."

She went on talking and talking, bustling about meanwhile with the same zest and good humor.

"The poor child couldn't find anyone to take her place. . . . At her age, when you've been shut up all week you need a bit of a change. . . . I knew you'd be disappointed at finding a homely body like me instead of a pretty girl. . . ."

She was probably in her forties.

"You'll see, we'll get on all right together. . . . For one thing, I know a bit about you, because my brother works on your paper. . . . That's why I offered right away to give up my Sunday. . . . My brother's called Thévenot, Xavier Thévenot. . . . He's a compositor. . . . You may not have noticed him, in a busy place like that. . . . He's got a broken nose and he stammers. . . ."

Thermometer. Pulse. She wore her watch not on her wrist but hanging from a safety-pin on her bosom.

The change of atmosphere that she brought in was so violent as to stupefy him. She rushed hither and thither, never silent for a moment.

"I see the penicillin's worked. . . . The Professor's going to be pleased. . . . He's got a stiff sort of manner, but you'd never guess how much he takes his cases to heart. . . ."

She was looking at him straight with her clear eyes, not watching him furtively as the others had done.

"Well, you don't get worked up, anyway. . . . It's easy to see you're an intelligent man and you understand. . . . The worst to deal with are the patients who don't believe what they're told. . . . However much you explain to them, they're as obstinate as mules and fret themselves sick with all the ideas they get into their heads. . . .

"And as for the women! . . . I'm in a women's ward myself, on the other side of the big staircase. . . . Near the mental cases. . . . At one time there weren't any women here at Bicêtre. . . . They were all sent to La Salpêtrière, and there were only men here.

"Now everything's changed, they're all mixed up, so that you don't know where you are: incurables, mental cases, men, women, there's a bit of everything in this place. . . ."

The rain had stopped. The air was calm. The sky, above the slate roof which was drying in patches, was a cloudless spring blue. When the bells fell silent the quietness outside was surprising, now that the heavy traffic and the weekday noises were hushed.

It was the peace of a Sunday morning, and in the hospital there was less bustling about than on other days. The matron had not looked in yet. He wondered if she would come or if she, too, had left him to his fate.

Why should he need less attention and care on Sunday than on other days? Besson, at his country house, was not worrying about him. Audoire had not come in the night before, which suggested that he was away for the weekend.

Suppose he had got worse instead of better. This stout nurse had never seen him, knew nothing about him except what was written on his chart.

"As I told Mlle Blanche, it's a pleasure to look after a gentleman like yourself. . . . Now I'm going to give you a wash and brush-up. . . . I know I've got to use eau-de-Cologne to rub you. . . .

"Are you still scared of me? . . . You'll see that in about an hour you'll feel as if you'd always known me. . . . People are scared of me at first because I'm fat and I never beat about the bush. . . . When you've been coping with a whole ward-ful of women, like me . . .

"I wish you could see them. . . . Some of them sulk in a corner all day, crying and refusing to eat, others throw regular hysterical fits and roll on the floor to get attention. . . .

130

"You wouldn't believe how jealous women can be of one another. . . . If I stay a minute too long with one of them, I can be sure three or four others are going to shout for the bedpan, and then do nothing after all. . . .

"I've got one who's over sixty and who's brought up five children. . . . You'd think that would have taught her some sense. . . . Not at all! . . . She demands the bedpan twenty or thirty times a day, and as soon as she was able to speak she complained to the Professor that she'd been neglected. . . .

"Luckily, Professor Audoire knows what they're like. . . . Of course it's no joke for them. . . . I can feel for them. . . . All the same, being ill oneself is no excuse for making everyone else miserable. . . .

"Try and move your leg. . . . The one I'm holding. . . . Go on, try! . . . It won't hurt you. . . . Mark my word, you'll be using both legs quicker than you think. . . . You can trust Angèle! . . . Even Monsieur Audoire knows that I've got an eye for these things and he sometimes asks me: Angèle, what d'you think of No. 7? . . .

"I've had so many of them pass through my hands! . . . In our job, we're with sick people from morning till night. . . . We see more of them than the doctors, who have only a moment with each of them. . . .

"I shouldn't be talking to you like this. . . . I wouldn't do it with anyone else. . . . I know you won't get worked up. . . . When they bring us in a new case, well, after a couple of days I can tell whether the bed's going to be occupied for a long time or not. . . . And nine times out of ten I warn the nurse on night duty that Mrs. So-and-So won't be there next morning. . . .

"By and by, when the sun gets up a bit, I'll open the window. You must have some air. . . . You oughtn't to be living in a stuffy atmosphere. . . ."

She handled him like a baby, took particular care about washing his genitals, and made no bones about joking on the subject.

"We've got to look after this thing. . . . You'll be wanting to use it again. . . ."

Were the other women who worked in the wards like her, or had he happened on an exceptional phenomenon? He was beginning to understand why Besson had congratulated himself on securing Mlle Blanche for him.

And yet Angèle was quite right. He was growing used to her vulgarity and outspokenness, so overwhelmed by her vitality that he forgot to brood about himself.

"Good! You're nice and clean now. . . . I'll send for the barber, so that you'll be looking smart in case you have visitors. . . ."

The old barber shaved him while two cleaning women scrubbed the room. Only one of the Italian girls was on duty. The other woman was sullen and silent, never even apologizing when her broom knocked against the legs of the bed.

The bells started ringing. They would ring, now, for every service. The barber, on leaving him, went off to the main ward, and from nine o'clock onward all the shadows trooped past in the same direction.

"They're going down to the chapel," Angèle explained. "Are you a Catholic? Has the chaplain been to see you? . . . He's a nice quiet fellow. . . . Not like the one we had before, who used to scare the patients by rushing to their bedsides without being sent for. . . .

"It's very upsetting, when you're not well, to see a priest appear at the foot of your bed as if he were bringing you Extreme Unction. . . .

"I don't believe in God or the devil myself, and it wouldn't worry me. . . . But I've had some women who were convinced their last hour had struck, and whom you couldn't get to listen to reason. . . .

132

"There's no risk of that with this chaplain. . . . He only comes if he's sent for, and he smokes a big pipe that makes him look like one of the little old men in the infirmary. . . ."

The matron had still not put in an appearance. He had not caught sight of her silhouette behind the glass.

"I'll go and get your orange juice. . . . I'll be back in a moment. . . ."

The sky was bluer than ever, a clear light blue. The air outside must be light too, now that last night's downpour had cleared away its dust and dankness.

Without asking leave, Angèle had thrown out the yellow carnations, which were withered, and when she returned with the orange juice she brought him a rose.

"I don't like seeing a vase left empty, especially a pretty vase like that. . . . I pinched a flower from one of the bunches in the other private room. . . . The patient's not likely to notice, for he's not in his right mind. . . ."

Who was this other patient? For the first time he felt curious about one of his hospital neighbors. She raised the head of the bed and held out the feeding cup, from which he drank without effort.

Everything was perplexing. He missed his familiar routine. The intern surprised him too. It was not the one who usually came, and he wore such thick glasses that his pupils looked as big as marbles.

"He's taken his orange juice nicely, Doctor. . . . He's being very good. . . . We're getting to know one another and we shall soon have become good friends. . . . His temperature's a little below normal, ninety-eight point four. . . . His pulse is good, quite steady. . . ."

Generally such things were not mentioned in front of him. The others would exchange glances, whisper in a corner, or go out into the passage to talk in low voices.

Was it just that this dumpy woman was not treating him like a private patient but like one of those in the wards? The doctor himself, moreover, was not content with asking him to open his mouth and muttering a few reassuring words:

"I read your paper, like everybody else. . . . The gossip column is what I like best. . . . Am I hurting you? . . . No? . . . Raise your left arm. . . . A little higher . . . Again. . . . That's right. . . . Now try to move the fingers of your right hand. . . .

"I suppose it's not the same person who writes all the gossip under the signature Dorine? He'd have to spend his earnings running from one theater to another, his nights at night clubs, and in the afternoons be at the races and in the Chamber at the same time. . . .

"I'd be awfully interested, one day, if it's not too much to ask, to visit a big newspaper office and see how it works. . . . Now breathe. . . . Through your mouth. . . . Deeply. . . . That's fine! . . . The trachea's quite free and the bronchial tubes are clear. . . ."

The intern went on, as much for Maugras's benefit as for the nurse's:

"I don't see the point of keeping him any longer in an uncomfortable position. . . . He can lie flat again. . . . If the mucus starts troubling him we'll have to lower his head again. . . ."

She gave him an impish look, as if to say: "Wasn't I right?"

The doctor went on, standing relaxed, as if he were talking to a normal person:

"I shall be on duty all week and I'll have a chance to see you again. . . . I'm delighted to have made your acquaintance, though I'm sorry the circumstances are so unpleasant for you. . . . Is this your fourth day?"

He looked at the chart.

"Sixth. . . . You're well ahead, and your progress should speed up from now on. . . . Well, have a good day! . . . If you should need me, Angèle knows where to find me. . . ."

134

As soon as he had gone, she explained:

"That boy's done very well, he's been working and studying at the same time. . . . He's even done some baby-sitting
in the evenings, while parents have gone to the movies.
. . . They say he'll end up as professor, and I shouldn't
be at all surprised. . . . You're not cold? . . . Shall I open
the window? . . ."

He had shrunk back instinctively, dreading sudden contact
with the fresh air. And not only the air; it was his first contact
with the world outside, and all at once he heard footsteps on
the gravel paths.

"If you could see how the old fellows are enjoying themselves! . . . On rainy days they're glum and sulky, they don't
know what to do with themselves. . . . This place is so
crowded! . . . Did you know there are over two thousand
five hundred invalids and incurables? Not to mention nurses
and doctors and kitchen staff. . . .

"You must agree it's a pleasure to breathe. . . . This
morning it felt like spring. . . . Yesterday, everybody was
ready to go off the deep end, and they were having trouble in
all the departments. The rain never stopped, and worst of all
there was that wind that gets on your nerves. . . . And then
overnight . . . You're sure you're not cold? . . ."

"No. . . ."

He had not shaken his head. He had *said* no. With his
lips. Without being asked to. The sound had been practically
normal. He was shaking with excitement, felt the need to test
the thing still further, uttered the words:

"I'm not cold. . . ."

He felt like laughing; tears were in his eyes. He had spoken!
He could speak!

"I say, my dear monsieur, you *are* coming on! . . . What
did Angèle tell you? . . . Wasn't she right? . . ."

Mlle Blanche was being punished for her decision. It was
not in her presence that he had uttered his first words, for his

135

stuttered syllables the other day didn't count. He would surprise her tomorrow, to get his revenge.

And Audoire? Would he be told?

"D'you know what I'm going to suggest? I shall ask them to make you some nice mashed vegetables with some gravy, and I promise you that you'll eat it, and that by tomorrow at the latest you won't need this apparatus any more. . . ."

He spoke again, to prove to himself that it had not been a fluke.

"I'm not hungry. . . ."

"You'll be hungry by and by. . . . Even if you haven't got much appetite you'll enjoy being fed with a spoon and not with a needle and a rubber tube. . . ."

He did not know what to think. When she left him by himself, he stared at the window intently and felt overwhelmed. Everything was altered. Nothing was happening as he had foreseen, as he had felt so sure it would happen. He said out loud, to himself alone:

"I'm speaking. . . ."

He repeated two or three times, in the silence of the room:

"I'm speaking. . . . I'm speaking. . . ."

He was afraid his voice might give out. It did not give out.

Not only was he speaking, but he was going to eat, Angèle had given him her word and he believed her.

Lina was at the Château de Candines with Marie-Anne and her gang. Besson, at La Bluterie, was playing with his grandchildren. Clabaud had probably taken advantage of the weekend to shut himself up and work. Where had Mlle Blanche gone? With whom? Audoire himself was away, and so was the matron.

He had taken this opportunity to speak. He would have to get used to the idea. He had not been prepared for it. It had happened suddenly, in a strange way, while he was not thinking about it.

"Well, there we are, my dear monsieur. . . . I hope

136

you've no objection to carrots? . . . That's the only vegetable they've got in the kitchen today. . . . They're making
you a purée of potatoes and carrots, with veal gravy. . . .
Is the sun hurting your eyes? . . . Am I tiring you? . . ."

"No. . . . It's . . ."

It was not his voice that failed him. It was the words, the
answer that eluded him. He needed to close his eyes, to lie
still without speaking, without thinking.

He had been so sure it was all over!

CHAPTER EIGHT

It may have been mere childishness, but such childish matters sometimes seem at the time more important than serious concerns. It was Monday. He had wakened up in time, just as the church clock was striking six.

Joséfa was asleep on her folding bed. His half-hour was his own. He could think about whatever he liked without being disturbed. Why was he not happy?

The evening before, he had intended to ask Angèle not to tell anyone that he had spoken, so as to surprise Mlle Blanche. He had kept putting this off, until Joséfa had arrived, ten minutes late, in a between-season red coat she was wearing for the first time, which still had the smell of the store about it. The beret on her coppery hair was the same red. She was out of breath, as if she had been running.

"I'm sorry, Angèle. . . . I'm late. . . . I've kept you waiting. . . ."

"Oh, well, since my daughter got married and I've been living by myself . . ."

"And what about you, Monsieur Maugras? Did you have a good day?"

Angèle gave him a mischievous look and he hadn't the heart to disappoint her.

"Very good," he replied.

But it no longer gave him the same pleasure. Toward the end of the day, his voice had seemed to him less natural than he had thought it at first, rather hoarse, as if he'd had a bad quinsy. He had difficulty in uttering certain syllables, and tended to slur them.

"What d'you say to that?" Angèle exclaimed. "I'm so glad!"

He disliked remembering it. On waking up, he found himself faced with more problems than ever. Would they go on looking after him as much? Would they still leave him Mlle Blanche, who might perhaps be needed for another patient?

Angèle, the night before, had told him they were short of nurses, not only in the wards, but still more for those patients who could afford the luxury of a private nurse.

"You see, it's not easy to find girls willing to work twelve hours a day. . . ."

Of course, it was work. He tended to forget that Mlle Blanche spent her days with him only because it was her job. And Besson, too, would no longer feel obliged to cross Paris every day to see him.

He felt apprehensive lest the little world that had formed around him might start to disintegrate, leaving him more alone than ever. Now he had lost the resource, as he realized this morning, of withdrawing into the depths of himself. He tried in vain to recover a certain state that he could scarcely define.

Lying in his warm bed, he had undertaken a sort of assessment, of revaluation, which was far from complete, and he could not go on with it in cold blood.

Surely everyone must have experienced what, from time to time, had happened to him? You go to bed, thinking of nothing in particular. You try to sleep. You turn over and

139

over in bed without knowing whether you're awake or half asleep. Your thoughts become more and more unlike your daytime thoughts. You become intuitively aware of truths which, fully awake, you had never faced, and there is almost always a brief moment during which everything seems clear and luminous.

Next morning you try to remember it in vain, unless, remembering it, you try to forget it, because it would upset your everyday life.

He cast a listless glance at the sleeping Joséfa, he listened to the noises inattentively and without pleasure. Wouldn't Audoire need his room, since he had only two private rooms at his disposal?

He had scarcely had time to get used to things. Angèle had chattered too much. She had ended by telling him her life story and her daughter's with the same wearisome zest. Perhaps he, too, had talked too much, for the first day? Once the initial astonishment had passed, he got no further joy from it.

Joséfa threw off her blanket, rubbed her eyes, and looked at her watch.

"Good morning! . . . It's funny that you always wake up before me. . . . Are you used to getting up early? . . ."

"Yesterday I slept late. . . ."

"On *my* day off I stay in bed till ten. . . . It feels so wonderful to sleep at night like everybody else. . . ."

She stood up, fastened her brassière, tidied her uniform and her hair. She went to the door just as Mlle Blanche, in uniform, pushed it open. Didn't she seem livelier than usual? Was that the result of a day spent away from hospital?

"Good morning!" she remarked in her turn, planting herself in front of the bed and looking at him expectantly.

He hesitated, wondered whether she knew, and finally, in a sulky child's voice, brought out the words: "Good morning."

"Go on. . . . Say something else. . . ."

She showed no surprise. She must have been told.

"Say what?"

"That you're not cross with me for having taken the day off without warning you. . . ."

It was quite true that he was behaving ridiculously. He realized this, and returned her smile.

"I'm sorry. . . ."

"Are you pleased?"

"Yes . . . I think so. . . ."

Joséfa had said good-by and left the room. The routine began again: urinal, thermometer, pulse. . . .

"I hear you had some purée to eat. . . ."

She hadn't learned that from Joséfa. And she wasn't likely to have met Angèle. That meant that what had happened in his room had gone the rounds of the hospital.

"I ought to have warned you on Saturday. I wondered if I should. I was afraid you might have a bad night. Invalids don't like new faces. I was sure you would be all right with Angèle. What did you think of Angèle?"

If he made no reply this time, it was because he had nothing to say.

"She's a bit noisy, but I wish I knew my job as well as she does. They can trust her with the most difficult wards. . . ."

Did she guess what he was thinking about, as he watched her with anxious eyes? He wanted to ask her how she had spent her Sunday. He didn't dare. Then she herself broached the subject indirectly.

"I forgot I'd got a little present for you. . . ."

She drew from her pocket a cone of glossy blue cardboard, decorated with gilt arabesques and bearing the name Yves. He could not understand, grew worried, wondering whether she had a child. What business was that of his?

"They're sugared almonds. . . . Yesterday I went to my sister's at Melun for the christening of her third boy, who's a month old. . . . I'm his godmother. . . ."

141

He had tortured himself unnecessarily. Last night, then again this morning before she came, he had deliberately imagined Mlle Blanche in erotic postures, with a man. Just as in the case of Mme Remage long ago, he felt the urge to sully her. Ought he not to ask her forgiveness?

"My sister, who's younger than I am, married a schoolteacher five years ago. . . . She was teaching herself then at Origny, a village close to Melun. . . . For two years, even after the birth of their first child, they both went on working and every evening my brother-in-law bicycled over to Origny to fetch his wife. . . .

"She had a difficult time with her second pregnancy, and had to give up her job. . . .

"Now they've got three boys, a tiny house in the school yard, and an old lime tree in front of their door. . . ."

It reminded him of Fécamp, only in brighter colors. Yesterday the sun had been shining as it was today.

"If I hadn't been godmother I shouldn't have taken the day off. . . ."

"Thank you. . . ."

She wrote down his temperature on the chart, and for the first time he asked:

"What is it?"

"Ninety-eight point four. I oughtn't to tell you. Your pulse is normal. Are you ready for a wash?"

She too, like Angèle, after having sponged him from head to foot, began handling his fingers.

"Move them. . . . Yes, you can. . . . Again. . . ."

This was his bad hand, the right one. He looked at it and saw the finger joints bend slightly. Next she asked him to move his toes, but he could not manage this so well.

"Let me do it. . . . Don't be afraid. . . ."

She seized his two legs and pulled them out of the bed, then, turning to face him, passed one arm around his shoulders. He felt anxious, but offered no resistance, and presently found himself sitting on the edge of the bed with his legs dangling.

It made him feel dizzy. If she were to let go he would fall over sideways or forward. She was so close to him that he could feel the warmth and shape of her breast against his shoulder.

He scarcely recognized his own legs, they had grown so thin in so short a time. He had almost no calves now.

"Try to keep straight. . . . This is the first exercise of the set. . . . Tomorrow you will put your weight on both feet. . . ."

Having the lower part of his body naked was more embarrassing than it had been before. Because of his contact with the nurse, he was afraid of having an erection, for which he would no longer have the excuse of being unconscious or feverish.

He had scarcely thought about it when it happened, and he stammered:

"I'm very sorry. . . ."

"It's nothing. . . . I'm used to it. . . ."

So his intimate reflexes, too, were part of a process in which every stage could be anticipated!

"That's enough for today. . . ."

She put him back to bed, drew up the sheet.

"Do you like cereal cooked in milk, or do you prefer it done with water?"

He did not know what he replied. She went to fetch a bowl of cereal, oversweetened, which she gave him with a spoon.

The matron appeared while he was being fed.

"I hear we're making great progress here. . . ."

Mlle Blanche told her:

"He has just sat on the edge of the bed for nearly five minutes. . . ."

"Very good! Very good!"

And pointing to the dextrose vessel:

"You can take that away. . . ."

He himself did not feel sure that they were not going too fast. He felt as if he could not keep up. They were in such a hurry to re-establish him in everybody else's world, which had for so long been his own. He was not ready for it; he didn't believe in it yet, and he suspected them of wanting to get rid of him.

The two Italian girls arrived with their buckets and their broom. A vacuum cleaner was functioning in the corridor. He had not heard it on previous days, and deduced therefrom that it was used only once or twice a week. A man thrust the apparatus into the room, and for a while his head felt full of its buzzing.

No sooner was the housework finished than it was time for the barber.

"Wouldn't you like me to give you a haircut?"

"Not today."

"I say, Mademoiselle Blanche, your patient's talking. . . ."

And to Maugras:

"It makes you happy, doesn't it? . . . I've seen some people weep buckets out of pure joy. . . ."

Not necessarily out of joy. Hadn't those others, like himself, felt frightened at the sudden disappearance of that barrier? It was the first step toward a forced return into the world of men. What would they force him to do next?

The intern who had come yesterday, with his big round eyes behind thick glasses, came striding in and spoke to the nurse first.

"Have a good Sunday? . . . How did the christening go? . . ."

"We had great fun in the afternoon. . . ."

"And you, how are you feeling this morning?"

Maugras was sulking, even more so during the last few minutes, since the intern had come in. A short while ago, when Mlle Blanche had told him about her sister at Melun, he had asked her:

"What about yourself? Don't you intend to get married?"

"In the first place, there have to be two of you to get married. . . . And then circumstances have to be favorable. . . ."

She'd had a wistful look as she answered this, and now, perhaps, he understood why. He thought he noticed, between herself and the intern, a kind of familiarity, of understanding, which was not due merely to their working in the same hospital. They addressed each other with the formal *vous*. But it looked like a game. Maugras was convinced that their eyes were saying:

"You didn't find the day too long? . . . Did you think of me sometimes? . . ."

"The whole time, you great silly. . . . And you? Did you have a lot of work? . . ."

He could not be sure he was right. Their attitude none the less reminded him of certain couples one meets in the street, which had always fascinated him. They don't go arm in arm, they walk like the rest of the crowd, and yet one can sense at a first glance that they are in perfect harmony and that they form a small solid core amidst all the rest. He had sometimes actually followed them with a jealous eye as though to discover their secret before they vanished down the subway or into a movie house.

"So that aphasia of yours is nothing but an unpleasant memory. . . . Aren't you glad? . . ."

They all wanted him to be glad. Was he telling a lie when he said yes? Could he possibly explain the truth to them?

It was, in fact, true that he was glad in a certain sense. None the less, he was determined to defend himself and he would not allow them to rush him prematurely back into life. He wasn't even sure that he wanted to return.

145

"The Professor will see you a little later; he's very busy this morning. . . . Two urgent cases turned up almost at the same time. . . ."

They exchanged glances over his bed, and each glance seemed to cause a thrill of delight. Why should this affect him, since he was not in love with Mlle Blanche? Her private life was no concern of his. He was convinced Joséfa had lovers and this did not disturb him, although he had practically decided that, if he recovered, he'd like to make love with her.

"Has he had something to eat?"

"Some cereal. . . . Without any difficulty. . . ."

"Well, there's nothing for me to do but wish you both a pleasant day. . . ."

She went to the door with him, but did not follow him into the passage, on purpose, Maugras felt convinced, because she had understood that he had guessed their secret. The proof was that she wasn't quite herself when she came back beside him, looked at him curiously and finally murmured:

"He's a good fellow. . . . Professor Audoire thinks he's his best assistant. . . ."

And so deserving, too! He had worked to pay for his studies! A professor-to-be! . . . Angèle had already told him all about it. What did he care? He had no intention of getting divorced so as to marry Mlle Blanche.

"There have to be two of you," she had said.

There were two of them.

". . . and circumstances have to be favorable. . . ."

Perhaps he was married? Maugras had not thought of looking to see whether he wore a ring. She was not. Were they waiting for the young doctor's position to be more settled? Were they lovers?

Everything was speeded up this morning. You could see it wasn't a Sunday. It looked as if, in order to atone for yester-

146

day's absence, there was being twice as much of everything. People were bustling about. The doors never stopped opening and shutting, the nurses scurrying along the passage. Here came Audoire, who was also in a hurry, but seemed more relaxed than on other days.

"How are you?"

"All right, Doctor. . . ."

"I hear you've been sitting on the edge of the bed. . . . That's fine. . . . I'm glad, too, that the touch of inflammation in your respiratory tract subsided so quickly. . . . That will enable you to start rehabilitation all the sooner. . . . Our friend Besson hasn't been around this morning? . . ."

Mlle Blanche, out of habit, answered for him.

"Not yet. . . ."

Besson, too, must be making up yesterday's lost time at Broussais.

"I see you've begun to take food. . . . Life is going to be pleasanter for you. . . . Have you any appetite?"

"A little. . . ."

Actually, he answered without conviction. Hitherto they had not asked his opinion. He felt bewildered at being consulted, awkward and uneasy. He needed to set his thoughts in order, but it seemed as if he would not be allowed leisure to do so.

Already, they seemed to have changed. Audoire had become commonplace, he was just a doctor like any other, mechanically feeling his patient's pulse, leaning over with his ear to the stethoscope, saying, in a tone of indifference, the words he repeated a hundred times a day:

"Cough. . . . Breathe in. . . . Cough. . . . Very good. . . ."

Then Audoire, too, wished him a pleasant day, and went off to minister to another patient, then another, and so on until it was time for him to go home.

147

Twelve o'clock, and René had not had a moment's peace. The trolleys passed along the corridor and the saucepans clanked noisily. Mlle Blanche went out for a minute and came back with a soup plate full of pale green purée, then, sitting down beside him, she began to feed him with a spoon.

Besson chose that moment to appear, and Maugras was annoyed at this, feeling just as embarrassed as when the nurse gave him an enema.

"What did I tell you, my dear René?"

Of course he'd told him, of course he was triumphant!

"I suppose you understood why I didn't come yesterday. . . . You know what Yvonne is like. . . . If she had to spend a Sunday away from La Bluterie and her grandchildren, she'd be terribly upset. . . . Now that you've recovered your speech, your life here is going to be transformed. . . . I see no objection, for instance, to your editor, who's got a funny name that I always forget . . ."

"Colère. . . ."

"I see no objection to Colère's coming in every day for a few minutes to keep in touch with you. . . . Mlle Blanche will see that he doesn't stay too long or tire you. . . . I know how keen you are about your paper. . . ."

Besson was wrong: he didn't really know him.

"There's no question of your seeing people from morning till night or turning your room into an editorial office, but two or three visitors a day . . ."

Who? Why? Was Besson thinking of Lina? Had she called him up again?

"I see there's a telephone connection beside your bed. . . . I suppose they've got an instrument that can be hooked up there. . . . I'll have a word with the matron. . . ."

Maugras shook his head, because his mouth was full. It reminded him of the very recent time when that was the only way he could express himself.

"I don't wish . . . ," he brought forth at last.

148

More precisely, what he said was:
"I don't bish . . ."
That would happen with Besson, of all people!

At last he was left alone. Mlle Blanche went off to lunch
in the nurses' dining room. She exhorted him, as she left:
"Have a good rest. . . . You've had a tiring morning.
. . . I'll try to come back quietly and not wake you. . . ."
He did not intend to go to sleep. Nor did he want to lie
with his eyes open staring at the sunlit roof on the other side
of the window. He knew exactly what degree of drowsiness
he must attain, even though he could not reach it at will.
Besson, on the point of leaving him, had turned back.
"Guess who turned up for lunch at La Bluterie. . . .
Marelle and Nadine. . . . They were trying out their new
car. . . ."
Maugras had been present at the dress rehearsal of Julien
Marelle's first play in 1928, and he remembered it better than
more recent events. The older he got, the less impression the
months and the years made on him, and there were gaps in
his memory, facts that he could place only within two or
three years.
Since that time, Marelle had written a play a year. In fact,
it was basically always the same play, the same formula which
he had perfected and which had brought him to the Academy.
Was he aware of this? Did he feel any regrets at not having
taken a different path?
For the past twenty years he had lived in the same flat in
the Rue Blanche, a little beyond the Casino de Paris, but
practically each new play found him living with a different
woman. Either he set up house with his leading lady or he
wrote a part for a new mistress, always as much in love, as
dramatically passionate. As a matter of fact, this succession
of women, some of whom might be reinstated after an interim,
involved him in innumerable complications.

Maugras did not think about Lina, he refused to think about her. He would do so one day, he knew, and then he would exhaust the subject once and for all, he would probe the truth to its depths. The time had not yet come.

He did not want to think about the paper either, nor about Colère, still less about the three Schneider brothers. The pictures in his mind did not necessarily follow the thread of his ideas, and it was the pictures which, so to speak, were in the right. It was they, he felt convinced, that represented his deepest preoccupations, as dreams might. He remembered vaguely some discussion about dreams and somebody putting forward a fascinating theory on this subject.

What puzzled him was that most of his mental pictures today were of women. Why was he preoccupied about Mlle Blanche, and why had her relations with the intern with the thick lenses put him into such a bad temper all morning that he had been surly with his friend Besson, who had gone away quite crestfallen?

He had not been in love with Pilar. Women had played only an accessory role in his life. It might even be said that they had no influence on him, on his destiny, that work alone had mattered and had excited him.

He was not a skirt-chaser, like Besson. Neither would he be capable, like Jublin, of carrying on a second existence, unconnected with his friends and his cafés, in a stuffy lodging in the Rue de Rennes. Nor was he tempted, like Marelle, to form a new grand passion every year.

Not once, since he had come here, had he pictured himself at his desk or at the printing press, or in any one of his professional activities.

And yet the caricature recently published in some weekly reflected the truth fairly accurately. It showed him with a telephone in each hand, a visitor in front of him telling him a story, a secretary taking down dictation from him, with

Fernand Colère, in the doorway, wondering whether he dared come in.

The only time he had thought of the office, it was the face of Zulma, the typist he had seen only two or three times, that had sprung into his mind.

Now, without rhyme or reason, the early days of his career recurred to him. He had arrived at the Gare Saint-Lazare carrying his two suitcases, one of which, being somewhat dilapidated, was fastened with a strap.

It had been a cold gray day. In the train, he had been shocked and depressed by the ugliness of the suburbs. He knew all this but he did not picture it. It failed to come to life in his mind. He had dragged his cases from one hotel to another without finding anything cheap enough, and so at last reached the Place Clichy.

Not a single picture in his memory, not one thrill of recognition. On the other hand, as though to brighten this dreary period of his life, he recalled Pilar, the shop window in the Rue Auber, and the scene in the hotel.

If Abbé Vinage was right, this unconscious selection of images had its meaning. He took no delight in recalling this particular one, for, like his memories of the house between the docks, it was humiliating. Was that not also significant?

It was the afternoon of Christmas Day, his first Christmas in Paris, and he had spent Christmas Eve roaming the streets by himself, envying the couples cheerfully disappearing into restaurants.

He had as yet no friends. He had met Marelle once, in the waiting room of a newspaper office in the Rue de Croissant, and they had merely exchanged a few words.

Although he spent most of his time on the Boulevards and in the Rue de Montmartre, which were the home of the press at that time, he had gone on living in the Hôtel Beauséjour, Rue des Dames, in the Batignolles district, where he lived in the same room for three years, first alone, and then with his first wife Marcelle; indeed, their daughter was almost born there.

He had brought enough money with him from Fécamp to last two months, and the two months were nearly over. He had succeeded in placing only half a dozen news items, paid for at the rate of ten or twenty francs, he could not remember which.

Perhaps it was because he was lying in a bed, because he had been so close to death, because he was not sure, in spite of what they kept telling him, that he would ever become normal again, that these details meant so much to him. It struck him that he had gone one better than Artaud, his reporter; Artaud had died on the fourth or fifth day, and René had now reached his seventh.

Of that Christmas Eve he remembered one restaurant in the Rue du Faubourg-Montmartre, with a broad streamer saying: "Late night supper—Music—Dancing—Free gifts." The curtains were drawn. Shadows could be seen moving against them, as here against the glazed door, and music and laughter could be heard.

He had gone back to Batignolles on foot. He had slept late. A cold gray veil hung over the city, as if it were about to snow. He'd be able to paint that sky, flat-tinted, without luminosity, those houses with their slightest cracks clearly etched, and the sharply defined rooftops.

He ate some lunch, or some rolls, somewhere or other, he'd forgotten where. At three o'clock in the afternoon—a big clock showed three—he was standing with his hands in his pockets in front of a shop window in the Rue Auber, the very wide shop window of a steamship company in which the model of a transatlantic liner was displayed.

Why had he been gazing, fascinated, at that yard-long boat with its portholes, its various decks, its lifeboats slung from their stands?

152

The streets had been empty. Only a few family parties were to be seen, children in their Sunday best being taken to visit a grandmother or an aunt.

At one point, somebody came to stand beside him, whom he first saw hazily reflected in the glass. It was a girl with black hair, who seemed to be feeling the cold in a thin over-coat of an acid green color.

For three weeks, for reasons of thrift, he had been resist-ing the temptation of the professional streetwalkers who haunted the Boulevard des Batignolles, a stone's throw from where he lived. Was that what made him brave?

They looked at one another in the glass, with the black, white, and red ship between their two reflections. One or the other of them must have smiled first.

He had no idea what they had said to one another before walking off side by side, without knowing where they were going, mechanically strolling down the almost deserted Grands Boulevards.

In uncertain, lisping French she told him that she was Spanish, that she had come to Paris with the family of a South American diplomat, whose children she looked after.

He would find it hard to describe her face. She was not pretty, as he had understood prettiness in those days. On re-flection, he discovered that Lina bore a certain likeness to her.

He had made her repeat her first name, Pilar, several times; he thought it harsh-sounding.

He did not guess that he would be thinking of her thirty years later, in the solitude of a hospital bedroom. Even at the time, it had been an unimportant encounter.

He could scarcely recognize himself in the young man he then was. He had wondered, for lack of money, what he was going to do with her, glancing at movie posters yet unwilling to suggest a visit to the movies. He had almost taken refuge in one of those brasseries with steam-clouded windows that suggested friendly warmth.

Then a gap. How had he come to take her to that cheap hotel in the Rue Bergère? He was amazed at having been so bold. Pilar's first kiss, when they were alone in the bedroom, was so adept, so unfamiliar to him, that it shocked him.

She burst out laughing.

"You not know?"

They must have been about the same age, but she acted as the elder. How many times he gave her reason to repeat, with that curious accent of hers:

"You not know?"

He had watched her undress, but it had left no trace in his memory. All he knew was that she was rather thin and had very pointed breasts. He had never before seen such pointed breasts, with nipples that were almost brown.

When he had tried to take her in the way he was used to at Fécamp and Le Havre, she had protested, still in the same comical fashion.

"Not make love like brute, René. . . ."

She was enjoying herself. The more surprised, the clumsier he showed himself, the more pleasure it gave her.

"Lie down. . . . You lie down and shut eyes. . . ."

For three hours they remained shut up in the room, and it was pervaded with their odor. She took all the initiative, laughing at his embarrassment and shyness. When they were dressed again she asked him:

"How much you pay for the room?"

He did not understand why she wanted to know. She hunted in her bag, and drew out some money which she gave him.

"Yes. . . . Yes. . . . You your share. . . . Me my share. . . . As in bed. . . ."

He dared not hurt her by refusing. Once again they walked along the streets, where the gas lamps were now burning. They had gone all the way up the Champs-Elysées and he wondered, now, what they had found to say to one another.

It was night when they reached the Avenue Hoche, where

154

Pilar stopped in front of a private mansion whose façade was decorated with a coat of arms and a flagstaff.

She gave him a swift kiss before hurrying off, not toward the main doorway but toward the tradesmen's entry, without bothering to ask him where and when they should meet again.

It was to be never. Probably she had not wanted to. Twice he had prowled around the mansion. The kitchen, in the basement, was brightly lit up, and the second time he had caught sight of Pilar, in uniform, chatting gaily with a manservant.

That was what he remembered of his early days in Paris, and not his ventures into editors' offices, the waiting rooms where he had cooled his heels, his first contacts with the men who were his friends today.

Then he remembered. There was one other picture, and this, too, was of a shop window, in the Boulevard de Clichy, not far from Graf's brasserie in fact, but before his Graf period, the window of a delicatessen.

Out of economy he used to eat at home most of the time, bread, cheese, sausage, sometimes a bit of tripe warmed up over an alcohol lamp, which he stood on the window sill outside so that the smell should not pervade the hotel, where cooking was against the rules.

Later on, Marcelle and he carried on the same method. They hadn't been the only ones to do so.

In the window of the delicatessen, ready-made dishes were displayed, lobster *médaillons* in aspic, roast chicken, shrimp in shells, *pâtés en croûte,* almost always adorned with a slice of truffle.

On his way home at night he used to stop and gaze at these inaccessible viands, pressing his forehead against the cold window while his breath clouded it.

Marelle had gone through the same ordeal, and so had Couffé the novelist. They both liked to talk about it sentimentally, at the Grand Véfour lunch parties.

There was no self-pity in Maugras's attitude. He thought

155

about it gravely, as if he were seeking some mysterious link between the past and the present. What, for instance, was the significance of his encounter with Pilar? He had never had another experience of that sort. It had disconcerted him, particularly to begin with. As far as he could remember, he had not felt humiliated at the time.

Later on, things had never happened after the same fashion, either with Marcelle, his first wife, by whom he had had a child, or with Hélène Portal, who had refused to marry him, or finally with Lina.

What, exactly, was he searching for in that luminous haze, as he lay half asleep? He was conscious of the door being opened, of somebody closing it again quietly instead of leaving it ajar, of Mlle Blanche watching him from a distance and then tiptoeing to sit down by the window.

If he should venture to speak freely to her, to tell her what had been going through his head when she thought him asleep, would she not ascribe these ramblings to his illness?

It seemed only logical that an embolism should leave its traces in the brain. But then why, long before he went into hospital, while he was leading a normal life, did he sometimes find himself pursuing the same shadows, when he lay in bed at night?

That was not quite correct. He had not pursued them, as he was doing now.

He had shunned them, on the contrary, attributing them to insomnia or indigestion.

"Father, I accuse myself of sinning against the sixth commandment. . . ."

"In thought?"

"In thought and in deed. . . ."

The first few times, the muffled voice behind the grille had inquired:

"By yourself, my son?"

"By myself."

Lina had not called that morning, as she had promised without being asked. She must be back from Eure-et-Loir. If only she did not take it into her head to come and see him without warning, as she'd done on Saturday!

He felt less vexed with her than with anyone else. He wondered what Mlle Blanche might be thinking as she sat motionless, watching through the window the old incurables walking about in the sunshine in little groups, smoking their pipes, or sitting still on their benches.

For a long time, he had been afraid of being a failure. He knew a great many failures. Editorial offices attracted them, as they did lunatics. It wasn't always easy to distinguish between them, for they all came with far-fetched notions to expound.

The difference lay in the fact that failures are resigned, don't believe in what they tell you and end by asking for a few francs. Thus, old pals turned up from time to time to sponge on him, feigning joviality.

"You see, I'm going through a bad spell, but by next week . . ."

Where were the ones who had completely disappeared from circulation? Might some of them be found among the inmates of the infirmary?

He might have been a failure too. His early days had been like theirs. When he left the Lycée Guy-de-Maupassant, without attempting the exams which he knew he would not pass, he had no plan, no project, no idea what he would do in life.

He had nearly gone to work for Monsieur Remage, where he would have had the same career as his father.

He lacked talent, and his colleagues knew that he was incapable of writing a good article. Wasn't that why, from the very first, he had instinctively specialized in news items and gossip?

157

He was curious about the lives of prominent men, and asked himself questions about them. He had tried to find the answers to these questions.

Since the general public shared his curiosity, news items and gossip had made his fortune.

People spoke of his infallible flair, but others, more fastidious, described it as being in bad taste. Perhaps both were right. It was true that he had begun by collecting backstairs gossip, like a scavenger. . . .

Enough of that. He was coming face to face with depressing truths. He felt himself getting bogged down, and even before opening his eyes he said out loud:

"I'm thirsty. . . ."

It wasn't true, but he needed to come up for air, and to see once more the soothing face of Mlle Blanche.

CHAPTER NINE

He was nearing the close of his seventh day in hospital, Monday, February 8th, without suspecting that it was to mark the end of a slice of his life. The people around him knew it, and perhaps that was why he felt ill at ease. He had antennae. He guessed, from indefinable signs, that a change was in preparation, somewhat as the father of a family guesses that his wife and children have a surprise in store for him.

He felt uneasy and nervous. Several times, as he looked at Mlle Blanche, he was on the point of questioning her, of imploring her to speak frankly to him, as to a grownup. He was just about to do so when the telephone rang in the corridor. The nurse was called out to answer it. He felt sure it was Lina, and was glad he had refused to have an extension fixed beside his bed.

"Your wife's on the line. . . . She's sorry she didn't phone this morning. . . . She caught a cold in the country, and she's had to go to bed. . . . She's afraid it may be flu. . . ."

He felt neither surprise nor distress on hearing this. Almost every time she stayed with Marie-Anne, Lina retired to bed for two days, and she invariably talked about flu or bronchitis.

159

"She wants to know if you need anything, if there isn't something you'd like her to send you. . . ."

"Some underwear, maybe?"

"You've been sent a whole suitcaseful, and I've put it away in the closet. You've even got a dressing gown and slippers. . . ."

He hesitated, and was on the point of mentioning the red diary that lay on his desk at the Résidence.

"Some money," he said.

"They've deposited some in the office. . . . The people at your newspaper thought of that, and an account's been opened for you downstairs. . . ."

"Don't let my wife know I can speak. . . ."

She gave a smile of complicity. She had understood. Especially where Lina was concerned, she understood everything without being told. She disappeared once more and, when she came back, made sure by a glance that this telephone call had not upset him. He was already thinking not of his wife but of his diary.

He was not a man who went in for a lot of papers, for notes, memoranda, meticulousness. In spite of the complexity of his activities, he never had writing materials about him. He carried everything in his head.

None the less, since he'd been here, he had frequently felt a longing not to keep a diary, but to write an occasional word or two so as, later on, to recover the stages of his evolution.

That sounded pretentious. The truth, however, was quite simple. In the stillness of his room he had tackled so many subjects that he was in danger of losing his way among them. Several of these subjects bore on an essential truth, he knew that, even if he did not know how or why. For the first time he felt the need to give concrete verbal form to certain impressions, certain gleams of light that had appeared to him.

For a week, now, he had been seeking something. Not to

160

justify himself, despite appearances. He was ready to plead guilty. But of what?

He wanted this slow pilgrimage to leave some traces. Everything changes too fast. He dreaded further changes.

"If you should see a stationer's open on your way home, would you be kind enough to buy me a diary?"

He did not want the old one, which was at the George V, and in which he would find entries that no longer interested him. He would rather make a fresh start.

"Are you thinking of doing some work?"

"No."

She understood that too, of course.

"A big diary?"

"It doesn't matter. . . ."

He would not write much, just a word here and there, which only he would be capable of interpreting, and besides it was tiring to write with one's left hand.

"You know, Professor Besson d'Argoulet has a great admiration for you! . . . He's spoken of your wonderful energy, which has always amazed him. . . . He says you've an incredible capacity for work. . . ."

No more so than Besson himself, who managed to carry on several different lives at once!

"He also says you're an absolute slave driver to your staff, but that they don't complain because they worship you. . . . Is that true?"

"I'm not in a position to judge. . . ."

"It must be harder for you than for most people to be immobilized. . . ."

He merely murmured: "D'you think so?"

He felt she had something at the back of her mind. If she alluded to his paralysis in this way, didn't that mean that . . . That what? He could not tell. Mlle Blanche wore a disquieting smile. . . .

161

Once again, he would have liked to confide in her that he was not anxious to recover, that he was afraid of it. But that would have been unkind, since she was looking after him, and he was incapable of being deliberately unkind to anyone.

It was almost a physical characteristic. He could not bear to see suffering. It amounted to cowardice. When he was forced to dismiss one of the staff he always got Colère to do it. He was even more shocked to witness humiliation and distress than real grief or despair.

This was not his only reason for avoiding a longer conversation with his nurse. Although he was not reconciled to the idea of recovery, he was conscious, nevertheless, of certain slight signs of progress, and he would occasionally move his fingers and toes furtively under his blanket.

"When you need anything from town, be sure to ask me. . . ."

"Thank you. . . ."

It happened quite by chance, since he did not know that a change was imminent. If his Christmas story was not exactly a gloomy one, it was none the less somewhat crude and harsh in coloring.

Perhaps on account of the sunlight, glowing sumptuously red, which he could see from his bed, the two stories he told himself that Monday were brimful of light, warmth, and well-being.

The first of them belonged, like the story of Pilar, to the Rue des Dames period, a year or a year and a half later. Two years, since he'd been married a few weeks by then.

He was then working regularly for the *Boulevard,* writing about half its news items. Marcelle was not yet pregnant, and was taking Dullin's course on dramatic art at the Atelier Theater.

One evening, as they were walking home arm in arm, he suggested:

"Why shouldn't we go to the country tomorrow?"

162

What had caused that sudden longing for the country? He could not remember. Possibly a poster, glimpsed casually. He did not know the real countryside, being more familiar with the shingle beaches and cliffs of Normandy.

Even today, despite his property at Arneville, he felt indifference, even a certain hostility, toward the countryside, except for his kitchen garden, which he inspected every Sunday morning with the gardener.

As in the case of that Christmas afternoon, he could remember nothing about "before" or "afterwards," except that Paris had a dusty taste and a smell of apéritifs.

How had they chosen the goal of their expedition? They had set off very early in the morning and taken a train to Orléans, attracted toward the Loire because of its associations with French history. Nothing was decided beforehand. As they were leaving the station they caught sight of a local train and asked where it was going.

"To Cléry. . . ."

They got into it. They had started off warmly clad, for the mornings were still cool, and in the jolting coach they began to feel too hot.

Of Cléry he remembered nothing but the Basilica, which they visited, all gray stone and coolness. They ate in a restaurant where there were no cloths on the tables, and he remembered particularly some goat's milk cheese, hard and dry but very tasty, which he had never eaten before.

"Is the Loire far off?"

"If you take the highway, it's about one and a half miles."

"Aren't there any footpaths?"

"There are several, but it'll take you much longer. . . ."

Why had he, who never drank much, encumbered himself with a bottle of local white wine, which weighed down his pocket and bumped against his leg?

He remembered nothing about the footpath. They lost their way. Marcelle's feet hurt her. They ended up amidst reeds, on marshy ground, and they were annoyed because they could not see the Loire.

Suddenly it was there in front of them, cool and shimmering, with its pebbled sandbanks. From the spot they were in they could see nothing but the opposite bank and a man, very far off, wearing a straw hat, who was fishing, sitting on a campstool in a flat boat.

They were thirsty. They drank from the bottle of wine, which was lukewarm. They had already drunk with their meal at the inn. Drowsy with the heat, they lay down on the sand, amidst the whispering reeds.

He recalled the bottle of wine standing to cool in the river water, with only its neck showing. He had taken off his jacket and tie, Marcelle her shoes and stockings. She had paddled in the water, trying to splash him, and then had come to lie down beside him.

Was there a meaning in all this? Did this picture deserve to have found a place in his memory?

His skin, burning hot, had the wholesome smell of country sweat. Everything smelled good, the reeds, the earth, the river. And the wine, once it was cooled, had a taste he had never met with again.

He had chewed a blade of grass, lying on his back, his hands behind his neck, his gaze lost in the blue depths of the sky, where an occasional bird passed.

Did he sleep? Probably not, but his whole body was steeped in well-being and peace. He remembered one gesture, his hand groping at his side, touching sand and then Marcelle's body. He felt so lazy that he took a long time to make up his mind and slide over on top of her.

He had never really loved Marcelle. He had married her so as not to be alone, so as to have somebody else there, perhaps, too, so as to have somebody to protect. That was another question, which he was in no hurry to consider.

They stayed for a long time almost motionless, like certain insects you see mating, and he felt the sun on his back, heard the lapping sound of the water, the shivering of the reeds.

He was not drunk, but he had drunk enough for his body, from head to foot, to be more acutely sensitive. A smell of saliva and sex mingled with the other smells.

That was all. Afterwards, they finished the bottle. They tried to lie down again and recover the state of grace they had just experienced without seeking it.

The spell was broken. The air had grown cooler. The sun was clouded over, and they got lost again on their way back to Cléry. Marcelle was tired, and grumbled at him for taking the wrong path.

When their daughter was born, he did some reckoning. He would have liked it if she had been conceived that day, on the banks of the Loire. But the dates did not fit.

A luminous image, then, one hour, less than an hour, of what he was tempted to call perfect happiness, a gratuitous happiness, received in utter innocence and enjoyed unawares.

By hunting through his memory he might perhaps recover other recollections of the same sort. He had inevitably lived through as many summers as winters, as many days of sunshine as of rain. But it was not so much the light that mattered as a certain harmony with the light, with the whole world, a sort of fusion.

He had experienced that same fusion one other day, without Marcelle, without sexual excitement, and it had been so powerful that it made him dizzy.

Marcelle had been partly responsible for it, though. They were living in the Rue des Abbesses. Through the window they could see the white walls of the Atelier Theater, the shops, the bistrots, and the working-class life of Montmartre, with all its bustle and din, particularly in the mornings when housewives clustered around the vegetable carts.

Colette had been born. When she was only a month old Marcelle suggested sending her to an aunt's in the country. She was ashamed of the child's clubfoot, as if she were responsible for it, and she tried to lay the blame for it on the Maugras family.

"They say deformities are commoner when there are alcoholics in the family. . . . Your father drinks, doesn't he? And your mother died of TB. . . ."

She grew more and more irritable, particularly when the baby cried several times a night. At such times it was René who got up and walked about the room with Collette's head against his shoulder, in the light from the street gas lamp.

Marcelle had been incapable of bringing up a child. He had given in eventually, and their daughter had been sent away.

"In any case, country air is better for her health than the foul air of Paris. . . ."

He did not blame her for it, any more than he blamed Lina for being what she was. He did not try to justify himself. It was he who had made a mistake, and who was really responsible.

He had taken charge of a little seventeen-year-old dancer who wanted to become an actress, and he had thought himself capable of transforming her into a wife and then into a mother.

"Do you think we're really made for one another?"

She had practiced the drop-of-water method, just as in the case of Colette's departure. A single sentence that fell from time to time, like a drop of water, dripping from a tap, always in the same place. She was never insistent, but each time made her meaning a little clearer.

"I'm sure people wonder why we live together. . . . You have your own work and I have mine. . . . We're not free at the same times. . . ."

It was quite true. What was the point of going home to

find no meal ready, but instead a note telling him that his wife would be back late?

"When we happen to be alone together we've nothing to say to each other. . . ."

This had gone on for several months. He had stubbornly refused to listen. He had worried about her, wondering what would become of her.

He had been mistaken, since she had made a success of her chosen career. They had each been successful in their own field. They had only gone a short stretch of the road together, for as long as they lived in the Rue des Dames, where they played at being young married lovers and often could only afford the price of a meal by selling back empty bottles to the store.

"Why shouldn't we try an experiment? . . . Living apart for a month or two. . . . We'll soon see . . ."

She was blonde and tiny and delicate-looking. To use one of his mother's expressions, she looked, when she danced in the quadrille at the Moulin-Rouge ball, like a bird about to be swallowed by a cat, and her pale blue eyes made one think of First Communion and Children of Mary.

Actually, she had an extraordinary will power and her physical stamina was amazing.

He had left her the flat and the furniture and had gone to live in the Hôtel des Anglais in the Boulevard Montmartre.

Another confused, featureless period followed: the Grands Boulevards, the luminous street signs, the stream of green silver-topped buses, the terraces of cafés. . . .

Just as he had felt a sudden longing to see the Loire, so the word "Mediterranean" gave rise to a compulsive desire, and when he had a little money he took the train at the Gare de Lyon.

Why had he stopped at Toulon? Why, afterwards, at Hyères? He discovered unfamiliar sunlight and warmth, the smell of eucalyptus, the inescapable chirp of cicadas, and finally the palm trees that made him fancy he was in the tropics.

By chance, as at Orléans, he had climbed, not into a little train but into a ramshackle motor coach reverberating with the lilt of Southern voices. He saw the great white squares of the salt pans, the pyramids of salt glistening in the light.

"Are you going as far as the Tour Fondue?"

He stayed in the coach, and at the foot of a rock a white boat with a yellow funnel was waiting to carry passengers over to the island of Porquerolles. The captain was wearing a sun helmet. Hampers full of cackling hens were stacked up on the deck.

When the boat slid away from its moorings he stood in the bow, leaning over the transparent water. For a long time he was able to see down to the bottom and for the space of half an hour he lived in music, as though at the heart of a symphony.

That morning was like nothing he had ever experienced since. It was his great discovery of the world, of a boundless, radiant world of bright colors and thrilling sounds.

Figures were lined up on the edge of the jetty. The houses were red, blue, yellow, and green. A joyful hubbub rose as the boat was moored, then he came to a village square drenched in sun, a toy church, café terraces where you could idle, drinking white wine.

He was drunk without the help of wine. He felt exultant all through. Here, again, he had a longing to touch water, and wandered off along a dusty path.

The outline of the stone pines against the deep blue of the sky delighted him, and so did the flowers that he did not know, the cacti and prickly pears, and the shrubs with a heady perfume whose crimson fruit reminded him of strawberries.

Later, he found out that they were called "arbutus," and

that "lentisc" was the name of the plants with prickly leaves that fishermen burned to grill their fish.

He had often been back to the Mediterranean seaboard. He had seen other seas equally blue, trees and flowers that were more extraordinary, but the magic had gone, and of all his discoveries, this was the only one to have left a trace.

As at Cléry, he had nearly lost his way, slithering over smooth rocks, clutching at bushes. And, again as at Cléry, suddenly the sea was there, with its slow deep swell, so different from the sea at Fécamp.

Just as Marcelle had done, he took off his shoes to run barefoot in the burning sand, surprised to find himself on a long beach with a border of pine trees and with both ends closed in by rocks.

He ran like a child, but as a child he had never felt such joy. He walked in the water. The sandy bottom, combed by the waves, was like golden moiré. He undressed and, keeping only his pants on, rushed in straight ahead until the depth forced him to swim.

A whole orchestra resounded in his ears, with triumphant cymbal clashes stressing its rhythms.

Then . . . things went wrong, just as they had done by the Loire. The sky did not become overcast. The water remained just as limpid. He let his eye roam around the horizon. He felt alone in that immensity and, seized with panic, he swam back to the shore as if he were in danger of being swallowed up and drowned in light.

He had quickened his pace to reach the village square where fishermen were playing bowls. He had eaten bouillabaisse and drunk the white wine of the island, but he had lost contact; the wires were cut.

"It's nearly time, Monsieur Maugras. . . ."

He gave a start, for he had forgotten Mlle Blanche and Bicêtre.

"Time for what?"

She realized that he had been a long way off.

"For your temperature. . . . And then your purée. . . . And soon time for me to go. . . . I promise I won't forget the diary. . . ."

The diary? Of course! What would he write in it tonight, if he had it there? How would he sum up those two plunges into the past?

Cléry. Porquerolles.

Water, both times, and sunshine, heat, fresh smells. And both times, too, irrational panic and a sullen homeward journey.

Perhaps one word would be enough for both these adventures?

Innocence.

Was twice in a lifetime enough?

The sound of bells for early Mass ushered in Tuesday, that eighth day of which he'd been told so much:

"The first eight days are the worst. . . ."

"From the eighth day onward, you'll make spectacular progress. . . ."

He had eventually conceived an almost terrifying notion of that eighth day, as if everything were going to change all of a sudden. The nights had already become shorter, and the windows grew light earlier. Joséfa was sleeping restlessly, her hand not on her belly but on her chest. Last night she had been afraid she was getting a cold.

He listened to a few noises, out of habit, and almost immediately began thinking about Marcelle. He was dissatisfied with the picture he had formed of her the day before. He felt he was becoming petty-minded through lying in bed with nothing to do. Wasn't he growing like his father, who with a self-important air went on counting and re-counting bales of cod and sacks of salt, obsessed by the possibility of an error?

170

It was not so much for the sake of having somebody to live with that he had married his first wife, at the age of twenty-two. He wanted to get down to the absolute truth, to achieve total sincerity. After all, when he first came to Paris, knowing nothing of the world outside Fécamp, Le Havre, and Rouen, he'd behaved like any country boy attracted by light and bustle. The proof of that was that he used to spend hours walking up and down the Grands Boulevards and that he felt dizzy with delight when, at nightfall, all the lamps lit up.

It was because of the lights and the swarming humanity, too, that he began to frequent the Moulin-Rouge dance hall in the Place Blanche. The long entrance hall, with its walls lined with mirrors, glittered with hundreds of lights. Up to a specified hour, a notice over the ticket window announced: Admittance Free.

You pushed aside a red curtain at the end and you found yourself in an enormous room, throbbing with life, where two bands faced one another in the gallery and played in turn, without ever letting the atmosphere cool down.

At hundreds of tables, people sat with refreshments before them, in couples, in groups, sometimes men or women by themselves, and there was a constant coming and going to and from the dance floor, reverberating incessantly with the sound of shuffling feet.

He liked to spend hours at his little table, watching, listening, observing people's faces and attitudes. Several times he had been tempted to accost one of the girls who were waiting for partners and who rose automatically when a man came toward them.

About half-past ten a drum roll announced the entertainment, the lights went out, and spotlights were focused on the floor, onto which, with whirling petticoats and a triumphant shriek, the can-can girls now rushed.

How many of them were there? About twenty, he seemed

to remember, and each of them was dressed in a different color, each performed her individual turn while her companions stood motionless around her.

The girl in red was a handsome, buxom brunette, with a full bosom and sensual lips; the girl in yellow, a tall adolescent with an immature face; the one in violet, an acrobat who performed a series of perilous leaps.

There followed a twenty-minute orgy of sound and movement, of many-colored silks, with naked thighs flashing white above black stockings.

The girl in green was Marcelle, a thin, anemic little thing whose individual number was the least elaborate and won the least applause.

If he had had the choice, wouldn't he rather have had the red girl with the full lips? Maybe not. He would not have felt at ease with her. He'd have been afraid of her.

Night after night, he gazed at the green dancer with compassionate tenderness. Then he lingered on the sidewalk after the show to watch the dancers come out. He was disappointed to see them, in their town clothes, neither more nor less attractive than the shopgirls and typists who frequented the dance hall.

Some were met not by a rich lover with a car, but by a young man who emerged from the darkness and on whose arm they went off. Others, such as Marcelle, hurried toward the subway station.

She wore a black beret on her fair hair, and a black coat of some shaggy material. He followed her, took the same subway as she did, and sat opposite her; she seemed to be thinking of nothing in particular.

She got off at the Bastille station. Half running, as if she were afraid of the darkness and the figures prowling about the sidewalks, she went off toward the Rue de la Roquette, where she rang at a door that closed again behind her.

Had he been in love with Marcelle herself, or with the

lights of the Moulin-Rouge? Or else with the contrast between those petticoats swirling to the blare of the band and
the scared little girl in the schoolgirl's beret, nervously ringing
at her parents' door?

The second hypothesis seemed nearer the truth, seen in
perspective after the lapse of years. What had mattered was
her fragile appearance, arousing compassion and protective-
ness.

He'd spoken to her, not in the Place Blanche but in the
subway. She looked annoyed at first, then mistrustful, and
eventually she smiled at his awkwardness.

For weeks he went through the kind of emotional experience one usually has at sixteen, and every evening he bought
a bunch of violets from the old flower-seller stationed in
front of the Moulin-Rouge.

Marcelle's mother was concierge to the block of flats in
the Rue de la Roquette, and her father was a policeman. At
twelve she had been sent to dancing classes because a little
girl in the neighborhood had become a ballerina at the Opéra.

She had no intention of remaining in the can-can group,
nor of going on dancing. Her ambition was to become a
real actress, and she went to Charles Dullin's classes in the
morning.

For two months nothing happened between them. One
afternoon, when he had persuaded her to go out with him,
he took her to his room in the Rue des Dames.

He wondered whether she was a virgin, and the thought
scared him. She undressed without demur, and lay down on
the bed, staring into space.

Afterwards he asked her: "Have you done it often?"

She frowned, not understanding.

"What d'you mean? . . . Oh, that. . . . I shouldn't be
at the Moulin-Rouge if I hadn't been through it. . . ."

"With whom?"

"With Hector, the tout, to begin with. . . . We call him

the tout; the funny man, who introduces the turn and tells stories. . . ."

A fat, baldish fellow, exuding smug stupidity.

"And then the band leader, although he's scared stiff of his wife. . . ."

"And who else?"

"You remind me of a priest. . . . What does it matter, and what business is it of yours? . . . If I hadn't known other men I shouldn't be here. . . ."

"Did you dislike it?"

"I don't know. . . ."

"And with me?"

"Is it true you write in the papers? . . . You didn't say it to impress me? . . . Then why don't you sign what you write?"

She formed the habit of coming twice a week to the Rue des Dames. He always waited impatiently for those days, and gradually the idea of being one of a pair occurred to him. Not to be all alone in one's room. To have one's meals with somebody else, even if the cloth on the little table was a horrible brown material with a floral pattern. . . .

One day as they were leaving his hotel together and he was walking back with her as far as the subway, a man with dark mustaches on a red face suddenly appeared before them.

"You get along home. . . . And you, my boy, I've something to say to you. . . ." It was her father, the policeman, threatening and stubborn-looking.

How did the two men eventually reach the Boulevard des Batignolles, where they walked between the rows of trees up toward the Place Clichy, then turned back and went down as far as the railway, and then up again? What stages did they go through before becoming friendly?

"It's a job, I suppose, but how much do you earn?"

He had cheated, revising the figures upwards.

"That's all very fine, but it's not as good as a regular job. . . ."

Had he been caught in a trap? Might he not have spoken of the funny man, with his scanty hair, and the band leader? Had they been treated to a display of paternal indignation?

Actually, he had been relieved by what had happened. He had not tried to escape. On the contrary, he had pleaded his cause, and an hour later the policeman and he were drinking apéritifs together in a *bar-tabac*.

And so he had got himself married to the lights, the Moulin-Rouge, the green dress, and to a sort of pitifulness that made him conscious of his own responsibility, his superiority.

That was enough about Marcelle. He had gone to the heart of the matter as far as it was possible to go. It did not make him feel proud.

He was relieved to see day break and to watch Joséfa waking up. It brought him back into the present.

"Good morning! Had a good sleep?"

"And yourself?"

"I got up twice, out of habit, to make sure you were all right. . . . You were sleeping like an angel. . . ."

She folded up her bed and put it back into the closet.

"You must be pleased with your progress, aren't you?"

Once again, he was aware of an upsetting, mysterious note. And why did Joséfa, when she said good-by to him, feel impelled to shake him by the hand?

"Have a good day. . . . Keep well. . . ."

She seemed disturbed. She went off, turning back once more at the door.

"Good-by," she said, waving her hand.

Did that mean he would not see her again? Were they going to give him a substitute? She had not bid farewell to him, because that was probably against the rules. Anything that might excite a patient was avoided. It was easier to confront him with a *fait accompli*.

"You were sleeping like an angel. . . ."

That might mean that he no longer needed anyone to look after him during the night. A nurse was permanently on duty in a corner of the passage. Maugras had occasionally heard bells ringing and footsteps hurrying off toward the main ward.

As he gradually became like other people, he was going to be treated like other people, he was aware of that, and he steeled himself in anticipation, determined to defend himself.

"Hello, hello!"

Mlle Blanche was excited, exuding open-air coolness even from the folds of her dress. There had been a frost, and traces of it still lingered on the slate roof, where the sun was absorbing it.

"Had a good sleep? . . . Feeling fine? . . . We're going to take your temperature and I'm almost sure it'll be the last time. . . ."

He had foreseen it. They were proposing to do away with his thermometer. He had seen the dextrose vessel disappear, and he was only given one injection a day. Then that would stop. What would they do away with next?

"Ninety-eight point six. Pulse seventy, like a grownup!"

He did not like her joking tone this morning.

"I nearly forgot the diary. . . . I chose one with two days to a page, and I've bought you two ballpoints, one black and one red. . . ."

The intern looked in while he was being washed, and merely gave him a cursory sounding, his eyes and his thoughts elsewhere. Maugras was no longer an interesting case.

"You agree with me, Doctor, about what I suggested yesterday?" the nurse inquired, mysteriously.

"Absolutely. I mentioned it to the Professor and he thinks it's time. . . ."

And the matron too, presumably? It concerned him, but he was the only person not to be told about it. Any other day he would have been delighted to be given clean pajama trousers as well as his jacket. This morning he read it as a fresh threat.

"By the time you've had your orange juice and cereal the barber will be here. . . . You know your razor's in the closet with your things? . . . When you feel like it, you can try to shave with your left hand. . . . It's a question of habit. . . ."

She did not add that it would take his mind off things. They persisted in trying to take his mind off things. As he looked at the door, which a draft had set moving, he remembered the patient in the purple dressing gown who had come to stare at him, and whom he had not seen again. He mentioned him to Mlle Blanche.

"Do you know who I mean? . . . He used to stand for a few minutes motionless, as though fascinated, and then go off without making a sound. . . ."

"The blockhead!" she exclaimed, laughing. "That's what they call him in the ward. . . . He's no longer here. . . . They've managed to send him back to his family at last. . . ."

"Didn't he want to go?"

"It was his daughter and son-in-law who didn't want him, on account of the children, they say. . . . But he's quite harmless. . . . I gather that on Sunday he ran away from Joinville, where they've got a small house, and got here, nobody knows how. . . . They found him sitting on the bed he used to occupy, where there was a new patient, and they had to take him home again. . . ."

The barber shaved him. Mlle Blanche opened the closet and took out his blue dressing gown with the white piping, which Lina had put into the suitcase with his pajamas. She

177

laid his slippers at the foot of the bed, left the room, and then came back accompanied by a male nurse whom he had never seen before and who saluted him, raising his hand to his cap in military fashion. Probably an ex-N.C.O.; he looked like it, and Maugras took an instant dislike to him.

"What does . . . ," he tried to protest.

"Didn't the Professor tell you yesterday that you were to stand up for a few minutes?"

They slipped on his dressing gown, they put his slippers on his feet. The male nurse passed a muscular arm around his shoulders, Mlle Blanche helped to support him, and there he was standing on the floor, dizzy with anguish at the thought of resting on his own two legs.

"Don't let yourself go. . . . Don't go limp. . . . There's no danger of falling. . . ."

The door opened. The matron. The scene had been prepared beforehand, unless it was the same for all hemiplegics. The eighth day!

Now he was only being held up under the armpits by the man on one side and Mlle Blanche on the other.

"That's fine!" approved the matron, as if she were encouraging a poodle to beg. "Put your weight on both legs. . . . It's important. . . ."

So that she should soon be rid of him? He hated being touched by another man and he was furious with them for having brought in the male nurse. He was equally resentful of the elderly woman's intrusion; she kept her eye on him and even came up to feel each of his calves in turn.

He was facing the window. Standing there, he could see a larger portion of the buildings and a few trees in a corner of the courtyard.

"Just a minute longer," ordered the matron.

She went out, leaving the door wide open, and returned a moment later pushing a wheel chair covered with shabby oilcloth, its padding molded into the shape of its previous occupants.

So that was their surprise! That was the big step forward promised for the eighth day! He dared not even betray his disappointment, for Mlle Blanche's face, close to his own, which had at first been radiant as though anticipating his delight, now clouded over.

"Aren't you glad to escape from your bed?"

The male nurse lifted him up and he found himself in the wheel chair, his arms on the elbow-rests and his legs half stretched out.

It must be part of the tradition to put the patient by the window. To take his mind off things!

She looked at him almost imploringly.

"I was so sure that . . ."

He thanked her with a glance, and pretended to gaze at the courtyard, which he scarcely noticed. The male nurse went off. The matron seemed to be expecting a word of thanks, but she wasn't going to get it.

He felt he was bending toward the right, that his body was leaning over, that he was going to fall and overturn the wheel chair.

Mlle Blanche laid her hand on his.

"You'll soon get used to it. . . ."

He forced himself to turn toward her and to smile.

"Thank you."

CHAPTER TEN

The diary was not red, like the one in his apartment at the George V. It was bound in gray-green imitation leather and had coarse paper. Had Mlle Blanche chosen a very ordinary one on purpose? If so, it had been a good idea, and he was grateful to her.

He had immediately turned to the page for Tuesday, February 2nd, and marked it with a red cross. He had hesitated before adding any comment and finally, with a slightly bitter smile, had written with his left hand the word *urinal*. A word he had always loathed. He did not use a more formal or a more familiar term.

More crosses for the following days, the 3rd, 4th, 5th, 6th, 7th, and 8th. Nothing else. It looked blank, and there was an ironic contrast between these half-pages marked only with a small cross opposite the date, and the very full days they represented.

It was precisely because they had been too full that he preferred not to write anything down. The hours he had spent lying in bed could not be summed up, because everything had counted, everything had been equally important, the nurse's hair brushing against his cheek, footsteps in the corridor, the rings of sound that the bells sent out into the sky, silhouettes behind the glazed door, a visit from Audoire or Besson, or just his thoughts, sometimes stretched out, sometimes on the contrary so condensed that they were like thoughts in shorthand.

A small cross. It was better that way. Later on, since apparently there was to be a later on, that would be all he needed. Unless perhaps he had ceased to understand, and merely shrugged his shoulders.

This day was as crowded with incident as the previous ones, even more so. Presently, however, he was simply to reduce it to three words: *Yet they're alive.*

Then, on reflection, he was to add, with a faint smile on his lips: *Pipe.*

Léon, he had discovered, was the name of the sergeant-majorish male nurse with the big biceps and the bluish chin. He had been sent for three more times, once to put René back to bed after a quarter of an hour in the chair, the second time, after his siesta, to install him once again in his wheeled seat, and finally to put him to bed again. Each time, on feeling the play of the man's muscles against him, Maugras had shrunk back, seized with revulsion.

Tuesday was the day of the doctor's official visit. That morning the Professor, followed by his pupils, spent a long time in the main ward before coming in to visit him, alone and preoccupied.

There must have been serious cases in his department, possibly cases that involved a difficult decision. He expressed satisfaction at finding Maugras in his chair, and spared time to feel his limbs muscle by muscle, and to try out every joint slowly.

"That's all going very nicely. . . . Our friend Besson will look in by and by. . . ."

Whenever he had to be told anything, Besson took charge of it. This had annoyed him at first. And yet it was only logical. Audoire, as specialist, looked after his present illness. Besson, who had been his doctor for a long time and cured all his minor ailments, knew him better.

He recognized now that this division of responsibility, this hierarchy which had repeatedly aroused his resentment against them and against the whole hospital, was indispensable.

If he had been able, day by day, to draw portraits of the two doctors as they appeared to him, he would have been confronted with a whole series of different faces. And if he had drawn his own portrait? Would not each hour have revealed a different René Maugras?

Besson d'Argoulet appeared relaxed today, and did not feel compelled to assume a jovial tone. He was almost natural, and if he was not exactly the Besson of the Grand Véfour lunches, neither was he the physician putting on his best bedside manner to cheer up a patient.

"Don't worry if you feel like a fish out of water for a few days. . . . You must understand that it's inevitable. . . . For a whole long week you've been dependent on those around you, as if you'd lost your own personality. . . . Little by little you're taking up normal life again, and you must expect fresh discouragements. . . . By the way, I must tell you about Joséfa. . . ."

"She won't be coming back. . . ."

"Who told you?"

"Nobody. . . . I guessed it when she went away this morning. . . ."

Long sentences were still difficult. He could not always find his words, whereas within himself he was capable of playing complicated games with ideas.

"She's sad about it, but she can't help it. . . . She's a highly trained nurse and she's needed for someone else. . . . You're sleeping well now. . . . You've got an electric bell within reach. . . . If you'd like I'll find you a night nurse. . . . It's up to you to decide. . . ."

"And Mlle Blanche?"

"She'll stay with you as long as you're here. . . ."

It was a sort of bargain. He was to consent to spend the nights alone in his room, and he'd be allowed to keep Mlle Blanche.

"Another point that I was going to forget. . . . If I mention it, it's because your wife's been worrying. . . . She's afraid the hospital atmosphere may depress you. . . . You're used to a different setting, to different treatment, to having people at your beck and call. . . .

"It's not essential, at your present stage, for you to be under Audoire's eye constantly. . . . You could go this week into a private nursing home of your own choice, at Neuilly for instance. . . . They're not equipped there for rehabilitation, as this place is, but that can be arranged. . . ."

His *no* was so spontaneous and so categorical that Besson laughed.

"All right. . . . That's fine! . . . Don't worry. . . . Audoire isn't intending to get rid of you. . . . Now there's still Fernand Colère, who called me again this morning. . . ."

Maugras did not wait for the end of the question.

"No!"

"In that case, I suppose you don't want to see any of our friends either? . . . They've been calling me up too. . . ."

"I'd rather be by myself. . . ."

His throat soon got tired and then the syllables grew confused. He did his utmost for Besson to go away satisfied with him, and then gave himself up to gazing at the courtyard, which fascinated him.

It was much bigger than he had thought. It was a huge quadrilateral surrounded by gray buildings whose windows he promised himself to count, when he was left in peace.

183

Opposite him, a vaulted entrance opened onto the outside world, and two men in uniform stood on guard.

Beyond, cars drove by, met, passed one another, and people walked fast and gesticulated.

The old men, whom he used to glimpse from a distance as he drove past along Route Nationale 7, all wore a very thick gray-blue outfit with colored braid down the seam of their trousers, and as though to differentiate between regiments, these braids were of two or three different colors. He had already picked out yellows and reds.

But the one thing that did not differ was their slowness, their immobility. From a superficial glance at the courtyard one might think that each of them was confined to his place, as rigid as a toy soldier.

Taking advantage of the sun, many of them were sitting on the benches, but they did not look relaxed like people on benches in Paris. You had the impression that they never spoke, that they had no contact with one another, that each of them was shut up within himself.

This expression, which he had always used as everybody else did, now took on a meaning for him. They were shut up within themselves. They were not sick men. Mlle Blanche had told him that in official parlance they were known as "institutionalized." She herself preferred to call them "our little old men."

Many of them were smoking pipes, like the old fishermen at Fécamp who spend their days watching the harbor, pipes often mended with wire or adhesive tape and producing a gurgling sound at every puff.

Did Mlle Blanche follow not only his gaze but also his train of thought?

"Did you smoke?"

"Yes."

"Cigarettes?"

"A pipe, when I was sixteen. . . . Then, in Paris, ciga-

184

rettes. . . . Eventually, both. . . . I gave it up three years ago, when they began talking about lung cancer. . . ."

It was paradoxical, for his newspaper had launched the campaign against tobacco in France. Maugras had been influenced by his own propaganda, whereas Besson, who was a doctor, went on chain-smoking cigarettes.

A disagreeable thought arose, as always when he recalled the life of the outside world. This campaign had led to telephone calls and personal visits from more or less official personages, and he'd been given to understand that it was harmful to certain very powerful interests, indeed to the interests of the State.

They had even brought him statistics aimed at proving that the damage done by cigarettes was not scientifically proved. The question of advertising contracts was raised, and he gave in. The campaign was called off.

He had not been ashamed of it at the time. It had seemed natural. He lived in a world where the rules that regulate ordinary mortals are waived.

Now his horizon was limited by buildings as regular and monotonous as those of a barracks, and his attention was concentrated on the courtyard and on those silent figures.

The old man who used to come and watch him in the mornings had been returned to his family, not without difficulty. Like a big dog that won't be shaken off, he had come back, heaven knows how, to sit on his hospital bed. Perhaps he would come back yet again, since he could not be tied up, and then he'd have to be taken home to his daughter's once more.

"*Yet they're alive.*"

This was the great discovery he had made that day. They were all over sixty. Most of them were older, or seemed so. Some of them limped, and others moved jerkily, flinging one foot out like badly adjusted automata.

They had worked for scores of years. They had been the

sort of men you see on scaffoldings, building the walls of a house brick by brick, or emerging from the mouths of sewers, or punching tickets, or carrying crates or sacks on their backs. They had probably belonged to every sort of trade.

He remembered the "small ads," so profitable to the newspaper.

"Pensioner, strong and active, seeks job . . ."

They would mingle with the crowd of youngsters on the sidewalk, studying the list of situations vacant, as soon as the newspaper, still wet from the press, was posted up, although they stood no chance.

They had been married, they had had children. They had run, exulting, to register the births at the Town Hall of their district or suburb, and stood drinks all around in the bistrot across the way.

Wasn't his own father one of them? Was he not still living a vegetative life at Fécamp, waiting long hours for the reward of a glass of red wine?

His father was alive! Only yesterday he had thought of him as an imbecile, passive and resigned. If he was alive, if the men down in the courtyard were alive, surely that meant that . . .

He did not succeed in completing his question. Still less in finding an answer to it. This disturbed him, for he felt he was on the verge of a discovery.

His maternal grandfather, on the other hand, had not stayed the course. He was a fisherman from Yport, a squat sturdy man, whose cheeks were colored brick red by the sea.

For twenty years, every spring, he had embarked aboard a Newfoundland fishing vessel, wearing high, heavy boots with wooden soles.

Often when he got back he found there was a new baby in the little house on the cliffs. He had had nine. Only one had died in infancy.

The girls had all gone into service at thirteen or fourteen.

One boy had joined the police force at Le Havre, another eventually became headwaiter on a transatlantic liner.

They had married, one after the other, while their father, grown old, gave up the Newfoundland banks and took to herring fishing.

When he reached retiring age, he and his wife were all alone at home, and he began to cultivate his bit of garden and to go out to sea in his dory to lay lobster pots.

Once a week he put on his blue cloth suit over his best sweater and went off to Fécamp for a drink with his old pals.

Wasn't it, on a different plane, the equivalent of the Grand Véfour lunches?

One morning when he was supposed to be working in the garden his wife called him to mend something in the house —not a faucet, for they drew their water from a well. She called his name in all directions, and an hour later they found him hanging in the shed where he kept his tools and nets.

It was never found out why. Here, the men were alive. They possessed nothing. They no longer had homes, nor wives or children wanting them. They got no pension.

To avoid the sight of old men dying on the sidewalks, society shut them up. They were not really shut up, of course. They had the right, at certain times, to roam about in front of the shop windows of Bicêtre. They were given a ration of tobacco. Their infirmities were cared for. They were washed. Their sores were dressed. They were shaved from time to time.

They were alive! This was the discovery he had just made, at which his friends would have smiled. It gave him an uneasy conscience, made him want to ask somebody's forgiveness. But whose? Wasn't this the world that he belonged to by right? The world into which he had been born, where he had learned, after a fashion, to live? Afterwards, he had betrayed them. . . .

Every day, in his paper, he chose the headline for the most

187

stirring news item, the mother who had drowned her four children before throwing herself into the water, the old woman who had once known fame and who had gassed herself in the Rue Lamark, the switchman who slashed his veins because he was summoned to appear in court following a railway accident. . . . There were plenty of them, and they helped to sell the paper.

It was he who had taught his colleagues the principle of selection.

"No. . . . That won't make anybody cry. . . ."

That famous flair of his! He knew by instinct what news item would excite compassion, which headline would catch the attention. He belonged to those who are outside, who judge from outside, without feeling involved.

He lived in the most luxurious, the most anonymous grand hotel in Paris, where, if the doctor is sent for in the middle of the night, it's to attend to a patient who has drunk too much champagne and whisky, indulged in too many drugs or an overdose of barbiturates, for no reason, for a joke, out of disgust, sometimes to impress a husband or a lover.

Mlle Blanche's little old men sat quietly on their benches, their eyes lost to the immensity of nothingness, drawing at their pipes from time to time.

It was because of them that he had now acquired a pipe. The nurse had asked him:

"Don't you miss it?"

He had missed tobacco, three years ago, and he had occasionally smoked a cigarette in a corner as if he were hiding the fact from himself.

"I don't know. . . . Maybe. . . ."

It was not only in order to feel closer to them that, somewhat later, he had murmured:

"I wonder . . ."

"Would you like a cigarette?"

No. Not a cigarette.

188

"Do you think the Professor would forbid me to?"

"Most of the men in the wards smoke. . . ."

"Would you go and buy me a pipe?"

"Tonight?"

"Right away. . . . There must be a tobacconist's in the neighborhood. . . ."

"Opposite the main gate. . . . What sort of pipe? . . . I'm afraid that in this district . . ."

"Any sort. . . . And ordinary tobacco, just shag. . . ."

Just as at Fécamp. Later on he'd smoked English blends, but it was the taste of shag that he wanted to rediscover.

She threw a coat over her uniform and went out. He watched her crossing the courtyard both ways, and as she came back she gave him a little signal from down below.

The pipe was a stubby one with a metal ring and a horn stem.

"There wasn't anything better. . . ."

An old man's pipe, like those they smoked in the courtyard.

"D'you want to try it?"

As he could use only one hand, she had to fill it for him. Her clumsiness amused him.

"Must I pile up the tobacco? . . . Like this? . . ."

He drew a few puffs, and was disappointed. He should have expected it. He had not thought his jaws would refuse to obey him. As soon as he let go of the pipe it fell from his lips and the nurse had to extinguish the flakes of burning tobacco that scattered over his dressing gown.

"For a few days you'll have to hold it in your hand. . . . Are you going to try again? . . ."

She took his wish to smoke for a good sign. This showed that, after all, she was not able to follow the train of his thought. The acrid smoke made him cough. He went on trying for a moment and then gave it up.

"That's enough for the first time. . . ."

"Did you find you enjoyed it again?"

189

In any case, there was a new smell in the room.

He was allowed some broth, mashed carrots, and red currant jelly. He had not tasted red currant jelly for over thirty years, and he wondered why.

He dozed, neither sad nor cheerful, neither hopeful nor despairing. It was his most bewildering day since he had been in hospital, and when they came to take away the folding bed he felt a void.

Lina had not called up. She must have found a friend, male or female, or perhaps several, to keep her company. She liked lying in bed and feeling herself surrounded. Quite likely she had eaten nothing for lunch but a bowl of soup and some fruit. About once a month, she thought about suicide.

He had thought about it too, less frequently. He had sometimes felt convinced that it would come to that someday, and instead of depressing him the prospect cheered him up.

It was the proof that whatever happened he had the option, the possibility of going away.

To his mind, there was nothing tragic about such an action. He would just throw up his cards. Nobody could deny him that right.

An hour later he would be leaning over the presses, rearranging the layout of the latest edition, or sitting in his office, just as in the caricature, with a telephone in either hand, his busy secretary beside him and Fernand Colère, as usual, with one hand on the doorknob.

In the courtyard, where the clipped trees formed geometrical patterns, in all the honeycomb cells where, in the uncertain light, could be seen serried rows of beds and nurses and doctors hurrying about, they were all alive!

And that man of about his own age with bent back and hanging jaw, walking straight ahead along the path as though hypnotized, with a male nurse keeping watch behind him, he too was alive.

Was it possible that all this signified nothing?

In the pale green diary he did not mention the two visits, as if they were to leave no trace, whereas on any other day they would have captured his attention.

The blockade around him and his room must have been relaxed, for Colette, his daughter, was able to come and knock at his door without any questions being asked. Mlle Blanche rushed to open it, and gazed with surprise at this squat, ungraceful woman, badly dressed and wearing an orthopedic shoe.

"Ask her in," he said.

He added, after a pause:

"Let me introduce my daughter. . . ."

Colette had grown stouter, and fuller in the face. She already looked like one of those working-class women who by thirty-five are of no particular age.

"Hello," she rapped out, looking at his wheel chair.

She did not call him Father, still less Daddy. As a child she had stubbornly persisted in considering him as a stranger, encouraged by her aunt who had always disliked him. However, she addressed him as *tu*.

"I'm not disturbing you?"

She was looking at him against the light, for he was sitting in front of the window, and it was only when she came to sit on a chair opposite him that she could see his face. The others, Audoire, Besson, Clabaud, Mlle Blanche, all who had come into contact with him, had avoided showing any surprise at his appearance. Colette was the first to betray feelings of shock, and hurriedly said:

"You've got thinner. . . . It was only yesterday that I learned, from Dr. Libot, who had happened to hear about it, that you were here. . . ."

She was more relaxed than when she used to visit him at the newspaper office. An unkind thought passed through Maugras's head: was it not a kind of compensation for his daughter to see him more severely handicapped than herself?

"Was it very painful?"

"No. . . . It's not a painful illness. . . ."

They spoke to one another like strangers, although they used *tu*. They had never had anything to say to one another, or had never succeeded in saying anything. She watched him more attentively than usual, less as an unloved father than as a man newly discovered.

"Are you well looked after? . . . According to my boss, Professor Audoire is the best neurologist in France, and it's a piece of luck to get a bed in his department. . . ."

She examined the rather shabby room, the flaking paint on the walls, the much-used wheel chair.

"You don't feel too much out of your element?"

And then she referred mockingly to herself. "I know it's not the custom to come and see an invalid empty-handed. . . . The visitors I met in the passages were all bringing oranges or grapes or sweets. . . . But I can't somehow see myself coming here with goodies. . . ."

She was looking less plain. Her face was still homely, but not unpleasantly so now that one no longer expected it to wear the bloom of youth. Why didn't she smile more often?

Her gaze, following her father's, rested on the courtyard, on the old men in their gray-blue uniforms who were once more sitting motionless on the benches or pacing monotonously up and down.

"It reminds me of our little nursing home. . . . There's no comparison, of course. . . . Our place is very humble and we get only the scantiest of subsidies. . . ."

He was watching her now more attentively than on other occasions.

"Are you beginning to understand why I'm so keen on my work? . . . Imagine that instead of old men you have children who've not yet had a chance to live. . . ."

Of course! None the less he harbored a long-standing mistrust of self-sacrificing people, men or women. At Fécamp he'd already felt an instinctive dislike for the patrons of the Church Guild, which he'd attended only one summer.

He did not care for missionaries, do-gooders, all those who revolved around charitable institutions. He suspected them of self-admiration and self-righteousness.

Was this the case with Colette? He used to think so. He had even been convinced that, in order to shame him, she had deliberately chosen to live in a sordid suburban street. She must have said to herself:

"I might get as much money as I wanted from my father, I might live in comfort, dress well, and frequent the same set of people as he does, where they'd make a fuss over me because I am his daughter. . . . But I made my own choice."

She had caught sight of the pipe and the opened package of shag on the window sill.

"You've started smoking again?"

"I've tried it. . . ."

"What was it like?"

"Rather odd. . . ."

"Have they started you on rehabilitation exercises?"

She knew all about it. Of course, she had to deal with abnormal children, and there must be some paralyzed ones among them.

On the whole, the visit went off fairly well. Their words had little resonance. She stayed for over a quarter of an hour and he could not have said what they talked about. They chiefly looked at one another, with unconcealed curiosity.

"I don't suppose I'm allowed to stay a long time. . . . Does your wife come to see you every day?"

Was that why she kept turning to look at the door? Was she afraid of finding herself face to face with Lina, whom she did not know? He replied with another question:

"How is your mother?"

"The last time I heard from her, she was all right. . . . I had a postcard from Lebanon, where she was passing through

193

with her company. . . . They've been touring the whole of the Near East and they've had a great success. . . ."

They broached no vital issues, even indirectly. At last she got up.

"I'll come back next week. . . . Unless I'm disturbing you?"

"On the contrary. . . ."

They did not exchange a kiss, nor even a handshake. He followed her with his eyes as she made her way toward the door. Mlle Blanche came back, but not for long, for she was sent for a few minutes later. This was ladies' day!

"There's a lady asking to see you. . . . Hélène Portal. . . . Shall I ask her in?"

Why not? Having reached this point, surely he might as well get used to things? She came in, smiling and beautiful, for at forty-five she was more beautiful than she had been at twenty. She pulled off her glove to shake his hand.

"Hello, René. . . ."

At the newspaper office, she called him Boss. They had ceased being lovers years ago. She was now married. She had married a lawyer, younger than herself, with whom she was passionately in love.

"I must point out that I asked Professor Besson's leave to come. . . ."

For years they had spent most of their nights together, in the greatest possible physical intimacy, and yet they had never used the familiar *tu*.

It had all started when, about 1936, he was running the "Paris page" of the paper of which he was to become editor-in-chief, and which had collapsed after the war. Hélène Portal had just passed her baccalaureate. She had a lively expressive face, a body that was never still, and she could be entrusted with any kind of interview.

The men reporters were jealous of her, for the most inaccessible people proved willing to see her, and she was accused of making use of her charms.

He had taken a long time to fall in love with her, to treat her otherwise than as a colleague and a comrade. One night when they had had supper together, after an exhausting session at the office, and when he was on the point of saying good night to her, he had murmured:

"Do we have to separate?"

"That depends."

"On what?"

"On what's in your mind. . . . If you're capable of treating it lightly and forgetting it by tomorrow, that's all right. . . . Otherwise, René dear, nothing doing. . . ."

He had a flat in the Boulevard Bonne-Nouvelle, near the Porte Saint-Denis, his fourth Paris home. She had left it at eight o'clock the next morning.

She was to come back there often, but, as she decided on the first day, the affair never assumed any importance. In the office, at the printing press, at parties where they met, their relations remained unchanged.

The war brought them closer to one another, for they were evacuated together, with part of the staff, first to Clermont-Ferrand and then to Lyons. Life had been precarious then, and the housing shortage obliged them to live together for a while. She was partly Jewish, through her mother, and he was anxious about her.

"What prevents you from marrying me?"

"Nothing, René. . . . Nothing at all. . . . If I ever marry . . ."

She did not finish her sentence, for fear of hurting him. He interpreted it:

"I don't love you. . . ."

It was true. She knew him too well. Confronted with the most illustrious or glamorous personalities, she could always find the chink in their armor, which made her the redoubtable journalist she was.

How did he appear to her? She had consented to share his bed, while refusing to share his life. When he was promoted she had taken over his Paris page, and at the Liberation she had joined him on the staff of the new daily he had been asked to create.

A few months later she had fallen in love. Everybody knew this, but nobody knew with whom she was in love, not even Maugras, who watched her changing, becoming excitable and aggressive, liable to burst into sudden tears.

Without warning, she had disappeared for a whole month, abandoning everything.

Later on, it was learned that she had taken refuge in a tiny village in the Morbihan, to try to forget; the man she loved was ten years younger than herself and had no intention of marrying her.

He had changed his mind, however, and gone after her, and she presently reappeared, transfigured, and the marriage took place a few weeks later.

"I needn't tell you that poor Colère is as bewildered as a dog that's lost its master . . . he says you've refused to see him and even to listen to him over the phone. . . ."

There was nothing forced about her manner. She was talking gaily because she was gay by nature.

"I took a risk in coming here and finding my way through this building, where you're apt to get lost and to meet the most extraordinary creatures. . . . So it's just too bad if you turn me out!

"I shan't ask you questions about your health, because I've heard all about it from Besson. . . . He's one of the most sought-after men in Paris just now, because everyone wants to know how you're getting on and he's the chief source of information. . . . Well then?"

She looked him straight in the eyes, as if she wanted to make sure that he had not broken down.

"Morale not too good, eh?"

"I'm not bored."

"It's not a matter of being bored or not bored. . . . You understand me quite well. . . . And what about Lina?"

"She went to Marie-Anne's on Saturday evening, caught a cold, and took to her bed. . . ."

She knew all about the relationship between René and his wife.

"Has she been here?"

"Once. . . ."

"You don't like having visitors?"

"No."

"Including me? . . . Don't be afraid to say so. . . . I'm old enough to stand the truth. . . ."

Half an hour earlier Colette had been sitting in her place, ungainly, carelessly dressed.

Whereas Hélène, who went to the best couturiers, was one of the most elegant women in Paris. It was she, for instance, who had defiantly launched the fashion for mink-lined coats.

He watched her as he had watched his daughter, as he had come to watch everybody, in the hope of making some discovery.

Hélène was not disconcerted.

"Well, are you satisfied? Got my likeness? . . . Good. Now tell me what you're thinking about. . . ."

He would have found it hard to reply, even if he had wanted to. Hélène had probably taken a more important place in his life than anyone else, and yet he felt like a stranger in front of her. Why?

Everything counts, our actions, our words, our thoughts, Abbé Vinage had declared.

How was it, then, that no trace of their intimacy remained

197

save a certain quality of friendship, of mutual trust, an absence of shame? For in her presence he did not feel ashamed of being incapacitated.

"I don't suppose you want news of the paper, or of our dear Monsieur Schneider. . . . You can expect to see him turn up one of these mornings, for he misses you terribly, and he's convinced that in your absence something disastrous will happen to the paper. . . ."

There had been three women in Maugras's life, not counting casual affairs. Of the three, Hélène was the only one who had understood. He could not formulate this more precisely. There were some ideas, such as this one, that he preferred to leave unsettled.

The same thing was true as far as Lina was concerned, although the case was different. Having Hélène Portal in front of him made him think of his wife and of the Hôtel George V.

"They'll soon be putting me back to bed," he said as he saw the little old men in the courtyard making their way toward various doors like school children at the end of recess.

He did not want her to see the male nurse lifting him out of his wheel chair and laying him down on the bed. Was she happy? Wasn't she afraid of growing old, living with a husband who was too young for her, and was her poise not somewhat artificial?

"I'm glad I came, anyway. . . ."

"Why 'anyway'?"

"It's not easy to make contact. . . . I don't mean any criticism. . . . Cheer up, *mon petit René*. . . ."

She said "*mon petit René*" as Besson had done. She had always called him that in private, although he was considerably the older.

"It'll pass, you'll see. . . ."

He did not ask what would pass, for he could guess at her

198

thought. He smiled inwardly, determined that it should not pass.

Nothing else happened that day. Only the note that he made so carefully in his diary:

"Yet they're alive!"

He, too, was alive. That night he would not have Joséfa beside his bed, only a bell-push within reach in case he was seized with panic. For he was liable to panic. Twice in his life he had felt in harmony with nature. Twice, he had almost been absorbed into nature. Nature had pervaded his whole being. He had become part of it.

And both times he had been afraid!

The first time had been on the banks of the Loire, in the gentlest and most reassuring of landscapes, the second time beside a picture-postcard Mediterranean, luminous and limpid.

On the Loire, where a man wearing a straw hat was fishing with rod and line, a cloud and a breath of chilly air had been enough to awaken his fear. At Porquerolles, the mere sight of the beach apparently retreating had set his heart beating faster and made him want only to escape.

Had Hélène understood that, in the old days?

"Good night, *mon petit René*. . . ."

His schoolfellows at the Lycée Guy-de-Maupassant used to shout at him:

"Fathead!"

He was fifty-four years old, and as he fell asleep that night he wondered whether one ever really becomes an adult.

CHAPTER ELEVEN

They had taken a blood sample from him, and contrary to his custom he had wanted to know why. He had also asked about his blood pressure, which Audoire declared to be most satisfactory.

On the half-page devoted to Wednesday there were only two notes, one above the other.

Breast.

I hate Léon.

Because of what this implied, he felt miserable the whole day. Actually, the second note ought to have come first, for it was, directly or indirectly, the cause of the first.

From their very first contact he had felt an aversion to the hairy-armed male nurse, and hated being handled by him like some inert object. Now it was even worse. He had been right in his assumption that something new would happen each day. He was being given massage, not only of the arms and legs but of the whole body, and the masseur was none other than Léon.

Maugras lay naked and defenseless on his bed while those hard hands manipulated him, and the man's sweat made him feel sick.

He loathed not only Léon, but all men of his sort, whom he described as triumphant he-men, men who always seemed to be proudly flaunting their male organ.

He had never envied other men's intelligence or skill. He was jealous of their muscle and their virility.

That was the truth, which he faced reluctantly. In a fit of ill-temper he had taken his revenge. Not on Léon. On Mlle Blanche, who, so he felt, had somehow handed him over to this man.

After the massage, the two of them together had helped him into his wheel chair. Maugras had his left hand close to the nurse's bosom, which was hidden from Léon.

Then, shamelessly and spitefully, he had grasped her breast and squeezed it as hard as he could.

She did not flinch. For at least an hour he dared not look at her. Even when they were left alone together, she made no reference to his behavior, and he dared not apologize for it, so ridiculous and horrible did he appear to himself.

Especially as certain fresh signs confirmed his impression that she was in love with the bespectacled intern, whose name was Gaston Gobet.

He might have added in his diary: *A bad day.*

The other two notes served the purpose. His thoughts had begun to lose some of the softness and mystery they had acquired in hospital.

Although that mystery had sometimes been a source of anguish, he regretted its loss. He felt all at sea. He belonged nowhere. He was hovering between two sorts of existence.

Lina had not telephoned. He had no news of her, for Besson had not come and he could no longer expect to see him every day.

The next day, Thursday, was so neutral that its page was almost left blank. The sky was gray, the weather mild and melancholy. In the end he wrote, halfheartedly: *Benches.*

Would he understand that if he should ever glance through

this diary, as though it were a photograph album? He always avoided looking at old photographs of himself, particularly those amateur snapshots that show one among people with whom one has lost contact, one's arms laid familiarly over their shoulders or around their waists, at the seaside or in the country, against some long-forgotten landscape.

Benches should surely recall a thought that had filled his mind for a while, as he sat by the window.

He had begun, from afar, to distinguish between the old men. At first, because of the distance, they had all seemed alike, like ants.

He had been helped by their beards or mustaches, their various disabilities, their way of walking. There were some who were always by themselves and others who went about in pairs, some who gathered in little groups, some who never stopped walking and others who remained sitting down.

His note referred to the latter. He had noticed that they stayed motionless, indifferent, like certain fish he used to watch in the clear water of the Mediterranean. As in the case of the fish, as soon as another old man drew near there would be a quiver; you felt that they were anxious, ready to defend their living space. Not until the intruder had passed by did the man on the bench, following him with his gaze, regain confidence and gradually resume his solitary dreaming.

Would the note have any meaning in a few months, in a few weeks, even in a few days? He had added, still under Thursday's date, the words: *Not corridors.*

Again, this referred to an anodyne incident. About eleven, when he had just been settled into his wheel chair, Audoire having looked in after the massage and prolonged his visit somewhat, Mlle Blanche had suggested:

"Wouldn't you like to go for a turn outside the room?"

He knew the corridor and the main ward only by their noises and by the shadows that filed past his door. He looked at the nurse with a kind of terror, as if he suspected her of urging him toward fresh dangers, and a protest broke from his lips.

"No!"

He added, ashamedly:

"Not yet. . . ."

For he guessed that they would no longer condone his sudden changes of mood. From now on he would be expected to behave properly, like a normal man. How could he explain to them that the time had not yet come, that he needed time to get used to things, to learn resignation? Would they even be able to follow the intricacies of his thought?

Beyond the door people formed a group, just as in the courtyard they formed a different group. He could watch both groups from afar, sheltered by a protective screen, without belonging to either. But what would happen on the day when he was taken along the corridor and when he would see the main ward with his own eyes?

Wasn't it a basic need, for man, to belong to a community? If his father had formed the habit of going to the café every day at the same time, it was less for the sake of drinking than in order to take his place among other people. They would wait for him before starting the game. They would bring his glass before he had ordered it. If he glanced at the clock over the counter, somebody would comment:

"Your son can wait another ten minutes. . . ."

This was true on all levels of society. At the Grand Véfour, they formed a group too. Who knows? Perhaps it was not out of vanity, out of a craving for honors and medals, that Besson was chairman of so many committees, that Marelle and Couffé belonged to the Academy and handed out literary prizes.

They accumulated membership in various social groups, and this gave them the illusion of possessing a multiple personality.

He, too, belonged to a number of groups. Lina hurried off,

each evening, to meet her own little set, and they got together again on Sundays at Marie-Anne's.

Still no news of her. He was reluctant to ask Mlle Blanche to ring up the Résidence George V, and if he eventually decided to do nothing about it, it was not out of pride or indifference.

Two or three times the nurse held a lighted match over his pipe, which had begun to taste better and which he was now able to smoke almost to the end.

If things went on like this, there would be blank pages in the diary. The fuller his days became, the shorter they seemed. He was able to stand up beside his bed for several minutes. He had begun to co-operate, and succeeded in shaving with his left hand. It was a slow business. He'd cut himself slightly on the upper lip.

On Friday morning he had a visitor. He ought to have been expecting this, for Hélène Portal had warned him. From his window he saw a Rolls emerge from the entrance and make its majestic way across the courtyard.

It drew up below his window, at a spot where he could have seen it only by leaning out. Not only was he still incapable of leaning out, but the window was closed, for the weather had turned cold again and it seemed as if there might be snow.

The matron herself turned out to show in François Schneider, impeccably dressed and smooth-shaven. He was a spare man, robust for all his sixty-five years, and his hair was scarcely graying.

In his private house in the Avenue Foch, he had set up a regular barbershop for his personal use, as well as a gymnasium with all its equipment. His barber called every morning, as did his manicurist and his Yoga instructor. He had the supple rhythmical walk of a gymnast or a dancer.

"So you've decided to take no further interest in the paper?

. . . Don't worry. . . . I haven't come to persuade you to run it from here. . . ."

He, too, belonged to a multiplicity of social groups, to the Stock Exchange, the turf, to fashionable drawing rooms and directors' boards, but the only set in which he was interested, the Jockey Club, had not yet accepted him.

His wife, who was the same age as himself, was a huge woman who carried her fat defiantly. She went nowhere with him, and was utterly indifferent to his having mistresses and giving them jewels, although the larger part of the family fortune came from her.

She ate. It had become her sole passion. She stuffed herself, particularly with candies, spent her time reclining on a chaise longue or playing canasta with other women as greedy as herself, never walking as much as a hundred yards in a day.

All this meant nothing. He no longer sought for a meaning in things. He made a note of them. Or else he extracted them from the depths of his memory, played with them for a moment, and then threw them away.

Why had François Schneider come? He could not have been more out of place. He was the very antithesis of the incurable cripples in the courtyard or the sick men in the main ward.

And yet he himself, too, would be a sick man someday, a dying man, connected by a tube to a flask of dextrose or shut up in an oxygen tent.

He had wanted to see Maugras with his own eyes, and maybe to plead on behalf of Colère, who was frightened by his responsibilities.

Knowing him, Maugras felt sure he must have insisted on seeing Audoire and on asking him specific questions.

When he went away, he left a faint trail of perfume behind him in the room. Mlle Blanche did not like him. Maugras guessed as much without her speaking, and was glad of it.

Actually, she probably found he-men of Léon's type just as distasteful. . . .

He'd been put back to bed, and it was close to lunch time, when he was brought an unstamped letter bearing the crest of the George V. He recognized Lina's handwriting. She had sent him this message by Victor, who had gone away without asking to see him.

René.

She did not write *My dear René* and he was glad of that. *René* by itself was more direct and intimate. One writes "my dear" to all and sundry.

I don't know what's to become of me. I've never been so unhappy. I need you. Please, please, send me a word!

I love you, René.

Lina

Mlle Blanche discreetly looked the other way while he re-read the note several times. The writing was shaky, which implied that she had not yet begun to drink. Until she'd had her first glass, her hands were always seized with an uncontrollable tremor.

Was she still in bed? He was the one who had nearly died. He had been so ill that it could be said without exaggeration that he had been at a turning point in his life. And now, although he had not yet fully recovered, it was she who was calling out for help.

That was just like Lina. She was never interested in anything outside herself. She needed other people to worry about her, as she worried about herself, from morning till night, for she had no lack of problems and was always ready to invent them.

She was frightened of life. She was frightened of solitude. She was frightened of crowds too, of people she did not know, of those she knew too well. And it was because she was frightened, even with someone like Marie-Anne, that she drank

206

and talked too much, trying to convince herself that she existed and that in spite of everything she was important in her own small way.

"Shall I bring your lunch?"

Why not? He was scarcely in a fit state to rush off to the George V!

"A bit later I'll ask you to telephone my wife and tell her I've had her letter and she can come whenever she likes. . . ."

Mlle Blanche foresaw complications but betrayed no anxiety.

However, when she was feeding him with a spoon shortly after, she could not resist asking questions.

"Have you been married to her a long time?"

He had already told her. Had she forgotten, or was it his mistake?

"Eight years next month. . . ."

If she had dared pursue her cross-examination further, it would probably have run as follows:

"Was she already like this?"

"Practically."

Except that she hadn't begun to drink.

"Where did you meet her?"

"In the corridor at the French Television Studios, in the Rue Cognacq-Jay. . . ."

That was quite true. That morning they had been recording a round-table discussion in which he had taken part as representative of the leading newspapers. On leaving the studio he had lingered in the corridor, talking to a former member of his staff. In front of the door of a neighboring studio some thirty girls, all about the same age, were queuing up.

"What are they waiting for?"

"Some supers are needed for a play, a couple I believe, and these are the applicants for the job. . . ."

They had gone on with their conversation, standing there, and eventually Maugras's eyes rested on only one of the girls, the last but one in the queue.

What was it about her that had attracted his attention? Was it her pathetic or tragic look? Her long white face was made to look even longer by the hair that hung down her cheeks and fell untidily about her shoulders.

She wore a shabby coat, her heels were worn down, and one of her stockings was laddered.

She looked poor and pitiful. Her eyes were fixed so intently on the door behind which her fate would be decided, that one felt a longing to reassure her.

"Do you know them?"

"A few, the regulars. . . . Some of them appear automatically as soon as a television play is advertised. . . ."

"The last but one? . . ."

"With the greasy hair? . . . Never seen her. . . . It's the first time she's been here. . . ."

Was she aware that they were talking about her? Did she understand that she had just awakened a response in one of those two men who seemed so completely at home here? Her eyes lingered on Maugras with a resigned and yet beseeching expression.

Two or three times he turned away his head, but each time he ended by watching her again.

"She seems to be at the end of her tether. . . ."

"Some of them faint because they've had nothing to eat for the past twenty-four hours. . . ."

"Do you think she stands a chance?"

"I'd be surprised. . . . It's a period play and I can't see her at the court of Louis XVI. . . ."

Bodin was puzzled by the interest taken by his former boss, and the latter almost went off without paying any further attention to the young girl, who was still waiting for her

208

turn. As it happened, Bodin was called back to the studio they had just left, and they shook hands.

"See you one of these days. . . ."

When he was left alone, Maugras hesitated. Several of the girls were now watching him hopefully, suspecting that he was somebody influential. Why did one of them break into a giggle, by which Lina's fate was, once again, almost altered?

However, he overcame his embarrassment, and once he drew level with her he whispered:

"Will you follow me, mademoiselle?"

"Me?"

They walked together to the end of the corridor, turned left, and then again left. He did not know where to take her. He was convinced he was acting purely out of curiosity or out of pity. Looking for some unoccupied office, he opened two or three doors in vain.

"Let's go outside. . . ."

She followed him like a sleepwalker. On the sidewalk, Léonard hurried forward to open the door of the car.

"Not yet. . . . Keep waiting. . . ."

And he took the girl into the nearest café.

"What would you like?"

"A *café crème*. . . ."

He gave the order, while she went on staring intently at him.

"You're not in television, are you?"

"No, I'm not."

"You're a newspaper owner. . . . I've seen your photo. . . . Why have you taken me out? . . ."

"They told me you didn't stand a chance in there. . . ."

"What d'you want from me?"

She seemed mistrustful and aggressive.

"To have a talk. . . ."

"Is that all?"

"I might perhaps find you another super's job or even a small part. . . ."

"You don't really think so. . . ."

"I might even find a job for you on the paper. . . ."

"I can't do anything. . . . I don't know how to type or write shorthand. . . . I can't spell and I'm very untidy. . . ."

She was staring at the basket of croissants on the table. "May I?"

"Of course. . . ."

"Is it very obvious that I'm hungry? . . . Was it because you'd guessed it that you brought me here? . . . I know it sounds like a soap opera, but it's true that I've had nothing to eat since lunch time yesterday. . . ."

"Where do you live?"

"Nowhere, as of this morning. . . ."

"Your parents?"

"I haven't got any parents now. . . . Only an aunt who brought me up. . . ."

"Does she live in Paris?"

"Lyons. . . ."

"Doesn't she look after you any longer?"

"I ran away from her home. . . ."

"When?"

"Last month. . . ."

"Don't you want to go back to Lyons?"

"For one thing she wouldn't have me back, because I took all the money I could lay my hands on. . . . It didn't amount to much. . . . The proof is that I've got no more left. . . . Besides, I want to live in Paris. . . ."

"Why?"

She shrugged her shoulders and reached out for another croissant.

"Why are you in Paris yourself? . . . Were you born here? . . ."

She ate eight croissants, and by the end could scarcely swallow the mouthfuls. She watched his hands while he was pulling his wallet out of his pocket and selecting notes.

"Have you left your things at the hotel?"

"I had to. They'll give them back only if I pay what I owe them. . . ."

"Will this be enough?"

"Much more than enough. Are you giving me all this money?"

"Yes."

"Why?"

He did not know what to reply to these direct questions, and, of the two, he was the more embarrassed.

"No particular reason. . . . To encourage you, I suppose. Come and see me at my office tomorrow. . . ."

"Will they let me in?"

She was used to waiting rooms and the haughty insolence of doormen. He handed her a card on which he had scribbled a few words.

"Preferably after four o'clock. . . ."

"Thank you. . . ."

Standing on the sidewalk, she watched him getting into his car, and until it turned the corner of the street she never moved.

That was how it had all begun.

The nurse was hurrying back and forth between the sick-room and the telephone in the passage.

"Your wife wants to know at what time she'd disturb you least."

He would rather she found him in his wheel chair. Last time he'd been lying head downwards.

"Between three and four. . . ."

Didn't Mlle Blanche consider it selfish and ridiculous of him to refuse to have an extension fixed up in the room?

211

He'd come to it in the end. He'd give in to them. He could foresee the time when he would do whatever they wanted and would resist only on principle.

And to gain a few days, too. He was not ready yet, he was torn between past, present, and future. He no longer even had the consolation of dozing. He would lie terribly wide awake during siesta time, staring at the ceiling, while the nurse at intervals turned the pages of her book.

Lina was going to come, and he did not know what he would say to her, what attitude he would adopt toward her. He loved her, that was certain. He had probably loved her unawares from the very first day.

The proof was that on the day after their meeting in the Rue Cognacq-Jay, while he waited in his office wondering whether she would come or not, he had felt distraught, with his nerves all on edge, to an extent that he had never known before.

He blamed himself for not having taken her address, he pictured her lost in Paris, and grew so impatient that he turned everyone out of his room and walked up and down smoking one cigarette after another.

She came, and when she was sitting opposite him he did not know what to say to her. At last, awkwardly, he asked her various questions, about her parents for instance, and she told him they had both been killed when she was quite small, in a railway accident near Avignon.

Had his feverish excitement died down then? He had taken her into the glassed-in office where they sorted the answers to the "small ads." It was the only place where he could find a job for her.

Several girls were employed there, looking through the bags of mail brought in several times a day by the mail truck and classing them according to the box numbers on the envelopes. An elderly female who looked like the hospital matron was in charge of the girls, who wore gray overalls.

"When am I to start work?"

"Tomorrow morning if you'd like. . . ."

Was he, or wasn't he, disappointed? Next day he merely gave the elderly female a ring to make sure Lina had turned up at work. He thought he would forget all about her. Then, three days later, after a long struggle, he went downstairs just as she was finishing work.

"I'll go along with you," he said as she got ready to leave.

He was quite aware that the other girls exchanged glances. He did not care what they thought. He took her out to dinner in a restaurant in the Latin Quarter where he was not known, and he asked her further questions, as though impelled to find out all about her.

What had attracted him in this fashion? Eight years later, he could still find no satisfactory explanation. Or rather he could find too many, and they were contradictory.

She asked questions too, specific and forthright.

"You must have a fine flat?"

"Not at the moment. . . . I'm still living in an old apartment in the Boulevard Bonne-Nouvelle while a new one's being redecorated in a former private house, Rue de la Faisanderie. . . ."

"Is that a smart district?"

"It's supposed to be. . . ."

"Are you married? Divorced?"

"Divorced."

"Have you a mistress living with you?"

"No."

"Do you sleep with your secretaries?"

He had said no. Actually, it was both yes and no. He had had casual affairs with some of them. If he had stayed on so long in his flat near the Porte Saint-Denis, where he entertained nobody, it was partly because he shrank from severing the last links with his past.

Not out of sentimentality. Rather out of superstition.

213

From his windows he enjoyed the sight of the vulgar, teeming life of the populace.

His position obliged him to entertain visitors and in two months, when the workmen had finished, he would move house.

"Was your family poor?"

"My father was a clerk. . . ."

She had gravely persisted, as if fully conscious of what she was aiming at.

"You want me, don't you? . . . Confess it! . . . If you didn't, you'd never have waited for me after work. . . . Where shall we go? . . ."

He took her to his flat and, first of all, she asked if she might have a bath. Late that night, while she lay naked on the rumpled bed and he, in his pajamas, sat in an armchair, they went on talking.

"I was twelve years old when my uncle started fondling me and forced me to fondle him too. . . . When I was thirteen and a half he took me and hurt me very much. . . . I couldn't say no, as they'd taken me in out of charity. . . .

"My aunt found out, because she used to look through keyholes. . . . She's a spiteful woman. . . . She made life hell for me. . . . For him too. . . .

"And yet he used to manage to get at me from time to time. . . . He couldn't do without me and sometimes at mealtimes, when he looked at me, he'd begin to shake all over. . . .

"I'm sure it was my aunt who killed him by slowly poisoning him, for he'd never been ill. . . ."

"When did he die?"

"A year ago. . . . After that my aunt never allowed me to go out, and locked me in when she went shopping. . . ."

A week later he'd had a report from his Lyons correspondent. Lina had had to show her identity card to the

214

personnel officer, when she applied for national insurance. Her address at Lyons was in the Rue Voiron, in the heart of the Guillotière district, an area as crowded as the Rue des Dames or the Porte Saint-Denis.

Her surname was Delaine, and at the address she'd given there did, in fact, live a Mme Delaine, who worked as cashier at a movie house in the Avenue Gambetta.

This was not Lina's aunt but her mother, with whom the girl had lived until her departure from Lyons the previous month; she was the widow of a foreman fitter who, ten years before, had been crushed by a crane. At Lyons, Lina had worked in a cardboard-box factory.

There had never been any aunt or uncle, only a little girl who, since she was twelve, had run wild in the streets with boys.

"Why did you make up this story?"

"So that you'd take an interest in me. . . . Nobody ever took an interest in me except my mother, and that was only to thrash me when I came home too late. . . . I don't count. . . . It's just as if I didn't exist. . . . Now you're going to turn me out, aren't you? . . . It's all my fault. . . . I oughtn't to be alive. . . ."

She was really unhappy, even when she was acting a part. After living with him for eight years, she still felt the need to seek reassurance. There seemed to be a gulf between herself and other people, which she could not cross, and therefore she shrank back into herself.

Had he wanted to protect her? Had he felt some responsibility toward her? Had he been fascinated by her strangeness, artificial though this was in part? He did not know. Now she was going to come, and he was not prepared to make a fresh decision.

Surely the fact that she would owe everything to him had played a part in that earlier decision? This had been the case with Marcelle, whom he had rescued from a concierge's lodge only to transplant her, actually, into a one-room flat in the Rue des Dames.

What was the good of hunting for an answer? He'd never find one that would satisfy him. Neither concerning himself, nor concerning Lina. She would lie, and then ask him to forgive her. She spent her life torturing herself, without realizing that she was torturing him at the same time.

She did not feel at ease anywhere, and she suspected everyone of misjudging her. For she referred everything to herself, even remarks made in casual conversation which had nothing to do with her, but which she interpreted as a personal attack. . . .

In her very first week she had quarreled with the elderly woman in charge of the mail sorting, and, instead of trying to find another job for her, he had set her up in the Boulevard Bonne-Nouvelle, where she had played at housekeeping.

She took it into her head to learn to cook, and to prepare surprises for him each time he came home, and he would find her in tears because she had let the stew burn. . . .

"The one time somebody tries to understand me I'm only a nuisance to him. . . ."

"No, no, Lina. . . . Listen . . ."

"Now you're going to talk to me again as if I were a little girl. . . ."

He could not get on without her, and at the same time he did not know what to do with her. He'd tried to give her an interest in life, to induce her to read, for instance, but books soon bored her, or depressed her because she discovered in them resemblances to her own case. He had even taught her, in the evenings, to play cards.

"What did you use to do after work before you'd picked me up in the street?"

"You know I didn't pick you up in the street. . . ."

"It comes to the same thing. . . . I'd have had to follow

the first man I met so as to have somewhere to sleep. . . . What were you doing before you had me?"

"I used to go out . . ."

"Why don't you go out any longer?"

"So as to stay with you. . . ."

It was quite true. He needed to be with her.

"What prevents you from going out with me? Are you ashamed of me? . . ."

He had promised himself to examine the problem at length, to probe it deeply, and now it was too late already. He should have done it while he was still imprisoned in his bed, before he had rediscovered the world through the window.

Perhaps the terrible thing about their eight years together had been that she needed to have attention paid to her just as much as he did. He had thought that he could turn her into a domestic pet that would obey the sound of his voice, and he had found himself tethered to a creature that insisted on going her own way.

She wanted him to be happy. She was sincere. He was practically certain that she loved him and that she'd be willing to die for him.

To die, but not to live!

It distressed her to feel herself a weight, a drag on him, and she tortured him by torturing herself.

Ten times, a hundred times, he had thought her a monster of selfishness. Then, as he held her sobbing in his arms, he had blamed himself for such a thought.

He had to be at the newspaper office at half-past eight, clear-headed, self-possessed, ready to make weighty decisions. And often he hadn't gone to bed until three or four in the morning, after some exhausting scene in which she had threatened to kill herself, and he, in the end, had felt like doing so himself.

He had gradually introduced her to his friends. She had

217

taken some of them up impulsively, and later refused to see them again. With others, on the contrary, she had shown herself needlessly suspicious and aggressive. Her attitude had provoked tricky situations, and involved him in quarrels.

"They only put up with me because I'm your mistress, and behind our backs they wonder why you've saddled yourself with a slut like me. Yes, I *am* a slut. . . . You said so yourself that evening after the play when you slapped me in the street. . . ."

He'd shouted so many things at her, when he was at the end of his tether, and then had begged her forgiveness a few hours later. Which had not prevented him from making her his wife, once they were settled in the Rue de la Faisanderie.

He had hoped to train her gradually, to teach her how to run a house and initiate her into the Parisian way of life. . . . He had shown her how to dress, how to plan meals, how to welcome guests around a dinner table. . . .

"What do you expect me to do, when you leave me alone all day? . . ."

"Darling, I've got my work, which doesn't allow me . . ."

"I know. . . . You exist. . . . You give orders. . . . People listen to you. . . . You're doing something interesting. . . . Everybody knows you and respects you. . . . Whereas your friends who come here consider me a freak. . . ."

This had gone on until she discovered Marie-Anne's gang, where she felt at home because no rules existed there, because anything was allowed.

It happened more and more frequently that she was out when he came home at night.

"Madame left word for Monsieur that she wouldn't be in for dinner. . . ."

"Do you know where she's gone?"

"She had herself driven to the Champs-Elysées. . . ."

They had tried hard, both of them, for it was only fair to say that she had tried too. It was more than she could cope with, like a drug addiction. She could not resist the free-and-easy atmosphere of the fashionable bars, where she was greeted with:

"Why, hello, here's Lina. . . ."

She knew that it led nowhere, that she was gradually ruining herself, that drink was undermining her.

"We'd be better divorced, René. . . . You'd get back your liberty and you wouldn't have to worry about a crazy woman. . . . D'you believe I'm really crazy? . . . I wonder. . . . Your friend Besson is convinced I am. . . .

"When I had that nervous depression and he prescribed sleep treatment, he wanted me to spend six months in a Swiss nursing home where they look after people like me. . . .

"Really, it would be better if I went completely mad. . . . It'll come. . . . I hope it comes quickly and then you'll be rid of me. . . . But I love you, René. . . . I swear I love you and I've never loved anybody but you. . . ."

While he was recalling these incoherent scenes, his eyes rested on the gentle, serene profile of Mlle Blanche, who was deep in her book.

It was time. Léon came in. He was lifted up, set on his feet. The nurse suggested giving him clean pajamas, as if he ought to make an effort for Lina's sake, and although it seemed absurd to him he consented.

Now he was back in his armchair, and they wheeled him in front of the window, and he gazed once more at his old men, who seemed melancholy and slower-moving in the gray light.

"Are you worried?"

"No."

"Try not to get upset. Your private life is no concern of mine, but at the stage you've reached now the psychological factor is tremendously important. . . ."

He reassured her with a smile. There would be no scenes. He would be very gentle and tender with Lina.

Wasn't that what she had repeated most often: that she needed tenderness? He had given her everything else, his name, dresses, furs, jewels, friends. He had given all the love of which he was capable. Indulgence, too. And pity, which infuriated her so.

What did she mean by tenderness? Surely there was tenderness in his attitude to everyone, above all to her, who seemed to him an epitome of every sort of weakness?

Occasionally he would grasp her by the shoulders and look at her with compassionate curiosity. At such times she would seem to be expecting something. What could she expect? If it was words, he could find none.

And surely he himself, from time to time, needed someone to . . .

He must not grow bitter. He had to feel relaxed when she came. He saw the Bentley cross the courtyard, and he could make out Léonard's small mustache.

She came up. Soon he heard her footsteps, and he felt a pang, just as when he had waited for her that first time in his office and thought that she would not come and that he had no way of getting in touch with her again.

When she knocked, Mlle Blanche's hand was on the door-knob.

"You're sitting up?"

That disconcerted her. Her eyes were glittering. Since writing the note she'd had time to drink. She was tense, her nerves on edge, unable to keep still, not knowing where to look or what to cling to.

"I'm sorry to have bothered you. . . . How are you feeling? . . . So you're still willing to see me? . . ."

220

"Sit down. . . ."

"May I smoke?"

She smoked so nervously that she seemed to be biting her cigarette.

"Let me look at you. . . . You're calm. . . . You don't seem angry with me. . . ."

She was trying to control herself, but he realized that she was on the verge of tears. She wept, her face against the arm of the chair, her thin back shaken by sobs.

"I need you so much, René! . . . And I was so sure you'd never want to see me again. . . . It's so stupid! . . . I don't even know how it happened. . . . We'd been drinking a lot, as we always do at Marie-Anne's, and I got all worked up because I thought they were laughing at me. . . ."

He looked at her as though fascinated. He felt no desire to know what had happened at the Château de Candines, nor why she was so ashamed. He looked at her, reflecting how each of them . . . It was difficult to state precisely. . . . They had been groping, each of them, trying to find out where they belonged. . . . He seemed to have found his own place . . . everyone was convinced of it. . . .

"So then I took off all my clothes, because Jean-Luc dared me to. . . . Then . . ."

He lifted his left hand and laid it on his wife's head, against the smooth hair, no longer greasy now.

"Hush! . . ."

"No! I want you to know. . . . Jean-Luc carried me off over his shoulder and the rest followed carrying lights. . . ."

"Yes, yes, I know. . . . Hush! . . . Stop thinking about it! . . ."

She was weeping as if her tears would never cease to flow, and he, with his hand on her head, stared straight in front of him at the peeling wall.

CHAPTER TWELVE

There were more and more blank pages. It seemed as if this new period had begun to resemble his former life, since it included days devoid of significance, tasteless and odorless.

None the less he set a small red cross beside each date, and on almost every half-page a black capital L.

That meant Lina. Was this something definitive, or only an experiment? She would come in the afternoon, on the stroke of three, and sit down beside him, at an angle, so that she could see his face.

"I'm not complaining, René. . . . I admit that all the fault's on my side. . . . I'm only going to ask you a question: Have you ever really talked to me, except, in the early days, to question me about my life? . . . I'm a fool, I know, and I've had no education. . . ."

They were both trying hard. There were long silences during which she crushed out her cigarette in the ash tray and lit another, and to keep their composure they stared into the courtyard, or pretended to take an interest in what was going on in the passage.

Beside the date February 16th he wrote: *They only seem weak.*

Would these words, too, lose their meaning? While he was

writing them in his diary, it was clear enough in his mind. An hour before, she had said with a sigh:

"You're a strong person! You don't need anybody!"

Did he give that impression? It was misleading. Or else his strength existed only in contrast with others' weakness. And the weak were the ones to be envied, since they depended on the strong.

The latter got no help, encouragement, or sympathy from anyone. A strong man's fall would arouse no pity, it would rather be welcomed as a sign of the immanent justice of things.

Was he one of the strong or one of the weak? He asked himself such questions without endeavoring to answer them. He knew only that there had been a touch of resentment in Lina's voice, in spite of the gentleness that she displayed during these almost daily visits, and which gave a sort of muted quality to these conjugal tête-à-têtes.

Physically, in spite of her fragile appearance, her excesses, her periodic wish to die, Lina was tougher than he. The proof was that he lay in hospital and she was only visiting him there. His illness would leave its aftereffects. One day, he would have a relapse, from which he would not recover. She would be left a widow.

No contact.

That was written beside the date February 19th, but it must have taken place on the 18th, a Thursday. Mlle Blanche had pushed his wheel chair into the corridor and he had discovered that section of their floor of the hospital.

He had seen the ward, as big as he had imagined it to be, with some patients lying down, others sitting on the edge of their beds or on chairs, and some in wheel chairs like his own.

Every stage of hemiplegia was represented, so that he was able at one glance to visualize the different phases of his illness, what was past, what was happening now, and what lay ahead of him.

He had not been taken beyond the threshold, but most eyes were turned toward him. He retained a rather bitter memory of this experience.

They knew, no doubt, that he was the patient from the private room. They were seeing him for the first time and their faces showed no friendliness, no trace of welcome, no attempt at contact.

No hostility either. Indifference. Mlle Blanche was so well aware of it that she hastily pushed him in the opposite direction, where there was a consulting room and a rather gloomy little space that served as dining room for the nurses.

Had he been wrong about the occupants of the main ward? During the short time he had watched them, he had not noticed any contacts between them either. They seemed to be immured in their sickness, as he himself tended to be.

Buds.

A few pages further on. Once again, a spring sky and birds singing at half-past five in the morning, for the sun rose earlier and earlier. The famous chestnut tree on the Boulevard Saint-Germain must be beginning to flower.

The last few weeks had been exceptionally mild. For the first time in his life he had seen buds swelling, on the trees in the courtyard.

He had watched their hidden unfolding, the endeavor of the frail leaves to throw off their brown husk. He had spent so many hours observing them that he retained an animated mental picture of them, like those films that show the opening of a flower.

It was the first time, and the last. Soon he'd no longer have the leisure to observe buds. He would stop thinking about them.

The days were going by faster and faster. Besson seldom came to see him, and then only for a flying visit. As for Audoire, he went on studying him as he would have studied the progress of a culture in his laboratory.

Apparently he was getting on faster than had been anticipated, or than the normal evolution of a case such as his, and on some days he deplored this, whereas at other times he would grow impatient at the slowness of his progress.

He was able to put his weight on his right leg, and to move his fingers, which he looked at with slight emotion, as if he were rediscovering a piece of himself.

He was vexed with Mlle Blanche, and did not always hide his resentment. She tended increasingly to leave him alone, not only during lunch time but at other times of the day. Did she go and gossip with the other nurses? Or hurry off to meet Dr. Gobet, the intern with the thick glasses?

She was in his service, she owed him all her time. Her good temper was no longer so even, and he came near to regretting the high opinion he had formed of her. She was just a woman like any other. As soon as he felt a little better she began to neglect him.

Beside the date of February 26th there was a reference to her, summed up, like all the rest, in an enigmatic word: *Mother-in-law*.

They had exchanged confidences. It had all started with Lina, who seemed considerably calmer and was drinking only in moderation.

"You're doing the right thing," the nurse had told him, as if she knew all about his relations with his wife. "She needs to be reassured. . . ."

"What about yourself?" he retorted.

She blushed, then she laughed.

"Has somebody told you?"

"I've been told nothing."

"You guessed all by yourself?"

"Why doesn't he marry you?"

"We shall have to wait for years. . . . He lives with his mother, whose health is poor. . . . His financial situation isn't too good, because in order to devote himself to hospital work and to research he refuses to take private patients. . . .

"Like many women who have had a difficult life, his mother is jealous, and she's incapable of living alone. . . . And she couldn't bear, on the other hand, to be a burden to a young couple. . . ."

He listened, without drawing any conclusions. Everything found its niche somewhere in his mind, and it might be that one day all these trivial facts, all these impressions, would come together to form a coherent pattern.

Then he would understand! What would he understand? What was he groping for? Wasn't it too late?

He ceased to resent the nurse's occasionally leaving him to his fate. But he did not feel sorry for her.

In the queue.

February 27th. It should have been a great day. They had talked about it too much beforehand and he had got no pleasure from it.

On the contrary. They had pushed his wheel chair into the huge elevator in which he had been carried up, unconscious, on the first day, and which he had taken to visit the X-ray department.

This time they had taken him into the courtyard, and he could see the little old men at close quarters, the little old men who paid no more attention to him than had the patients in the main ward.

What struck him was the size of the buildings, in which he occupied only a tiny cell. Did this not somehow make him feel less important? He had been, he still was, a single unit amidst a multitude.

He had promised himself to count the windows when he had an opportunity. There were too many of them, too many doors, numbered staircases, patients waiting outside different departments, white-clad men and women rushing hither and thither.

He was taken across part of the courtyard and under one

226

of the vaulted entrances, for there were several of these, and he found himself in a smaller courtyard, in front of a building that looked like a gymnasium.

It was, in fact, a gymnasium. It was the rehabilitation center, where he was supposed to recover the use of his limbs.

Had he assumed that this would take place in private, as in the initial stages of his illness? Beside the door, a nurse sat at a table, and for every new arrival she ticked off a typewritten list.

"Maugras? . . . Wait a moment. . . . Is this your first session? . . ."

Mlle Blanche talked to her in a low voice, leaving him in the gangway, and he was afraid that the patients who passed close to him, limping, flinging their feet out or leaning on crutches, might knock over his wheel chair.

He was wheeled up to some parallel bars in the middle of the room. Large black and white squares were painted on the ground, like a checkerboard. Men and women were queuing up.

"We have to wait for our turn," she whispered to him.

So he queued up too, a thing that he had not done for over thirty years.

Some of the patients around him had come there unaided and behaved as if they were used to the place. Most of the women were elderly. He noticed only two young ones, both ugly.

A doctor, or a male nurse, he didn't know which, steered the patients one by one between the parallel bars, to which they clung, while trying to walk straight ahead, and what struck him particularly was their gravity, their look of concentration.

It might seem like a game, but it was no such thing, and they were all aware of it. They would elbow one another aside to get a place, and watch each other's progress with cold detachment.

As far as he could judge, most of them belonged to the lower ranks of society, even to that poorest class with which he had long since lost touch.

"Maugras," somebody called out.

And Mlle Blanche, helping him to get out of his chair: "Your turn now. . . . Good luck!"

Here, she had no part to play. She had come to bring him, and she handed him over to the specialists.

"Your hand on the bar . . . like that, yes. . . . Your thumb spread out wider. . . . Yes, of course you can stretch it further. . . ."

Don't children experience the same anguish when attempting their first steps? A pity nobody remembers. . . .

He moved from one square to the next, with just as much concentration as those who had gone ahead of him. Farther on, a bicycle was fixed to the floor and a man with a gray mustache was pedaling on the spot, oblivious of his surroundings.

Maugras was afraid that he, too, would be hoisted onto this apparatus. But that was for another day. Then they took him even farther away from his nurse, leading him up to a wooden wheel which had to be turned by means of a handle.

"Not your left hand, your right. . . ."

He cast his eyes around for the nurse, to summon her to his rescue. Here he was not an exception, as he had been upstairs. Here there were no private patients and ward patients. He was back in the ranks. He had never been a soldier, but this was how he imagined life in barracks.

When he left the place he was bathed in sweat, less from the exercises than because this first experiment had disturbed him violently. If it were up to him, if he had the right to choose, he would never go back there.

Beside the date of February 28th: *Initials.*

His pajamas were of silk, with his initials embroidered on the left side. This embarrassed him when he visited the rehabilitation center, and he tried to pull his dressing gown across to hide them.

The people here were not the ones who led an abnormal life, and their poverty was not an exceptional phenomenon. What was exceptional, what was immoral, was his own way of life and that of others like him, who led a privileged life, and even more that of men like the Schneider brothers.

He had nothing in common with the Schneiders. Why had he chosen their camp? Wasn't this a sort of treachery?

His uneasiness lasted all that evening. He felt it recur next morning, on hearing the bells, which he had not heard for several days. They had not been silent. It was he who had ceased to pay attention to them, who had lost interest. So he added in his diary: *Eye of a needle.*

That went back to Abbé Vinage, whose voice he would have recognized in a crowd, particularly the intensity of his speech, which made his words sink into one's heart even more than into one's head.

"It is easier for a camel to go through the eye of a needle, than for a rich man to enter into . . ."

What did he care about the kingdom of God, in which he no longer believed? Had he really stopped believing in it? In any case, he felt a sense of guilt, and henceforward he gladly took his place in the queue, even allowing other patients to go ahead of him.

He did not belong here; he was the intruder.

Where, exactly, did he belong? Not to the Résidence George V nor to the Château d'Arneville.

Sometimes he felt a nostalgic longing for the Rue des Dames, not because of Marcelle, whom he never missed, but for the pleasure of eating, or drinking a *café crème,* at some counter, of gazing longingly at the display in a delicatessen,

229

of treating himself to some little, long-anticipated pleasure.

And yet, when he lived in the Rue des Dames, he had dreamed only of escaping from it!

Where did the rational, permissible threshold lie? At what point did one lose one's appreciation of smells and sounds and bursting buds?

Did the old fellows in the courtyard watch the buds? And weren't these men and women, who dragged themselves from one apparatus to the next, solely preoccupied with the life that was being reborn in their muscles?

Of course, all through the ages, men and women had given up everything to become hermits or to undergo the discipline and poverty of monastic life.

He mistrusted them, he had no more faith in saints than in those people who devoted themselves to good works.

He could not go back to being a humble sub-editor on his own paper. Nor could he, the head, lead the life of his employees and travel by subway. . . .

Tuesday, March 6th. It had not occurred to him that he had been here for more than a month. His friends thought about that in his stead, when they met at the Grand Véfour as on the first Tuesday of every month.

Besson must have informed them that he was now convalescent, and explained to them that rehabilitation demanded a great effort of will.

In order to encourage him to get well quickly, they had sent him the menu of their luncheon, signed by all of them.

They did not realize what a patient in this place would feel on learning that elsewhere people were eating:

> *Bisque d'écrevisses à la Nantua.*
> *Paupiettes de saumon aux huîtres.*
> *Tourte de ris de veau Montglas.*
> *Salade de laitues aux truffes.*
> *Bombe glacée royale.*

A messenger had brought him this menu, printed on fine paper, and without showing it to Mlle Blanche he had torn it into little bits, overcome with shame.

And yet it was in the Bentley, driven by a liveried chauffeur, that Lina came to see him every afternoon, and that he would leave Bicêtre.

And was he not sometimes seized with impatience when he watched life noisily flowing by outside the vaulted entrance of the hospital?

Two days later, he consented to having the telephone installed in his room. Ostensibly in case his wife wanted to speak to him. She had asked him to do so.

"At night, when I feel I can't get in touch with you . . ."

The telephone stood on his bedside table. He had never used it. It was still merely a symbol.

CHAPTER THIRTEEN

The first Tuesday in April. They must have met once again
at the Grand Véfour, where his place would be unoccupied.
There would surely be other absentees, for this was the Easter
holiday. Nobody, this time, had thought of sending him the
menu. Perhaps one of the guests asked, all of a sudden:

"By the way, how's René getting on?"

And another may have muttered:

"Will he ever be the man he was?"

What had Besson replied?

There were an increasing number of blank pages in the
diary. No capital L's these days.

"She keeps on calling me up, René. . . . I don't know
what to say to her. . . ."

"She" was Marie-Anne, whom Lina had avoided for six
weeks, to punish herself or to atone for something she'd done.

"Why should you not see her again?"

"D'you think so?"

Now Lina was at Cannes for a few days with Marie-Anne.
They had gone off together like bachelor girls, as they said.
He had thought a great deal about his wife, although he felt
increasingly unable, if not unwilling, to concentrate.

When Lina woke at noon, with a thick head, a sour mouth, and agonizing cramps shooting through her chest, didn't she, too, see the kind of pictures he had seen when he woke here in the early days and listened for the sound of the bells?

Just as he had recalled Fécamp with self-pitying nostalgia, she probably recalled the crowded streets of the Guillotière district, where a small girl had begun to learn about life.

Each of us has his Fécamp, his sharp, pitiless, black-and-white pictures.

On April 10th he wrote in the diary: *One for each.*

Yet another note which, in a few months' time, he would no longer understand, or of which he would feel ashamed.

Although he did not believe in self-sacrifice for mankind in general, was there not a possibility that each of us might love a single being and make that being happy?

These ideas had already come to seem so naïve and ridiculous that he searched for mysterious words to sum them up.

Spring was at its height. On Saturday and Sunday, cars drove past, two hundred yards from his window, bumper to bumper. In another hour, less than an hour, in spite of the traffic jams, their occupants would be out in the country.

He had also written: *Joséfa.*

On account of a touch of sexual desire that reminded him of the night nurse. Already he was no longer able to recall her face. He could picture her body stretched out on the folding bed, her full lips, the curve of her bosom, her hand hidden in the warm hollow of her groin.

He had promised himself to make love with her, and he had never seen her again. In what hospital or nursing home was she spending her nights now?

Because of Joséfa and the rebirth of his sexual life, he wrote next day: *Barbès.*

The name of a boulevard, of a crossroad, of a subway station. For him, it suggested Dora Ziffer, the only woman who attended the Grand Véfour lunch parties.

233

It had happened twenty-five years ago or more, and he had been working with her for part of the night, at the printing press, over the dummy of the women's magazine that he still ran.

In the street, they looked for a taxi, and when they had found one at last he proposed:

"Shall I drop you at your flat?"

"No. At Barbès."

He had not understood. What was she going to do at four in the morning in that unsavory district?

"I can tell you, René. . . . I'm not ashamed, with you. . . . Tonight I need a man. . . ."

Quite simply, she explained to him that she never had love affairs because, once the sexual act was over, she felt nothing but hatred and disgust for her partner.

"Perhaps it's pride? . . . I don't know. . . . As I don't have lovers and yet am strongly sexed, I sometimes hang about in certain streets, in front of certain hotels. . . . Do you understand?"

Not at the time. Now he understood.

But what if some man undertook to change Dora Ziffer, to rescue her in spite of herself?

Did he have a greater right to change Lina? For surely that was what he had tried to do? Sometimes she had co-operated and sometimes she had resisted, even to the point of hating him.

He would have to accept her as she was.

She had sent him a trunkful of clothes and personal possessions. As the closet was too small to hold everything, the trunk stood upright in one corner of the room.

At first he had worn flannel trousers and a house jacket. He had walked holding on to Mlle Blanche's arm. He still found a certain difficulty in lifting his foot, and he dragged his leg.

234

Many others in the rehabilitation center walked in the same way, and he had begun to recognize their faces. There was, in particular, one old woman who had only a few teeth, who was nearly bald, with one shoulder lower than the other, who smiled at him as soon as she caught sight of him.

She seemed to be watching for his arrival. He would smile back at her as he went to take his place at the apparatus.

For a whole long week he felt discouraged, for instead of making marked progress he seemed to be losing ground.

"All our patients have the same experience," Mlle Blanche assured him.

He was tempted not to believe her. He held them all responsible, convinced that they were not doing their best, that the staff at the rehabilitation center had taken a dislike to him and devoted less time to him than to others.

He even reached the point of keeping watch on them, of counting each one's exercises, like a child counting the sweets given to his sister.

And he got over that, too. He got over it so completely that one afternoon, when Lina was sitting beside him in a patch of sunlight, he said to her:

"Help me to get up. . . ."

It was the first time, and she was much impressed. He had her help him to the bed, and he lay down there, while she still failed to understand.

"Come here. . . ."

"You want to . . . ?"

She looked at the door, which had neither key nor bolt, and which anybody might push open at any moment.

"Am I to take my clothes off?"

"Just your panties. . . ."

He had not expected to make her so happy. True, she

235

had to be the active partner, and it was she who watched for the signs of pleasure on her husband's face.

Who could tell? Perhaps things would work out between Lina and himself. He was patient. He showed all the tenderness of which he was capable.

Ballets.

That note was for April 27th. There had been a new arrival at eleven that morning.

From his window, even from the courtyard sometimes, he had watched a number of arrivals and as many departures. Things always took place in the same fashion. New patients were brought in an ambulance and the staff were always waiting there in the courtyard, the male nurses with a stretcher, the intern with his stethoscope around his neck, the matron . . .

It reminded him of the ritual at grand hotels, the hall porter, the luggage porters, the reception desk, the concierge, the busy bus boys. . . . Everything took place with the precision of a ballet, and they would start hunting through the wards for Professor Audoire, they would prepare the syringes and set the dextrose vessel at the head of the bed. . . .

As for those who were leaving the hospital, they were often accompanied by their wives and children. The patient would limp off crookedly, while his family carried his bundle of clothes. Some people had taxis waiting for them. The rest crossed the courtyard on foot and went to wait for the bus at the street corner.

He had exchanged his flannel trousers for a lighter pair, and they brought him the papers every morning. At eleven o'clock he would telephone Colère.

He found it hard to endure idle hours. Five minutes before going down to the rehabilitation center he would grow impatient and blame Mlle Blanche for making him late.

236

The last entry in the diary was on May 18th. A name. A Christian name, rather, as in the case of Joséfa. This one, however, aroused no erotic thoughts: *Delphine.*

Delphine was the enormous Mme Schneider, who was so fat that she could scarcely walk and thought about nothing but eating.

He wrote her name in self-mockery, for he was growing like her. It was not so much that he was putting on weight as that his first waking thoughts concerned the meals he would get. As the hospital menus were tasteless and monotonous, he supplemented them with provisions that were brought in from outside, which he commissioned his wife to buy.

It started with a sudden longing for a sausage. He soon formed the habit of adding something to his menu every day, and the parcel became too heavy for Lina to carry.

Now Léonard came up with her. It no longer embarrassed Maugras that other people should see his chauffeur on the landing.

The wine served in hospital was discarded in favor of the Bordeaux he had been used to drinking. Oliver, the proprietor of the Véfour, sent him a terrine of pâté from time to time, so that he monopolized a whole corner of the refrigerator.

"How much longer, Doctor?"

"Can you take it for another six weeks? Otherwise you'll have to come back every day for your exercises. . . ."

That was hardly practicable. One couldn't combine two such different lives. He repeated:

"Six weeks. . . ."

It was the end of May.

"Five, maybe. . . . It depends a lot on yourself. . . ."

If he had had his own way, he'd have stuck to the rehabilitation apparatus until he was utterly exhausted. He could not understand why the exercise room was closed on

237

Sundays and holidays. What right had they to make him waste one, sometimes two whole days a week?

The holidays would have begun when he got out. Now that he was no longer immobilized his daughter had stopped coming to see him. Fernand Colère, on the other hand, came several times a week, bringing files and proofs, so that the room grew more and more crowded, and two hours might go by without Maugras's seeing Mlle Blanche.

Out of superstition, he went on marking crosses in the diary. Audoire had told him six weeks or maybe five, and like a prisoner he counted the days.

They were probably planning to welcome him back to the office, with all the newspaper staff assembled to drink champagne in his honor.

The doctors had warned him that for several weeks he would go on jerking his foot sideways as he walked, and that his right hand would always be clumsy.

Why should he feel ashamed of that?

The end came. Four weeks. Three. There were arrivals and departures. The old men in their blue-gray uniforms went on sitting on the benches, seeking the shade, and for them there would be no departure, save the final one.

"Where shall we go, René? To Arneville? . . ."

No. Nor to Porquerolles, either. He didn't know. It didn't matter. Perhaps he would not go anywhere.

There was no Tuesday lunch at the Grand Véfour during July or August. So he would not meet his friends again till September or October.

Would they find him changed? And his staff, who had not seen him for so long?

At the newspaper office there would surely be speeches, at all events a toast.

An ambulance drew up under his window. There was a great commotion in the corridors and in the ward. It was a new arrival, a man in coma, who knew nothing about the up-

238

heaval he had caused and who was about to go through all he himself had gone through.

Oddly, this made him frightened and melancholy, both at once.

He had almost left the place. Even his room, full of personal possessions, no longer quite belonged to the hospital.

For a space of time he had listened to the noises in the corridor, the sound of the bells, and lying motionless in his bed he had waited to see the "blockhead" who came every morning to gaze at him in silence.

For how many mornings? Actually, for very few, but none the less these constituted a considerable, if not the most important, part of his life.

He had felt close to the old men in uniform, smoking their pipes on the benches in the courtyard. Now he merely threw them a casual glance, and the pipe Mlle Blanche had bought him had been put away in a drawer.

Lina now brought him cigarettes. She had presented him with a gold case and lighter engraved with his initials.

He was growing impatient. Sometimes he was seized with panic.

Would he still know how to? He meant: to live like other people. For he was no longer quite like other people, and he would never be.

Audoire, who looked at him so gravely, realized this too. Did the patients whom he watched leaving with their families . . .

Even if he had not found any answers, he had asked himself questions, too many questions perhaps, and these would always be with him.

Hadn't they been there already?

He would lead the life that he had led before, drowning them in restless activity.

It had started already.

"Hello, is that you, Colère? . . . Who's the idiot who . . ."

239

Lina was beside him, watching him and listening to him, waiting for her turn. Yes, he would be kind! Wasn't his heart brimming with kindness?

If only it had been possible . . .

But no. You do what you have to do, and that's that. You do what you can.

Someday he would go and see his father at Fécamp, with Lina.

Noland,
October 25, 1962